# THE CLEANING WOMAN'S DAUGHTER

## ALEXINA DALGETTY

Published by Liquorice Fish Books
an imprint of Cinnamon Press,
Office 49019, PO Box 15113, Birmingham, B2 2NJ
*www.cinnamonpress.com*

The right of Alexina Dalgetty to be identified as author of this work has been asserted by her in accordance with the Copyright, Designs and Patent Act, 1988. © 2023 Alexina Dalgetty.

Print Edition ISBN 978-1-911540-22-9
Ebook Edition ISBN 978-1-911540-23-6

British Library Cataloguing in Publication Data. A CIP record for this book can be obtained from the British Library.

All rights reserved. No part of this publication may be reproduced, stored in a retrieval system, or transmitted in any form or by any means, electronic, mechanical, photocopying, recording or otherwise without the prior written permission of the publishers. This book may not be lent, hired out, resold or otherwise disposed of by way of trade in any form of binding or cover other than that in which it is published, without the prior consent of the publishers.

Cover and interior designed and typeset by Liquorice Fish Books.

Liquorice Fish Books is represented by Inpress.

## Acknowledgements

Thanks to Andrew Dalgetty and Renee Lehnen for their encouragement and willingness to read early drafts.

Thanks to Jan Fortune and all at Cinnamon Press for making things possible.

And thanks to Adam Craig—mentor, editor, designer, and publisher. Your support and encouragement made this book the best it could be.

*For Greg, Edward, and Jean,
who rarely interrupt and
always support my writing*

# Part One

I am Eve.
>   Collector of words.
>   New words.
>   Startling words.
>   Unexpected.
>   Exposed in books and heard from strangers.
>   I define words,
>   I write words down.
>   In notebook
>   after notebook.
>   Collector of words for thirty-five years.
>   (Notebook number eight.)
>   I look them up. I write them down. I knead them into sentences.
>   Define. Record. Shape and wield.

I have trespassed back into the stories.

All safety gone.
>   Eyes open.
>   Laid bare in starched sheets.
>   Relaxed.
>   Echoes of warmth lingering warmth in the sunshine, good-food warmth.
>   Unafraid, not compromised.

Skin smooth, heart pumps, heart hushed, coffee air, perfect fried butter smell.

Mind's eye empty. Clothes, my clothes, small pile in the corner. Neat.

When I peeked through the peephole a tiny eye stared back. It made me all over uncomfortable.

Stephanie's eye.

I know she sat in the painted-white cupboard under the stairs.

I know she tied knots in string. Eight knots because eight was her lucky number. Eight gave her strength. Eight knots in a string. Power.

I know she pinned the strings to the ceiling in the cupboard under the stairs.

I don't want you going in the cupboard under the stairs, she said.

I went anyway. You only say *I don't want you going in there* if you truly, seriously, in the middle of your heart want that. The strings hung from the ceiling. Thirty-seven strings. Eight knots each. Two hundred and ninety-six knots.

I didn't want you in my house, said Stephanie, but I never meant to hurt you. Yes she did. Yes she did.

I am d'Urberville's Tess no Alice no Hetty Sorel no Susan not Susan; I ride shotgun with Pony Boy, John Shipley, in a truck on a bridge. Falling into train through fire, past trestle, through water, searching Heathcliff.

I have trespassed back into the stories.

All safety gone.

Today. I stretch into soft sheets and brace for small amends and gallant celebration. Curious, not fearful, not raging. Thin midwinter light dribbles into the room.

I close my eyes and hear music. That loud proud piece Lucy hears in the *Dawn Treader* when she wants to be Susan. It swells big and overwhelming and my blood runs fast, my mind crowds with unsecured thoughts. Hope, glory, joy, forgiveness. My inside body grows larger than this thin skin it squats inside, buoyant, as if I could float, drift beyond my boundaries, search out a new chronology. I am filled with cautious lightness.

Coffee. Good coffee smell curls in on me, gently, gently until I am sharp for the day. And something else, more glorious than coffee. A smell golden in my nostrils, a toasty buttery smell, cheddar with spice, it tangs in my nose. I lean over the side of the bed. A steaming cup of coffee in a thin china mug with a picture of the mountains, *A gift from Bluff Falls* written on the side. Coffee. And a grilled cheese sandwich. I sit up and my brains collide with the inside of my skull. Too fast. Vertigo, giddiness, excitement. The sheet is wrapped tight around me. I breathe deep and focus on the orange comforter stretched across the foot of the bed. Orange. Colour of meditation. I meditate. Not really, don't know how. I empty my mind, try not to think, I have years of practise.

Gently, gently I reach for the coffee. It's hot and

strong, not burnt, not bitter. I sip and set the mug back on the floor—gleaming but damaged wood boards, thin with ancient style—and ceremoniously lift up the perfect grilled cheese sandwich. Golden at its lightest and a medium to dark brown—but not burnt—at its darkest. Cheese bubbles out the side. Real cheese from a solid block, not a slice or spread. I inhale the sandwich, cheddar and pepper and the bread shaped like a giant kidney, ridged like an old fashion record. Good bread, rye bread. On the side of the plate a loonie sized puddle of ketchup.

The first bite is always the best. Dipped in the exact and perfect amount of ketchup. Welcomed by heart, head, and belly. Crispy and melty with its stinging but delicious cheese. I chew and swallow and dip and bite and chew and swallow and repeat. Mustn't gobble, each mouthful deserves deliberation. With each swallow and the occasional sip of coffee my insides grow with a feeling that might just be joy.

I was a graceless child. Not clumsy. But I lacked dignity.

My first birthday party was hosted by Lucy, my best friend. I made Lucy a card and, knowing I should take a gift, asked Mum to buy one.

Do I look like I have money for gifts for other people's kids? Mum asked.

I figured not and wrapped up a school library book.

Orange leggings and a giant purple sweatshirt with black hearts all the way down to my knees. Excellent. Like a dress. Mum said skirts and dresses were a waste of money if you wore them over leggings. I tied my hair up in a ponytail a little to the left and on the top of my head.

I used a pink scrunchie. Pink, purple, and orange. Not bad.

Lucy's house. There were books everywhere. I'd done good, a book was an excellent present. I had birthday party instincts. Lucy wore a ballerina skirt over silver leggings.

I like your skirt, I said.

It's got sequins, said Lucy and skipped away to another kid, the netting glinting.

I couldn't believe how many rooms Lucy had. One after another. Doors everywhere. And red furniture. Red chairs, red chesterfields, red everything, leather and velvet and even wood. It was like a furniture store on red day. Maybe Lucy's family sold furniture. Could people walk in here and buy stuff? It all looked new. I searched for price tags. Nothing. Mum always said if you couldn't see the price tags you were going to get stiffed. Leave right away, she said.

And mirrors. You couldn't stop looking at yourself. There was a mirror in the hallway with a bunch of tulips in front, real ones with smell and everything, in a fancy glass jar. My face staring back at me through red and yellow tulips. I poked my nose into the flowers and breathed. I looked up and was in the mirror with the tulips and my back was in the room behind with all the furniture and a wooden floor with giant mats. We had carpeting, me and Mum. Lucy might have a hundred rooms and matching furniture but me and Mum had carpet. And we had smell, Mum and I had cooking smell and lemon cleaning smell but this house was smell-less. Even the tulips didn't smell.

Mum and I lived in a bachelor with a bed built in the wall. Beds in walls sound classy but it was creaky and scared me. I figured mice and bed bugs hung out in it. I imagined being trapped inside. I imagined mice nibbling my toes. It itched my arms.

Aren't you a vain little thing staring at yourself in the

mirror, said Lucy's mum.

No, I thought, I was looking at all your red stuff.

Come along and play. You're Eve from Lucy's school.

Yes, I said. Come along where? I thought. All I have to do is turn around and I'm there.

We played pass the parcel. I held my breath every time it was in my hands. I knew it was a book. It felt like a book. It was a book.

I didn't win.

Then we played musical chairs. These people had music and a cassette player. Mum and I didn't have music. I wanted to take one of the little boxes the tapes lived in but Lucy was my friend. Last kid sitting got a prize. Lucy's mum took away a chair, and another, and another. I pushed Zoe off her chair when no one was looking. Lucy's mum took another chair. I pushed Kristin off of a chair. Then it was Lucy and me fighting for a seat and I figured it was her birthday and all and didn't push. So much for me winning. The present wasn't a book anyways, it a little kit with nail polishes, not much of a gift.

Next, we dunked in a tub of water for apples. My hair fell down and got wet and when I shook my head I sprayed water and everyone got wet which we all thought pretty cool. Except Lucy's mum.

A little over excited, Eve? she asked.

Just wet, I said and shook my head.

Let's all settle down and colour. Then we'll eat, said Lucy's mum. Why don't you sit beside me, Eve? Show me what a good colourer you are.

Can we have music? I asked.

No, we'll colour in silence.

I hated colouring.

Eating was okay. Pizza. I ate five pieces.

I hope you're not going to burst, Eve, said Lucy's mum.

I often eat a whole pizza, I said.

After we ate we all sat in a circle around Lucy. I was worried I might explode. Once everyone was quiet, Lucy's mum checked in on us.

Does anyone need the bathroom? Eve?

Then came the serious business of present giving and getting. One by one we gave our present to Lucy who unwrapped it and sent it around the circle to oohs and aahs. Jigsaw puzzles, and Barbie dolls, and Polly Pockets. I figured I needed to have me a birthday party.

I was relieved to get up and give Lucy my present. Stretching my legs helped the pizza settle. It settled with a very loud burp. Everyone laughed and I took a bow. I had noticed that all the other presents were new, but mine was better. Mine was a book.

A library book, said Lucy.

Lovely, said her mum.

It's from school, said Zoe. Probably bitter from being pushed off her chair.

By the time the last present was opened parents had started to show up to take their kids home. Whenever anyone left they were given a little bag of goodies. Candy and small toys. This birthday party business was pretty good.

Is anyone coming to pick you up, dear? asked Lucy's mum.

I sensed that it would not be good to tell her I was taking my own seven-year-old self home.

I think Mum might be held up at work, I said. When that happens I meet her at the university.

Mum was a cleaner at the university.

I'll give you a ride, said a woman in a coat that looked like a pale pink puffball blanket.

To the university? I asked.

To the university.

We lived near the university, but I would have been quite content to walk from Lucy's house. I had arrived on my own though I'm guessing the other mothers thought

I'd been dropped off from a fancy car.

I travelled in Zoe's mother's car. Zoe was shy and very good at drawing and not particularly mean. We weren't enemies. But I had pushed her off a chair earlier that day. She looked out of her window and I looked out of mine.

Where would you like off? asked Zoe's mother.

English Department. I knew where my mother cleaned.

Maybe I should come in with you.

I do this all the time, I said.

When the car stopped I tried to get out but couldn't. I tried again and rolled down the window by mistake. I poked my head out the window ready to call for help. A student walked down the path.

Hi Eve, said the student.

Everyone knew Mum and I often waited at the university for her to finish cleaning. I sometimes thought the students had a competition to see who was nicest to me.

I smiled and Zoe's mum unlocked the car door after the woman spoke to me. I wasn't impressed. Zoe gets locked in every time she rides in her mum's car. It should be illegal, locking kids in a car.

From the university it was a few short blocks to my apartment.

Home free.

I opened the door to our everything room—kitchen-bedroom-living room all in one, only the bathroom separate.

Eve!

Mum sounded angry.

Did you steal a library book?

No! I was offended.

Lucy's mother phoned. Your daughter gave mine a library book for her birthday, she said. All snotty. The horror! said Mum, sarcastic but still cross.

I didn't steal it. I borrowed it. I took it out on my card. I needed a present.

Mum borrowed too. If I was Arriety she was more Pod than Homily. No, she wasn't Pod at all, she was a human bean, but human beans weren't Borrowers. I was Arriety trapped below the clock. I wanted to drink some milk from a thimble and settle all that pizza. I wanted to go to bed in a matchbox. (I was reading *The Borrowers*.)

What's going to happen when you can't return it? asked Mum.

It was a trick question.

Lucy's mum says she'll take it back. By the due date Lucy will have forgotten the book. She said you might as well keep the present you got to give to Lucy. Apparently, Lucy has too many.

I couldn't imagine a world with too many presents.

Does that mean you're going to buy me a present?

No.

Today. I roll out of bed and wrap myself in the orange for meditation comforter. Time to grow some emotional flesh on these forty-four-year-old bones. They are fierce with anticipation.

The floorboards bear my weight (not a lot) with a friendly sigh. They gentle my feet, my dried and blistered and calloused feet. Never burst a blister, said Mum. You'll heal sooner if you leave them be. There is no pain only puffed up skin full of liquid. I peer at my sensible and hardworking feet.

The grain in the wood planks on the floor is beautiful. Haphazard swirls and darts of oak tree fibre shine and flicker. I am delighted with the floor, treacle coloured with small hints of honey. Unadorned feet, bare on a beautiful bedroom floor. I step with care.

Wrapped warm inside the comforter, I edge towards the window, my window, my opening to a soft snowing and imperfect world. It is a plain street with stunted old trees, gnarled with black branches bare with winter. A thin ridge of snow rises along the edge, between sidewalk and roadway; in summer a small wedge of grass struggles for life. It is a forlorn street with houses plunked down in rowdy disorder, too close to each other, to the sidewalk, to the road. Planted a century. Mismatched teeth in a mutilated Halloween pumpkin.

I wore my neighbourhood like a proud scar protecting vulnerable skin.

Monday. Longboard under arm I race. Down the stairs, down the back fire escape of the apartment Mum and I shared. Longboard down and along the street, perched on deck, raspy rattle of wheels on asphalt, exhaust in the air. Lights, barriers, train.

*9842 94 Avenue*
 *9.30 Don't be late!*
 *You are going to work, dress accordingly.*
 *Did I say don't be late? Don't be late.*
 *Mum.*
 *P.S. No need to take a lunch, she has agreed to feed you.*

I was already late.

I hug my longboard, found behind a dumpster, worn out deck but wheels still perky. Covered with words in thick black indelible ink. Wuthering. Poltroonish. Tempestuous. Malarky. Etiolate. I read, I smiled, I hesitated. I changed direction, through the doors, down the escalator to the indoor outdoor train platform with a roof like giant umbrella.

Last night Mum was beside herself with anger. One mother, another mother, a third mother, a fourth. All lined up with flashing eyes and stout work bones grinding me down, bristling inside their skins, a merciless gang of polyester-clad anger.

I'd bounced into the apartment, my mind sifting a thousand reasons why I'd returned early. (I'd left a dumb message on Mum's answering machine telling her I was on a school trip for a few days.) Bus broke down, hostel booking messed up, kids too out of line for the teacher to handle, storm. Storm would be good. Very late winter storm. Storm, yes.

School says you're playing hooky, said Mum. Her words sliced into my stories.

They phoned?

I phoned.

You checked up on me?

Going on a field trip and not paying for it. I can pay my way. And yours!

She's enjoying this, I thought, smiling during the weighty pause. There's worse to come.

They don't want you back till September. Maybe not then. Not if you're going to lie and skip classes, said Mum.

And still more. She was too calm, almost smiling with a gotcha good, superior kinda grin. Wait for it.

I've got work for you. Cleaning.

A scream itched in my throat, thickened, spread upward, prepared to surface, magnificent as necessary. One crazy out of control, I didn't do anything, scream. I swallowed it down. I had, after all, taken off to the mountains.

But, I didn't want to clean.

One of the profs at the university, said Mum. (I hated it when Mum called them 'profs'.) Needs help around her house. Cleaning.

Let me out, whispered the scream. Not yet, I replied. Timing is everything.

You start on Monday.

I was squished, a mouse in an infinitesimal mouse hole, over there behind the tile in the kitchen, the tile behind the avocado-coloured stove, a mouse searching for crumbs.

Tomorrow Monday?

Shit! Was that me speaking? So much for strong and silent.

You betcha, tomorrow Monday.

I could be a bathroom mouse, lounging in steam, reading meagre mouse books. Mrs Titmouse, fully illustrated.

How could you do this to me?

I did nothing, I thought. You phoned the school. You checked up on me!

Working on my hands and knees, day after day.

Not you, I thought, not you crawling around the hallways.

I have to trust you, Eve. Off to the mountains with men.

She doesn't know I went with Don. She's guessing. The school didn't know.

You're not old enough for a decent job, she said. I tried to get you on early. Maintenance workers union say you're too young.

I'm a mouse in a grave, six feet under. Save me,

someone. Please, save me.

Working my way through your lies with the school. Them shrinking me down to size on the phone, said Mum.

That turned the oxygen off at my heart. She'd never done well with snotty school people. I leaned towards the door in defeat. It has only ever been Mum and me. Other people have families stretching backwards and sideways and even forward. Not us.


I jumped on the train, seat to myself, stretched out. The train lurched.

I counted bluebirds. Bluebird, scarecrow shacks, abandoned cars, bluebird, *Stormy Loves Prince,* bluebird, abandoned car, kid in a playground, his arms and legs wrapped around a broken swing, seat hanging almost to the ground, bluebird, *Stoker was here,* bluebird, broken wall, bluebird, boarded-up house, bluebird, bluebird, bluebird. Lanny Tell, two years ahead of me in junior high, tagged the bluebirds. He had a template, sprayed them everywhere. Prince and Stormy, I'd never heard of Stoker.

Fast, faster, fastest. We tilted full speed through the concrete tunnel with pipe-lined walls. Slower, slow, station. Repeat. Repeat. And then, a crack of light, walls still moving, sunshine, tunnel's end. The best part of the train ride was always when it bursts out of the tunnel onto the bridge, best in sunlight, best in spring, in May. Trees everywhere. Like  handsome preening boys, all leafed out and primped in a come and get a load of this, kind of way.

Tickets, said a voice. Excuse me. Excuse me, Miss.

He was a gaunt, bristled man, wearing his uniform like a weapon.

Ticket, Miss. I've already asked once. It's like you're delaying.

He cradled his ticket book, which was really a fine—not promising fine, penalising fine—book, in his hand.

You do have a ticket, don't you?

He licked his finger and fanned the pages of his triplicate paged ticket writing book.

I checked my front jean jacket pocket on the left. Then the right. I pulled out a wad of folded paper. He licked his finger again and fanned through the pages. They rustled louder than the low whizz-grind of the train's metal shell on the squealing track.

Bus pass, I said.

School bus pass?

Yes.

Bit late for school aren't you?

No.

I gave him a this is none of your business look and sorted through the folded up small enough for a jean jacket pocket papers. Notes for an essay on the sense of place in *The Stone Angel* by Margaret Laurence, a tiny orange book for collecting new words, a religious comic book handed out by the youth cult group that lurk in the train tunnels. Too polite to throw it away. I set it down on the seat beside me.

I hope you're not leaving that there, he said, voice as bony as his face, enjoying the moment.

No. I pick up the religious tract comic, cram everything in my pocket. Check my front jeans pockets, my back jeans pockets. He watches, too close, too careful. I pull the wad of papers out again. It has to be there. He licks his fingers and rustles through the pages of the ticket book.

Do you know the cost of riding the train without a ticket?

Twenty bucks.

Don't pay it on time and we can arrest you.

He couldn't arrest me. Not personally. He had no power. This was his only power, asking for my ticket, and he was enjoying it. I knew my bus pass was somewhere close. The train stopped.

Okay Miss, let's you and me get off here.

I know it's here. I'll find it.

After you, Miss. Off the train. Let's not make a scene for all these good people.

They learned these lines in ticket checking school. Only one good person was interested, a round man—round face, round eyes, round head, round belly, round glasses. He had a shopping bag of groceries and was eating chips the way you eat popcorn at a movie. Eyes on my starring role. Eating on the train was against the rules.

I leapt off the train.

Not so fast, said the ticket inspector. He had to protect his ticket book.

People rush past. Nobody, nobody cares.

I'll be late.

For school with your school bus pass?

He licked his finger and flipped a page.

I took out my small pile of papers.

Name?

Eve Sullivan.

The train was gone, the platform empty. He looked very slowly at his watch and filled out the time and date.

You are damned, said a speech balloon in the mouth of an innocent girl with horns… and my bus pass for a dress, attached to the comic book by some gum.

Found it!

He looked disgusted at the gum and took out a plastic glove. His bony knuckles threatened to pierce the black rubber. He turned my bus pass over, turned it back, turned it over again. It had my name and school printed on the back. It was initialled by Ms Chernyshevsky, the guidance counsellor. I meet with her for five minutes every month to receive a pep talk—you have potential, think about your future, read a pamphlet on university/

technical college/careers in the army—you name it she'd foisted it on me. She hadn't met Mum.

Address, Miss Sullivan?

I have a bus pass.

You said you found it. How can I know it's yours?

Figure of speech.

He folded his arms and stared. Baiting me, baiting me some more. I folded my arms and stared back.

Had it all along did you?

Phone Ms Chernyshevsky and check.

ID?

I pulled out my wad of papers.

Bit of a nuisance pretending you didn't have one when all the time it was there, he said. Tucked into your little… breast… pocket.

I held up my ID. Can I have my bus pass now?

He held it out but when I reached he pulled it away. Creating quite the disturbance, aren't we?

My bus pass, I asked. Polite. Determined. The platform was filling up again. Faces with bodies and briefcases, feet with brogues and runners and high heels.

Not so fast, he said.

What did you say about my breast? Not loud, not yet.

You know you can't ride that here. He nodded at my longboard.

I wasn't.

I saw someone riding one. This station. I might have to confiscate—

That's wrong, I said, louder than expected. Three pairs of brogues stopped and turned. An elderly woman smiled in our direction. I looked at her. I opened my mouth. I held her gaze. He hesitated. The train arrived. I snatched my bus pass and got on. I pulled out my papers and tore up the religious tract, tore up the essay outline, scraped the gum off with the papers, slipped my bus pass and ID into my word book.

Ticket Miss.
I stared at him and took out my bus pass.



Today. A woman with a thick woven basket on wheels—there's a name for the basket, what is it?—makes her way down the street at a crawling pace. One foot painfully plodding in front of the other and again and again and one day I will be that woman. My steps are still strong and fast, as speedy as is necessary and more so. And I do not fear the inevitable slow down.

I unlock the catch and poke my nose out the window. Crazy on a whim thing to do. Open wide to the crisped, shortest day of the year air, breezing in and out of the softness wrapped around my naked body. I stand back and eye the window sill with its cream paint blistered from the summer. I am tempted to prod and chip with my fingernail. I taste the pleasure of peeling a blister of paint. A glorious relieving and unravelling. But am unwilling to lay the dry wood grain bare. The wood stays protected.

I shut the window with a friendly thump. I lick my lips, their moisture already sucked out. I will rescue them with balm.

I sit naked on the toilet. I shiver, naked, in front of the mirror. Contemplate the stray hairs and small natural thickets of my body. I flinch to action. Cold water splash, puckered face, soaped armpits, shower later, rough towel, toothpaste, brush, brush, deodorant—eco friendly, skin friendly, natural, honeysuckle.

Bare foot in the hallway, blanket tight wrapped. I pause. Light hallway, white painted walls, white painted floorboards, like a blizzard, lost in a blizzard, except for the pictures, photographs, postcards, coloured frames, all on the wall and I think of Destiny, Chasity's sister. Destiny. Destiny's photographs of Jason. But these are deliberate, hers were an accident.

Hey! I said. You're in my light.

Half light. I had just settled down on a bed of sweaters: mine, Nikki's, Chasity's, Lisa's, and Tamara's. Leaf shapes jigged on the pages of my book as the shade tree bristled with wind gusts. We'd eaten pizza. Me and Chasity had babysat Jason (her nephew) and got paid, Lisa snuck change from her dad's dresser, Nikki saved and returned empty bottles, and Tamara had money from her mom's new boyfriend who was generous and thought giving treats to her kids would keep him in Tamara's mum's bed. We sat in a circle and ate an extra large Hawaiian and an extra large everything and drank pop till we were ready to burst.

Afterwards, the others flipped and puffed up their hair and strutted across the park, around the wading pool, across to the ice cream cart, back to the rose garden where the roses weren't ready to be roses, not yet, all the time humming their song of the moment. 'Walk like an Egyptian'. Our words:
*All the boys in detention hall say*
*All the girls with the uppity smiles say*
*All the boys with the whispering eyes say*
*All the dads with the angry hands say*
*All the teachers with the easy assignments say*

Anna Ambrosia (real name, Ms A. Ambrose), junior high English teacher, gave me books to read for summer. When I graduated she handed over the high school reading list. I was working my way through it for fun and in anticipation. In *The Stone Angel*, Hagar was just about to… when the lights went out.

Don. Blocking out the light.

I knew Don from the neighbourhood. He went to outreach school. He was thin and from a distance looked like he'd blow away in the wind. Up close he had a metal foundation and grasped his space in the world. He was wearing jeans and a white T-shirt.

What's up, Pony Boy? I asked.
Whatcha doing?
Reading.
Why'd'ya call me Pony Boy?
It's from a book.
Don't read.
I do.


Today.

I dress. Practical and prudent, cotton underpants large enough to fully cover both cheeks. I fasten my bra at the front and twist the band around so the fasteners are efficiently placed on my back, almost centred. A hold over dressing gesture from a rotator cuff injury, lurched on grease in an unfamiliar kitchen, saved myself, wrenched my shoulder, wrenched again when I reached behind. Long gone, the pain, but still I dress this way.

My camisole covers most of the bra strap today and reaches down to the tops of my thighs. A good defence against the breeze of a chilling mid-winter's day. It closes in on my body, a polyester and cotton hug in black rib knit. Black sensible.

I pull on my T-shirt. Black T-shirt, black camisole, old colour habit dies slow but does die, will die. Soft T-shirt. Long sleeves, warmth on a freezing day. Over top the soft caramel like sugar-treat sweater, neckline high up, almost at my chin. If too cold I can dip my chin behind the neckline. Solid, covering, welcoming, startling, not anonymous.

Last, cords, dark brown like purest chocolate with a hint of cream. They cling and separate from my legs with their not yet familiar looseness. The harsh toughness of youth's tight fitting, skin rumpling denim armour against the world, gone. New gone. Not long gone.

I am dressed. I am ready. I am ready for everything.
I am ready.
Remember.
Not yet.
Remember.
Not now.
Remember, the door.

Big trees, old houses. Arrogant, their windows winked in my direction, clean in the sun, polished and sparkling. Wood of the walls painted pink and purple, green and yellow. But Stephanie's house groaned and shivered with ill will. Weeds grew between the front steps. The windows were dark and un-curtained. It was my Lowood, I was Jane. It was my Branfield, I was Rosemary. This was the Dump, I was Barneyella. It was uncertainty seeping into my gut.

I was seventeen.

I walked up the steps and peered through the peephole. A tiny eye peeped back.

What was the eye doing in there? Uncomfortable. Wriggle, squirm, my Nina Simone T-shirt had stopped fitting. I dressed to meet my punishment. Blue jeans, knees worn by old age not by design; an orange T-shirt, never heard of Nina Simone, High Priestess, assumed she's a one woman band, her face on the T-shirt. Reduced to 99c in Value Village. T-shirts with faces on are always priced low in second-hand stores. I liked hers, I liked hers a lot, High Priestess, must listen, couldn't find 'Bird on a Wire'—maybe Mum hid it.

I propped my beloved longboard against the wall, not wanting it to fall. I leaned over from the waist and combed my hair with my fingers, pulled it into a top-of-the-head ponytail and squeezed a tie back out of my blue jeans pocket.

I adjusted my love bead and rubber tubing bracelets, birthday present from Chasity and she'd notice if wasn't wearing them. (Accidentally, we'd run into each other that evening, although I was 'grounded', like this penal colony house wasn't enough of a punishment, but we would meet near the train and I'd snatch a moment of youth from my cleaning world.)

Holding tight to the longboard, wood warm against my skin, I rang the bell. Nothing. I peeked again, the eye remained. What sort of person doesn't answer their door when they're right there? I checked the address. I rang again. The eye stared. I scrunched up my eye so it fit my side of the peephole. I rang. No answer. I rang and rang, relentless, frustration still flowing from my ticket inspector encounter. Nothing.

One last ring—for a count of one hundred—then go home… thirty-three, fifty-four, still ringing, sixty-one. Shit!

The door opened with an angry rattle.

Today. I take the stairs. Pictures. All the way down. In red and yellow and blue and green, bright like Lego, frames. Fragments of the world. A postcard called Elk Stalled in Snow. What happens when elk stall in snow?

I touch the cool glass, the child coloured frames, the loose cards, stuck on top and behind the frames. I return to Elk Stalled in Snow, lives stalled in snow, but the elk aren't dismayed. Almost grinning if elk grin. Confident this stalling will pass. In snow, emotional drift, like woman stalled in small rented rooms and dingy diners. Am I these elk? Not content but tolerant. Willing to wait for the snow to melt. Maybe the Elk are too far north for melt snow, maybe they are stalled for ever and always.

Destiny had slivers of ideas in photo frames all across her wall. Pictures of Jason, her son. An ear in one frame, his nose in another, his hair in a third, a gurgling baby smile in another corner and little fat legs on the other side of the chair, all separate and so much better than one picture of an ordinary little baby.

Cool, I said looking at the photos.

Thanks, said Destiny.

Accidental, said Chasity. Stoned when she took the pictures, missed the baby.

I like them, I said.

At the end elementary school Mum and I moved. I was charmed and delighted. Our new home was a one bedroom apartment in a walk up. Mum and I shared the bedroom and it was a hundred times better than sleeping in the bed in the wall. Best of all the living room was a real living room, free of the smell of night time despair (feet, farts, old socks and smelly armpits) that snuggled into bedclothes. A new and certain joy replaced the fear of the bed falling down and banging me on the head.

Don't sit under the bed wall, Mum would say.

And then we moved.


Off the living room in the new apartment there was a space for a table and Mum and I found a dining set at Value Village. Red Formica with four matching chairs and shiny chrome legs.

I suppose you can even have a little friend over, said Mum.

Like I had a little friend.


That summer I hung out on the balcony. It wasn't an honest to goodness balcony; the back of the building was crisscrossed with staircases that led to back doors and these platforms that were almost balconies. Okay so they were fire escapes. Mum had set an old wooden crate, 'Pepsi-cola' in curly writing on the sides, upside down beside our door. That way we didn't have to bend too far when we picked up the groceries after we unlocked the door. That summer I sat on the crate and read and dreamed.

That's how I met Chasity. Chasity didn't live in the building but her sister did. Destiny, was seventeen and had a baby, Jason of the accidental photographs.

I sat in the shade reading *The Lion, The Witch, and The Wardrobe*. I was Lucy hurt by Edmund, confronting the White Witch. I looked her straight in the eye and grabbed an arrow from the quiver on my back. My magic was stronger than hers. I slowly, slowly drew my bow. Edmund's allegiance to the White Witch faltered. The White Witch flinched. Fear, I assumed. I drew back the string. I had her in my sights, Edmund softened in my direction. The nock on my arrow radiated magical warmth. The air around us warmed, the White Witch melted, tears on her face were her ice skin dissolving.

I'd read the book before, in free reading at school, and had just discovered it was part of a series. I had a boxed set from the library, starting with *The Magician's Nephew*. I was eager to get back to Narnia. I read and dreamed in unison and this time Lucy fished, Edmund set the table. I hadn't noticed the table setting first time round but now things were different, I was Lucy.

I ignored the footsteps. Edmund was eating Turkish Delight. I quite liked how he was evil. (I would have stopped reading if Lucy or Susan had been evil.) I liked even more my plan to rescue him. I used to think the book would have been perfect if Lucy had been called Eve. I'd considered writing to C.S. Lewis and asking him to change her name. Except he was dead.

I heard a slapping plopping sound and sneaked a peak. Two feet wearing purple flip-flops and pink nail polish parked themselves across from the Pepsi-cola crate. I turned the page and read some more. The feet were still there. I looked up, no longer Lucy. Chasity was wearing a short skirt in pink T-shirt material and a purple *Little Mermaid* tank top. I was wearing cutoffs and a John Lennon T-shirt. When I found the shirt in Value Village Mum rolled her eyes but it was cheap. Chasity was wearing makeup and had gold polished fingernails. Her hair was cut short. My hair was long and tied behind. I had considered cutting it but decided, as I sat cross legged half in Narnia and half on a Pepsi-cola crate on the not quite balcony, to postpone in case short hair was connected with wearing pink.

Wanna hang out? asked Chasity.

No one had ever asked me to hang out before.

Sure, I said like people asked me to hang out every day.

I'm Chasity Mendelson.
Eve Sullivan.
Wanna come to my sister's place?
Sure.

I'd never been to anyone else's home. Not since Lucy's birthday party. I followed Chasity down the stairs never imagining that she was one of the tough girls. She looked like one of the wimps.

Where did you come from? asked Chasity?
Near the university.
Fancy.
Not where I lived. This is much nicer.
Seriously?
Yep!
But there are cool stores and a market and places to get ice cream and fancy coffee.
You drink fancy coffee?
Sometimes.
I drink mine black.
You drink coffee?
Every morning.

It was an exaggeration. I'd just started. A little coffee now and then. The taste was growing on me. I thought it was tougher to drink it without sugar and milk. Black coffee suited my personality.

Chasity's sister lived in the apartment with twinkle lights. They were on the back balcony platform at the top of her staircase. I'd seen them every night since we'd been here. She turned them on after dark. I wasn't a big fan of decoration but I wanted twinkle lights. I wanted to sit outside at night and read by twinkle lights.

Inside the apartment was even better.
This is… what was your name again?
Eve.
Right, this is Eve. She lives upstairs. This is Destiny and Jason.
Hi Eve, said Destiny. Want some lemonade?

Yes please.

There were more twinkle lights over the windows and Destiny had white wooden blinds instead of curtains. They were open so you could see out and made the apartment look bright. She had little origami birds hanging from the ceiling by coloured threads. The birds were all different colours and I knew they were ordinary and easy to make—we'd made them in grade four when we studied Japan—but they looked classy up there. She had a jam jar with flowers on the kitchen table and a tablecloth with embroidered flowers. And she had the pictures of Jason.

There was a dark red rug with a fancy pattern on top of the sludge green carpet. This apartment had to be exactly the same as ours but it felt like wonderland. Best of all, Destiny had books.

I knelt by the bookcase and pulled out *Wuthering Heights*.

I've read this, I said.

Liar, said Chasity.

I have.

What's it about?

A boy named Heathcliff who is taken to live with Cathy and her brother and dad. And Cathy and Heathcliff are best friends but then she goes to live with fancy people and even though she's in love with Heathcliff…

She's read it, said Destiny.


Heathcliff.

Sometime after Lucy's birthday party everyone in my class caught chicken pox. My first spots were on my tummy.

Go to school anyways, said Mum. No one's going to know. Just don't scratch.

The bumps were red and puffed up. And itched. I

wanted to scratch real bad. I went to the toilets, locked myself in a cubicle and scratched away. At first it felt wonderful, then a bump popped and puss came out. I freaked out. I stopped.

By the time I got home at night I had a spot on my hand.

Tell them it's a freckle. And don't scratch, they'll get infected and scar, said Mum.

Everyone's going to know I don't have a freckle there.

Rubbish, said Mum and I assumed she meant no one cared enough about my hands to notice. I tried to imagine other people's hands and if they had freckles or bumps or even six fingers. I couldn't. Mum was right. People didn't notice hands.

When I woke up the next morning I had two spots on my face.

Shit, said Mum. You're going to have to stay home.

I can stay home alone, I said. I knew she was worried about taking time off work. She lost money when she didn't work and if you took too much time off you could get fired. I knew these things. I was eight, I could look after myself.

Maybe you could get me some homework from school?

Mum went to the school before work and I looked at the bump I'd scratched until it popped and wondered how big the scar would be and how far it would stretch.

Teacher wouldn't give me homework, said Mum. She says it'll give the others a chance to catch up.

I'm tired, I said. I think I'll sleep.

That night when Mum came home from work she brought me a book. It had crushed banana inside, sticking the pages together.

Where did this come from?

Tossed in the garbage, said Mum. Somebody failing probably. Give me that, I'll scrape the banana off.

Mum scraped the banana off and washed the book. Then she set it to dry in the oven along with a tuna casserole. (The casserole cooking, not drying.)

Don't scratch those spots, said Mum before she went to work, next day. You're funny enough looking without scarring up your face.

I read and slept and looked in the bathroom mirror, trying to figure out what was funny about my face.

The book was *Wuthering Heights*. A note inside the cover, in the neatest and smallest handwriting, said 'wuthering' meant for the wind to blow loud. I liked the sound of the word. Wuthering. I wrote it in the notebook from my Lucy's party loot bag. It was a blue sparkly notebook and I'd been waiting for something important enough to write in it. I wrote down the word wuthering and copied out the definition. I had found my sparkly, patiently waiting notebook's purpose. I was a collector of words.

*Wuthering Heights* was mostly about grown-ups and houses and angry people to start with but it got better as the people got younger and soon I wished I had a friend like Heathcliff. Then he got nasty and I thought I might like a friend like Linton but he was a wimp. I thought Isabella was mean and I liked Catherine most of the time, Cathy some of the time. By the time I finished the book I decided I'd marry Hareton and live on a moor.

Mum sent me back to school too soon. I was still tired and fell asleep in math class which is odd because I had a fond spot for math. I liked the way the numbers fit together and the patterns always worked out if you thought about them long enough. Of course, it wasn't so much math as arithmetic but I liked it all the same. It was surprising that I would fall asleep. If anything would keep me awake it should have been the lovely number patterns.

The school phoned Mum and she was furious. She had to leave work to collect me early.
I understand the need to work, said the teacher to Mum, but Eve just isn't ready, she's still weak from the chicken pox.
Patronizing bitch, said Mum on the way home. And who do you think you are, falling asleep in class? Don't give in to these people, Eve. Don't let them see your weakness.
I was eight. I didn't know how to stay awake when I was tired, and my head ached. It wasn't my weakness; it was the chicken pox. I felt like Heathcliff when Hindley was mean. Then I remembered, Heathcliff won.

Today. I pick up the card from the floor. HOMEWORK HOME WORKERS, 1977. Acrylic paint, printed paper, linen, graphite, woollen scarf (I need a woollen scarf. Good idea), three metal brooches, household glove, twenty-nine plastic buttons (I can't see them, they are too small in the postcard. I search for the twenty nine plastic buttons. Nothing), and wood on canvas. 220 X 240 cm. It is huge. Taller than me. Wider than me if I was laying down. On the postcard it is tiny. Reduced in size. Homeworkers, 1977. I search some more for the plastic buttons and can't see them. They are too small in the photo on the postcard. The household glove is all too familiar, household familiar. Of the kind used by cleaners.

Orange and sometimes yellow.

A person painted this not long after I was born into this world. I never knew there were secrets like this, explanations of the daily grind, the bones beneath the surface of the world, with plastic buttons that I still can't see, with household gloves and a woollen scarf. Was my mother already a cleaner before this painting, not really a painting, was made? Did she clean before my birth? I only knew her as a cleaner. I never paused to ask this question, I can't remember her rubber gloves. I never paused in growing to ask after her life before my time and she was not a woman to encourage such questioning, to speak about herself. Too wistful, too restrained, too bitter, too stalled. I never paused in my mourning for her. I never contemplated her invisible mind and history, not for all those years when I was broken, shot down, like an elk stalled in deep deep snow.

My own life as a cleaning woman was brief and had an inauspicious start. I almost escaped it entirely.

My hand grasped my longboard. I was turning, turning, imperceptibly turning. The muscles in my feet flexed ready to take the stairs and jump on deck, they tightened with the joy of a raucous and unruly ride. The board always sounded loudest and bounced highest on old sidewalks.

But the door shuddered open with a creak, the angriest door opening sound I'd ever heard.

And there she was. Rosemary. Her name was Stephanie; she was Rosemary, the woman who chose to suckle the devil. I looked at her eyes and I swear they were golden. Rosemary stared at me. I searched the hem of her black minidress—dusty and outdated—for a tail hanging down, then raked up to the fair wavy hair searching the suspiciously low forehead for horns. Her eyes twitched from golden to brownish but she was not redeemed. I cradled my longboard and waited for her to speak. She didn't. Probably casting in-head spells.

I'm Eve, I said.

The cleaning woman's daughter? It sounded like a curse.

Yes.

Her voice dropped. Don't you ever ring my doorbell like that again!

Pardon me, I said. Shit! Shouldn't have poked the devil.

Leave that outside. Stephanie glowered at the longboard.

No.

What did you say?

She wanted it as a talisman. It was mine, she'd use it for spells, she'd send me into a coma, she'd blind me, curse me, kill me.

It'll get stolen, I said.

We both stared at the step. The paint was peeling and curling in front of my eyes.

Take it round back, leave it in the yard.

I looked. I couldn't see the back.

There's a path, she said.

She lied. There was no path. I couldn't see it.

There, right there. I'll meet you at the back door.

The path was a jungle. Completely overgrown. I had to hack and chop my way through Venus Fly traps all the way to the back. Creepers creeped up my arms, stuck to my clothing. Was there a village in this jungle? Was there a yard? I journeyed on, holding creepers and vines, pushing back a very tall daisy with my trusty longboard. Better than a machete, I figured. A twig stuck in my ponytail, my ponytail stuck in a vine. Ambushed! Pure malevolence. I suffered and continued, I had to save the longboard. Too much work had gone into its reclamation to let it be stolen. Besides, if I was suspended from school there'd be no more bus passes. (Free for honours students, average of 80+. Did I mention I did well at school?)

And then the longboard and I broke through. The trees stole the breath from my lungs. I'd never had feelings for this sort of outside before. It was the first time I fell in with nature.

I moved into a small flat of grass. It was what some people might call a lawn but it was tiny. There were daisies and dandelions, both pretty, and it had been raining. Not on me, must have been in the night. I could feel the grass underneath my feet. It was like the ground was pushing up from below, trying to infiltrate me. It cushioned me. Was this how a baby felt in its mother's belly? All I could see was green, trees and bushes or maybe they were small bushy trees. And blue flowers, straggly but somehow blue and green at the same time, reaching all the way up to my waist. And lilacs, white lilacs, it wasn't all green. In one nostril and out the other, the lacy lilac smell and more, a garden scent rush. I knew lilacs, don't know why. I looked around and the house was gone behind greenery.

I stashed my longboard under a bush. Invisible. Perfect.

I was in foreign territory. I could only see green and flowers and nature and the sky acting very blue. Birds sang. I'd never heard birds singing. Magpies cawing, yes. Birdsong no. I shuddered at the thought of being unable to see people or houses and only green stuff and blue stuff and nature stuff. And the shudder was delight. All this outside-ness and me the only person who could see it.

And then the banging started, Stephanie was banging on the window.

What are doing standing there? Get in here!

Stephanie wouldn't have broken me if I'd got away. But first she bolstered me up.

Today. I go down the stairs. They are steep, with a turn in the middle and ridged stair grips, nailed snug on each wooden riser. My hand grazes the bannister, the spindles holding it in place sturdy and practical like my mother in middle age, like countless women in middle age, dressing for comfort and no longer painting their faces. Unless for special occasion. For tonight, for winter solstice night, I will paint mine just a little.
*Dinner with guests and music and warmth. Nut loaf and corn casserole, baked squash and beets. Salads. Desserts.*

I go into my kitchen, run warm water into the sink, dish soap, whisk bubbles with my fingers. And stop, remembering my new sweater. Slip the apron on, apron old and faded, much washed, from Dollarama, carefully roll up my sweater sleeves so they don't bag. Dishes in hot, hotter water, my hands used to the heat.

Music afterwards. All my favourite poets sing their words. I arrange my thoughts and silences. I flatten out my secrets. Not secrets—histories, memories, stories, relations.

I stand still in the centre of the living room—walls have been removed, this is the whole main floor; thick posts still standing and a staircase that twists in the middle—stand in the sunlight crossing from window to window and think, *Home, this is home*, because it's still strange, to be here, in this house, this house which is mine, which is my home.

Memories come. Memories stoppered when I was

seventeen. Old injuries and past offences, left to curdle and ferment.

Some days Stephanie and I sat in the living room. It had bare floorboards that I washed and infrequently oiled. There was a red velvet couch with faded fabric and the springs misshapen and straining to burst through the fabric. There was a pink velvet armchair, the seat bulging upwards, arms slackly stuffed. I brushed this velvet furniture regularly with a brush bought at the hardware store. (Stephanie, in turn, bought the receipt from me, so it wasn't my money.) And everywhere books, which I dusted regularly. Great piles of books.

Stephanie perched on the bulge of the armchair. She wasn't heavy enough to push it down. She perched like a bird. Some days dressed in magpie black dress and nylons. Who wears nylons inside their house? Who wears nylons? Who? Stephanie, that's who. Other days, in her tweedy brown suit inherited (she told me) from an ancient relative, she was all sparrow. In Mondrian cubed dress she was all male cardinal.

Read something, she'd say.

I remember a short story about a girl who was older than me but not a lot. She worked as a chambermaid in a motel and took three buses to visit her husband in prison. He had killed their children in a fit of pique because he couldn't control her. The story ended with the girl going home, on a bus. The bus drives by an accident and the girl gets off the bus and saves the person who was in the accident. At least I thought the girl saved them. She administered CPR. For a moment I thought this girl was like me, then I didn't want to be that girl but I got pulled into her story all the same. By the end it was me doing CPR. I looked up and Stephanie was watching me. I read big, I clawed my way into the story. Maybe that day I read in recovery position or used my hands to administer compressions, leaned in close and offered the book recovery breaths. I wouldn't want someone bringing my books back to life with recovery breaths. Soft damp air fogging up the page. Or maybe I read in anger, in rage at her husband for killing her children, for marrying her, for changing her.

Sometimes I watched Stephanie, counted time between page turns. Some afternoons she never turned a page. Sometimes she sat with a notebook and pencil, chewing on the pencil, staring at the page. Sometimes I looked up from a book and she was staring at me with an intensity that bewildered and worried me, as if she was leeching my energy, my thoughts, my living in the story.

Most days she sat there and stared. I watched her lean into the pencil, pushing it towards the page. I willed it to make contact, I willed it to write. And then at the last minute the pencil swerved and swayed away. Other days she'd make the smallest mark on the paper and smile, almost beautiful. Light did lurk beneath her skin, hiding, rarely developing.

Can you paint? asked Stephanie, one day.

I remembered the stick people I'd drawn in school. Me and Mum with a sun and prickly green flower.

Why don't you use pink for the flower? said the teacher.

I don't want to.

Flowers aren't usually green.

Mine is.

Do you have any pets?

I painted a brown blob. A mouse. The small furry creature who lived under the stove.

We walked into the den and I thought of the man who painted surfaces, any surface, who stole for paint and couldn't not paint. I imagined wild jags of colour. I was excited. I could do abstract, I knew I could do abstract. I thought of my longboard, safe under the stubble trees and spiky bushes in the yard. I had covered it with words. It was art.

The den was small for Stephanie's house but had it been my bedroom I would have been space rich. It was likely ten foot square and had a very nice window, with a broad ledge but an unfortunate view of the neighbour's house. The next door siding was a dull mustard colour peppered with spots of sludge. I was fascinated by the sludge spots, were they trying to get out or were they burrowing to get in? Assault or escape?

In the middle of the den's ceiling a rose grew out of the plaster, carved in the distant past, realistic but lifeless. All around the edge of the room where the wall met the ceiling, more roses small and precious and, I thought, all frantic to escape. The floor was made of a particularly thirsty wood. I'd attacked it with cloths and a special wood floor oil, polishing, polishing, but the oil disappeared into the parched woodgrain, without change. It was beyond reclamation. No promise. No shine. But the grains in the wood were pretty, they wove towards each other and then away, making room for the knots.

It's just a floor, said Stephanie.

I was throwing paint around in my head. In my head, I was a young and female Gulley Jimson. Sara, Sally was young and male. Giant ribbons of black paint and splashes of primary colour, streaking brushstrokes against the ancient wall. (But clean, I'd washed it well.) At times my paint frayed away from itself, almost striped. And lacing into the black bright reds and oranges all the way to yellow and back again, a good yellow a solid yellow, not sunny but glowing.

Here, said Stephanie. She had paint can, rollers and paint dishes.

We painted. The walls. A blinding, boring white.

Is there any colour in this paint? I asked.
No.


Today. Ancient thoughts leak out my skin. I accept each memory as I stand in the centre of the downstairs. This room painted white, until you look close and see the slightest, infinitesimal (word from my early teens—word book two or three) pink. The kitchen is tiled, white tiled, has glossy cabinets white. The shelves are full of mismatched brightly coloured cheap from garage sales dishes. Assorted and each a small jewel on the shelf lined up and glittering. But the rest of the downstairs a white rose that, close up, is tinged with pink.

I stand in the middle of the downstairs firmly inside my body, willing to wander into the past, into the future, into the outside, towards amends, forgiveness, agency.


Is she a slinking, peering beast? asked Chasity.

No, she's a staring, heel clacking, clunk, clunk, clunk on the dry worn floorboards, beast, I answered.

No carpet? asked Chasity.

No carpet. (Chasity and I lived in a world where carpet was the height of class.)

Is there fear in her eyes? asked Chasity.

No.

Chasity stared—a flat no? We were playing The Village in the Jungle game. A grade eleven essay. Read the extract and comment on how the rhythm of the piece adds to the overall sense of pervading evil. I loved the way the words had strung themselves together. Beddagama. The words were music and I'd convinced Chasity to sing along. I found the book in the downtown library.

This can't be loaned, said the librarian.

But it's a lending library, I said.

It shouldn't even be touched by hands, said the librarian.

But I want to read it.

I sat in a small room, wearing thin white gloves gentle against my skin, and read. Private reading room. Perfection. Absolute silence. Me and a desk and a book. Three nights in a row after school. I wanted a private reading room.

Where have you been hanging out? said Mum.

Library.

I wrote down my favourite bits and shared with Chasity.

Is she an elephant remembering great rivers in the time of drought? asked Chasity.

No, she's a deer and angry eyed, on her guard, suspicious of everything especially me, reaching her neck into an almost dry water hole.

Does she sleep with her eyes open? asked Chasity.

I wouldn't know, but I suspect she does.

Does she recognise the hand that wrongs her? asked Chasity.

Hers is the hand the wrongs her, and no she doesn't know it.

Why do you say that? asked Chasity.

Instinct.

I asked, said Chasity, is there fear in her eyes?

No, I said.

Chasity looked curious and with imaginary steam coming out of her ears.

At first I thought her eyes were golden, like the devil

baby in *Rosemary's Baby*.

Devil child! said Chasity, in a growling meant to be creepy but a little too squeaky voice.

But they're brown, her eyes, a congealed sort of brown, sticky and greasy like fried eggs that are poorly cooked.

Fried eggs aren't brown, said Chasity.

Her eyes are.

Today. My coat is red almost leather, almost red, almost like an airman's jacket with phoney inside fur. I didn't choose black, I didn't choose leather, I didn't choose motorcycle style. It is a nod to fresh tranquillity, though I have had it longer than I think. A small and uniform jacket that has grown into my life.

I carefully flatten my cords against my shin and calf. Good calves. Muscled from step, step, stepping. Effective walkers, strong scaffold for this still slight body. I slip on my boots. A shred of stylishness and shape all the way up to the knee, fake frogging down the front, a zipper at the side. And black, only colour available. Not snow boots but traction delivering all the same. Perfect for today. My gloves are black and one step up from stretchy. I slip a thin mitt on top, woollen, knitted by Charmaine, friend along the way. I slip my wallet into my back pocket and pick up a basket. The basket. My basket. Don't dawdle. I am Red Riding Hood without the trust and innocence. Don't delay. This basket is new and perfect. Don't stall. I am going to market. Stop stalling. I am, after all, going to meet a non-wolf.

What happened in the mountains? asked Stephanie.
Why did you runaway?
Do you like school?
Your mother says you ran away to the mountains with a boy.
Can you read? asked Stephanie. Do you read?
Do you have a favourite book?
What happened in the mountains with the boy? asked Stephanie.
I ignored all her questions.


What happened in the mountains, asked Chasity.
Nothing happened in the mountains, I said.


Tell me about the mountains, said Stephanie.
What mountains?
Do you have a best friend? asked Stephanie.
Let me be your friend, said Stephanie.


What happened in the mountains? said Chasity.
Nothing happened.
Have you told her what happened in the mountains? asked Chasity.
Who? I asked.
Stephanie.
No.


Your mother said you ran away with a boy, said Stephanie.
Have you told Stephanie about the mountains? asked Chasity.
When you read your body goes all into the story, said Stephanie. Why?

And why do you write so much?
Why won't you tell me what happened in the mountains? said Stephanie.


Tell me, said Chasity. Tell me what happened in the mountains.


I hope what I think happened in the mountains didn't happen, said Mum.


I heard you got suspended from school, said Stephanie.
What do you and Stephanie talk about? asked Chasity.
Your mum said you ran away, said Stephanie.
Do you share secrets? asked Chasity.
Do you go everywhere on your skateboard? asked Stephanie.
Longboard, I said. It's a longboard.
What do you and Stephanie talk about? asked Chasity.
You and Don in the mountains, said Chasity. Give me all the details.


Nothing happened, I said.
Nothing.
Nada.
Nix.


Jeez, said Don when we arrived in Bluff Ridge. It's nothing but a two street town.
For days my skin had been tight with restlessness and this had seemed—while hanging in the foodcourt

bored with school and life—this had seemed the perfect antidote.

Been here before? asked Rod.

Yeah, said Don.

He hadn't.

This here, said Rod, is the Bear Claw Bakery. I'll be here from 4.00 to 5.00 this afternoon, drinking coffee and eating pastry. In the event you want a ride home.

Hope you like the premises, I called after Rod.


The car drove away, small, smaller, smallest. I watched it disappear then turned to the mountains, stretched up like giant versions of grown-in-science-class crystals. Surface leaning into surface, all angles, math and science sharp and hard against each other. Except the surfaces weren't transparent they were thick with colour, dark greys and browns with bits of snow, solid and dependable. I breathed, my skin stretched, the mountains were older than time.

In the event you want a ride home, mocked Don.

It was Jack and the Beanstalk in rock, all the way up. At the top there had to be magic. I was frozen to the spot.

Good luck with your premises, mocked Don.


Bedford was a place of small difference, north side, south side, distinct graffiti, better and worse houses, smaller apartments, larger apartments, rattier apartments, smarter shops, scruffier shops. All similar. Down the Bluff Falls street lurked wooden stores and houses, all Heidi, and I wished I had a few more layers of clothes.

Is this Dorfli already? Let's go find grandfather.

What the fuck? said Don.

Nothing, just a book.

Heidi was my first best friend. Now I was in the

mountains and their weight nestled inside my body.
 Could you at least close your mouth? asked Don.
 Pinch me, I said to Don and he did. Ow!
 You said pinch me. Such a hay seed.
 Don rolled his eyes and the adrenalin leaked through my skin. I knew I'd be at the Bear Claw between 4.00 and 5.00.
 I chafed at life, impatient but unready to scratch its surface.


Across the street was a train station with an old train outside, like a giant toy, plunked into the ground for kids to climb and play on. We walked by the wooden shops and hotels with pointy porches and pointier roofs, mini wooden mountains with doors to the inside.
 I'm goin' on the train, I said.
 No, said Don.
 Screw you, I said and crossed the road.
 I climbed up on the engine and smiled at the little kids and caught a small girl about to slide off.
 The air gripped my skin with chilly cuddles but I didn't care. Up close the mountains were the biggest rocks I'd ever seen and way up I could see tiny figures, tied together with string, edging slowly, slowly, upwards. Like paper dolls cut out of art paper only these were real people strung across the mountain. I closed my eyes, I couldn't watch in case they fell.
 If we want to make it to Vancouver by morning we should get going, said Don.
 Shit. I couldn't believe he still thought I was heading out west with him.
 It's kinda cute here, I said. I didn't mean cute. I meant magnificent and staggering but if I said that it would frustrate Don. Cute he could manage. Besides, maybe we should go back.
 *How to explain going back early to Mum? Bus broke*

*down?*

We just got here, said Don.

Yeah... but I've got a math exam tomorrow. I thought we were just coming to see the mountains.

*Lie. I could tell Mum some kid acted up and we all got sent back.*

I wanna see the ocean, said Don.

Me too but not this trip.

Pacific or nothing, said Don.

*I could stay with Chasity, make it home Sunday night.*

You go.

Alone? I don't think so.

I touched his arm as we walked away. He was vibrating with crossness but all I could think was how fragile his arm was inside the coat.

You know what my mum's like, I said. She'll go crazy if I take off.

Yeah, said Don.

He didn't know Mum. He'd never met her. But he liked the idea that I thought we were close enough that he knew her. He liked shared history. She was an excuse for him to go on and me to go back. Five at the Bear Claw bakery. I'd be there. I just had to disconnect safely from Don.

You go to Vancouver, I said.

Scout things out? Make arrangements, said Don. I shrugged. You going back with that premises guy?

Dunno. I can get another ride. There's lots of traffic.

Probably safer to go with the guy you know.

Probably.

Tell him I know you're riding with him. That'll make it safer. Walk with me to the end of town?

It was mid-afternoon and early May, snowflakes zapped and vanished in the sunshine. Light bounced from mountain to street to buildings, a little dilapidated, smarter in their postcards and every well-worn building existed again and again in its own four for a dollar postcard.

You really think I should go on my own? asked Don.

I watched our reflections in a souvenir shop window. Don and I didn't fit together. Destiny made people a good physical fit, like owners looking like their dogs.

Yeah, I said. You'll have a boy adventure and come back stronger, ready to take on life.

You'll be waiting for me?

Probably not, I said. No.

Don nodded.

I watched Don walk away, stealing glances at the mountain magnificence. He too was in awe but unable to admit to anything un-tough. The adrenalin leaked from my pores.

The trip was unfair to him, a monstrous mistake for me.


I walked with Don to the edge of town and then I came home, I told Chasity.


Today. Outside. My skin tingles. Colder than expected. Temperature dropping. The air smells cold but I am warm. The air sparkles in sunlight.

There are trees, black and leafless in a small square of not-quite garden. An unknown bush dusted with snow. Earth peeping through, brittle in the winter. No green. Black and whites and shades of grey like an old time reproduction.

I walk beneath a pale sky with clouds like unbrushed hair. My short road is deserted. Houses, small and old age solid, beating out the weather. A squawk. Magpies.

When did I first name them magpies? For years I called them squawky birds then suddenly they were magpies. No-one taught me the name, information absorbed without conscious instruction. Two magpies jangle and bicker over a half eaten, looks like bologna, sandwich. A throaty judgement bursts in from behind and above. A rattling crow in a tree.

Hawk, said Rod and pointed out the window.

The world was a puzzle that didn't fit together. Earlier that morning I lay on my back on a table in the food court of the local mall and smelled stale French fry grease laced with nail polish, Chasity painting her fingernails fluorescent fuchsia to match a miniskirt over leggings and work socks tucked into Docs. Straight blonde hair and a perfect oval face, soft blue eyes, soft mouth, soft nose. Me, I was all blunt edges, brown eyes, brown hair, sharp nose, thin lips. My mind bounced back to the afternoon's composition topic. Destiny and Tess. Tess and destiny. I eyed the bones of the mall, giant girders, an industrial roof and skylights. Big bolts. Blue sky.

I was restless and bad humoured, mad about Tess. Tess of the d'Urbevilles. Required reading for grade eleven English. Half the class didn't bother, watched the movie, got it wrong. I paged my way through the book, fingers crossed Tess would live, my breath captive in my lungs. Don't exhale and Tess will live. I exhaled. I was horrified.

Let's hitch to the mountains, Don had said.

Don, friend since fourteen, not a boyfriend. Tall,

broad, anonymous face because I've seen it so many times.

Sure, I answered. I'd never been to the mountains.

Chasity flinched and wrecked a fluorescent fuchsia thumbnail and had to start again. I wasn't kidding. I was not a prankster.

I want to see the mountains, I said.

You've got an in-class essay this afternoon, said Chasity. She didn't say if you skip you're for the school gallows. She didn't say you never skip English class. She didn't say she wanted me to write the essay, get Tess out of my system, she didn't say she wanted me to set a good example. But she looked it all. What about your mum? she asked.

Way to push my buttons.

I can handle my mum.

The hawk sat on a post made of ragged and mangled wood, guarding a muddy field with nothing growing, patient machinery in a puddle of water. Closer, closer, right beside me, like a bird carved from ancient wood and I peered into its eyes. It gazed back. Knowing eyes, its wings shifted, it lifted up and circled. This hawk understood my glorious whim; it circled, higher and higher, insisted I take care, warned against my mismatched confederate. It soared into the sky.

What does a hawk symbolise? I asked.

What does a hawk symbolise? echoed Don.

I'm serious. What does it mean?

Means you've seen a hawk, said Don.

Freedom, said Rod. Some people think they're messengers from the spirit world.

What's my message? I asked.

It's telling you you've seen a hawk, said Don.

I lifted myself off the table and Don grinned, Chasity shook her head, no she shakes, no, no, no, don't do it.

Great, said Don, maybe it's time for us to get back together again.

We were never together, I said.

Aw.


I should have said no. I was desperate to see the mountains. I should have said just joking. I wanted to hitch-hike like in an old novel from the fifties or sixties. I should have said I had an exam. I could smell change. I should have gone back to school. I had never been out of the city. I should have written about Tess. I could sense the world cracking open. My blood ran wild. I thought the wildness would last forever.

I tossed my homework into the garbage and left a message on Mum's answering machine. *Opportunity to go to the mountains with a group from school. I'll be safe. Love you.*

It was a rush. We ran to Stetson Trail holding hands which meant I ran faster than normal and Don slower. I could have beat him flat out if I'd been wearing runners but I was stumbling along with my jeans tucked into my fabulous new suede boots with their pointy toes and little high heels. Black, of course. (Once Ms Chernyshevsky—all my friends called her Miss C. but I like to get it right—asked me if wearing black reflected my state of mind.)

I shouldn't have held his hand.

It was like a movie, an almost warm wind blowing in our faces and my hair streaming behind. Don suddenly looked cool with a Pearl Jam T-shirt and scraggly hair and almost beard and that weird hat he thought was cool.

I was so full of spring air and warmth it made me light, I drifted like a balloon almost into the sky, everything seemed possible. Running to the highway I was a character in fiction, I was bigger than history. There were no consequences, only life and joy. The rest of the world staggered in slow motion. This was my story. The world outside my body was a grey country where nobody smiled.

Watch this, said Don and hung out his thumb.

A blue car stopped.

No way! I couldn't believe it. I walked up to the little bullet. It was as blue as never worn, never washed, blue jeans. And it shone. I slowed down, distanced from Don. I touched the car, it was warm from the sun and, I suppose, its engine. For me it was hot with freedom. Burning up. My life was starting, right there, right then.

Holy shit, said Don and sat in the front.

I got in the car thinking if it's this easy to get a ride I could go everywhere. All over. I could always feel ecstatic. Running with Don, getting in that car was a religious experience without a God. I was full of the power and the glory, I thought I might be invincible. Don smiled and then went all serious like it wasn't cool to be happy.

Where you guys going? asked Driver Guy.

West, said Don. Right, babe? He smirked and winked at Driver Guy.

I'm Eve.

Rod.

Nice to meet you, Rod, I said. We're going to the mountains.

As am I, said Rod, formerly known as Driver Guy.

To the mountains and beyond, said Don. To the Pacific Ocean.

I just want to see the mountains, I said.

And so you will, said Rod. Stick with me and you'll see them by early afternoon.

Don looked out of the window and Rod smiled at me. I smiled back and Don's shoulders stiffened. It's like he's got eyes in the back of his head, I thought.

Still, I leaned over the seat and watched Rod drive, hands comfortable on the steering wheel he darted from lane to lane, like the car was part of his own easiness, fuelled by his body, an extra limb.

Don rearranged his anger, grinned at himself in the car's mirror, his teenage arrogance searching for my eye. When I looked away he became fascinated by the square flat roofed industrial buildings that whizzed by the window.

My wild ebbed. My skin prickled. I searched for connection, to the wind in my face, to being a girl in a million, to owning the world.

You going to see the mountains, Rod? I asked.

I'm looking to open a Natural Foods restaurant. In Bluff Falls. Just heading up to look at premises.

Don yawned, in disgust, in boredom, in regret—best guesses. Don wanted to be a roughneck in the oilfield. No training necessary, big bucks on Friday. He pushed at the door with all his body; Don lived life through enemies, antagonistic towards everyone. He was my friend, I figured I could handle him but it was hard work. He'd get pissed off and yell or storm off. He wanted to do that now. He mumbled under his breath. I assumed he was swearing at Rod.

He evened out his temper. Still edgy but unready to attack Rod. Good. I'd stepped in and scooped up an injured but triumphant Don more than once and more often, more recently. He was uneasy in the world, we were all uneasy in the world, we were seventeen, but Don wanted his initials on a carved out slice of money-making independence. Right now. He was ready. And ready to fight. Increasingly ready to fight. Bad idea, never show your hand. Fight and be judged, graded, assessed, fight once and the whole world knows who can take you. Don never understood it's tougher not to fight. He scowled a lot, like he already knew he wouldn't make true liberty.

Hawk, said Rod. Again.

Another one, said Don. Double the freedom.

This hawk didn't look me in the eye. It circled.

I've never been to the mountains, I said.

Never been to the ocean either, said Don. Babe!

He knew how to niggle, sat there like he'd been all over.

Seriously? Where are you from? asked Rod.

Bedford, I answered.

And you've never been to the mountains? Weird, said Rod. And you grew up in Bedford?

Yup.

Was it so odd? Mum didn't drive, how would we get there? We weren't holiday people.

The best part of driving to the mountains is trying to figure out the exact moment you see your first mountain, said Rod.

Don snored. He wasn't asleep. He pretend to sleep, to see nothing.

I stared out the window. I'd been laid off from McDonalds in the winter and planned to start waitressing on Saturdays just as soon as I found a job. I'd heard tips could be good. I'd save money. Me and Mum could take the bus to the mountains. Stay overnight.

I didn't see where the prairie turned into mountain. I was too concerned Don was going to anger up again at Rod. If he thought I was enjoying Rod's company he'd shift into sudden antagonism. Next it'd be fists. Outside, the world moved. I was in a glorious mountain diorama—green and grey and brown and angles—and I was focussed on Don's potential anger. All the way. By the time we reached Bluff Falls I was mind tired. Tired of being on high anger-sensing alert.

Today. Corner of the road, steady hum of cars, a street of people, giant boots and scarves and hats and mittens. Heads down against the wind's cut, heads up for smiles and greeting, nods and eye contact. I shadow play, part of the crowd, walk into the wind, eyes down, nod slight to strangers, I am an unsocial bunny breaking out of my shelter, forging small contact with unknown humans. And one, once known. It is not as easy as it looks but I have practiced in the mirror. Oh, Mr. McGregor, you won't catch me! My nod. I have practised it over the years.

I turn the corner and am swallowed by the Christmas anticipating crowd. Every step another person and another. One becomes two, two becomes a gaggle. I thread my way through packages and baskets already full from market. The air rasps with car exhaust. Not unpleasant but with the power to gag.

This morning we are going to cut, said Stephanie.

I was terrified. Nikki cut. Her arms were a lacework of scars. The year she was fifteen, the year she was declared 16, we rarely saw her arms, she tried to keep them always covered. But I knew there were ridges up and down, hardened skin ridges.

Let's cut, said Stephanie.

Nikki and Chasity were best friends the year before I met Chasity, then Nikki moved a thousand kilometres away. That summer it was me and Chasity, Tamara and Lisa.

I suppose we better get you registered at this new school, said Mum.

It was a week before the fall semester started.

What new school?

You didn't think you'd be going back to that place across the river, did you? asked Mum.

Why hadn't she told me before? I'd been dreading September and everyone pretending I didn't exist. A new school, a new start.

I doubt I'll show up first day. It's junior high. You go alone, said Mum.

Where is it? I asked.

Why don't you ask that Chasity girl?


The first day was glorious. Classes were interesting but I didn't let on and at break me and Chasity and Tamara and Lisa walked back and forwards, heads high, evil eyeing the other kids. I could live with this. It was the safest I'd ever felt at school, at least since Lucy's birthday party. I had a pile of books at home and a bunch of friends at school. I was one of the tough girls (grade seven variety). Awesomeness or what?

The second day everything turned to shit. Nikki was back.

Who's that? asked Nikki.

Eve, said Chasity.

Tamara and Lisa lurked on the sidelines.

Who's Eve?

Lives in my sister's building.

Just moved in, I added.

Those apartments are pretty small, said Nikki, staring at me like I came from another planet.

There's just me and my mum.

Everyone nodded. It wasn't unusual to be just you and your mum.

But those apartments are one-bedrooms. My dad lives there. Do you sleep in the same bed as your mum? asked Nikki.

No, I lied. She sleeps on a daybed in the living room,

I said.

I'd learned the word daybed from Destiny. She was saving up for one.

And she leaves early for work, so it's almost like I have an apartment all to myself, I added.

Cool, said Nikki.


We walked down the hallway, Tamara and Lisa together, Chasity and Nikki arm in arm, and me behind. They were singing 'I Think We're Alone Now', and I was Susan when Prince Caspian blew the horn and summoned her to fight in battle. I have come to save you, Prince Caspian! I was riding a white horse, my bow was across my body; my John Lennon T-shirt had turned into a long, battle fighting tunic and my quiver bounced against my back. The horse and I jumped bushes and fences and small buildings like they were cracks in the sidewalk.

I didn't see the four giants walking in our direction. They were seriously tough and a year older. They were grade eight we were grade seven. They had breasts, we were flat-chested; they made out with boys, the others daydreamed about it and I saved Prince Caspian. I was reworking the novel into a version where I went alone and stayed brave. I didn't need boys or princes.

Whatcha looking at, Chasity Mendelssohn? asked Deirdre the first giant. She wore her name with disappointment, call me Deedee or I'll punch you in the teeth. Everyone wanted to be called Tiffany or Destiny in 1987. Deidre was a name to be proud of. Deirdre was a name perfumed with sorrow. Deirdre was brave and principled. I should have told her.

Mendelson, what kind of dumb name is that? asked Saffron, Deirdre's lieutenant.

Us tough girls stopped and eyeballed the giants. I walked into Tamara who walked into Nikki. I stumbled into the present and moved to the edge of my group. I was taller than the rest and looked pretty fierce. I brought on my war face and tried to remember all the self-defence Mum had ever taught me. It started and ended with keys between my fingers. Right about the moment I realised I hadn't any weapons in my fighting box I noticed all the giants were staring at me. I tried to make myself taller. I stared back. I prepared to be Susan. I hadn't a clue. I needed a horse. There were no horses in this north side junior high. I held their stares. Like I was an empty bottle, I stared back and kept pulling their stares in. I was absolutely still. They stared and stared. I looked meaner and meaner. I unfocused my eyes—the way you do—and made like I was a crazy woman. I was scared shitless until I realised they were scared too. Then I realised they were waiting for the bell. I was an unknown quantity. I must never fight. I must simply be there. I figured I'd solved a riddle.

The bell rang.

Later, said Deirdre.

Later, said the other giants.

Good job, said Nikki. Intimidating.

Yeah, I said, like I was learning to speak teenager.


I have photocopied paper with pieces of women on them, said Stephanie. They're old sewing patterns. I whited out the sewing instructions and enlarged them on the school photocopier.

School? She meant university.

All morning I cut out bits of women in old fashioned sewing pattern clothes. It was weird at first but I fell into a woman cutting out rhythm that soothed and lulled. I cut on the couch, Stephanie perched on the mushrooming and broken seat of her pink armchair. We had grown into a well brokered peace. We weren't so comfortable that Stephanie was able to tell me how much she resented my being in her house and I wasn't yet at the point where I could tell her I didn't wanted to be there anyway, how close I'd come to blowing the job off, heading back to the mountains on my own. But our relationship had grown beyond veiled hostility.

It started, like many good things, with a grilled cheese sandwich. Part of the deal between Mum and Stephanie was that Stephanie fed me lunch. Mum was an excellent finagler. Problem was, Stephanie didn't cook. First day she served me cereal for lunch, second day apples, third day granola bars. Sometimes when she was opening the pre-packaged food of the day she'd lean over and frown, it made her forehead grow and I could see the hair bursting out of her scalp. Stephanie had very large follicles, I would have liked it better if she had covered her hairline with a ribbon or scarf.

Do you want me to cook lunch? I asked. I was trying to be nice. Melt the silence between us. Sometimes I dusted or ironed in the same room where she read. We ignored each other in a shared contrariness.

What would you cook? Stephanie asked.

Grilled cheese sandwiches. You've got everything. I checked.

As long as you wash your hands first, said Stephanie.

To be generous I had been cleaning toilets. She watched me lather up and rub my bubbled hands together.

She stayed at my side as I buttered bread, grated cheese, placed the first slice of bread in the pan, buttered side down and with geometric precision, then the second slice, cuddled up beside the first. She leaned back to watch as I turned on the burner and we watched together as the butter sizzled. I piled the grated cheese on each slice with cautious balance, then added the top slices of bread, buttered side out. She leaned in when I flattened the sandwiches with the kitchen spatula and flipped—a bit like a juggler on the down town square. I added a lid like lunch was a burning torch, like a kitchen magician.

Her chin was almost on my shoulder, her breath was next to my ear, she was peering at the frying pan. The final reveal. Perfect looking sandwiches in my pan, her pan. So much better than a rabbit in a hat.

We sat at her red Formica table. It's exactly the same the one Mum and I found in Value Village. Identical.

We've got the same table, I said when I first saw it, and we've got chairs to match.

Of course you have, answered Stephanie. Stephanie's table stood in a nook in the kitchen, a built-in wooden seat either side, one green, one purple. The nook bulged out over the back yard and had a huge window, which suited me. I liked to watch the yard as we ate in silence. Stephanie always centred herself on her purple bench. I sat window side of mine so I could see the yard and didn't have to see those follicles.

Yum, said Stephanie. Delicious, I mean.

Yum works, I said. I almost fell under the table in the shock of her speaking.

I love grilled cheese sandwiches. That day's were golden crisp on the outside and packed creamy tight with cheese on the inside. When I bit into my sandwich the cheese blowsed its way to the edge of the bread. I thought it would run over but it stayed in place like an overstuffed golden pillow between two slices of bread. The sandwiches were excellent. My best. I suddenly realised I needed ketchup and pulled it out of the fridge. Stephanie looked in horror.

Where did that come from, she asked.

I brought it from home in case you agreed to me making lunch.

I poured a generous pile on the side of my plate and dipped. What? I asked.

Stephanie opened her mouth but nothing came out.
Try it, I said.
Stephanie shook her head.
There's a bit over here my sandwich hasn't touched,

I said.

Stephanie shuddered.

Experiment, I said. You don't know what you're missing.

I didn't think she'd do it. She stared at my plate, and stared, and then reached across with the slightest tremble. I have never seen so little ketchup, or such a small nibble. She chewed slowly, the follicles moved in slow motion.

Mortuusequusphobia, I said. It means fear of ketchup.


I focussed on the feet. Cutting out shoes, I thought, is a reflective business. Women had worn some seriously heavy shoes over the years. I appreciated the practicality of the solid high heels and square toes, but in photocopied outline and cut-out they looked like foot albatrosses.

How much did all this cost? I asked.

Don't know. I did it at the university.

It's fifty cents a page at Staples. I saw the sign, I said.

I have a card, said Stephanie, for the photocopier. It's like a credit card only it works the machine.

Why are we cutting? I asked.

Just cut, said Stephanie. You'll see.

Yes ma'am.

Sorry. It's a surprise, that's what I meant.

We cut and cut. I began to think there was no point. I began to think there was no surprise. She was delaying, trying to figure out what we were doing.


I took the pieces of the first woman and placed them together on the floor.

It's a 1930's tea dress, said Stephanie.

The dress had a square neck and a little white collar with a bow; there were short sleeves that puffed up on top; the top bloused over the waist; the skirt came to below the knee and it was kind of ugly. The model was bigger than Mum and had short hair with curls like ridges, and clunky shoes. But I was impressed. I was proud of how the shoes looked. I had cut carefully and stayed on the line. It had taken thirteen sheets of cut up copy paper to make Pattern Woman. She was life-size. She looked magnificent. It was like a woman from history, laying on the floor.

Now we glue her on the wall, said Stephanie.

It was the best idea I'd ever heard.

We must work slowly and very carefully, said Stephanie.

By early afternoon the woman looked out at me.

Today. I stop at the bookstore. A window of titles, old Christmas stories, mostly unexplored. I step close to the plate glass and peer beyond the book cover Christmas trees and sleighs, beyond the seasonal books to the modern classics shelf, the mysteries. I see the books of my childhood. Sold and resold. I cannot go in. You're stalling, I whisper to myself, get to the market and get it over with.

By seventeen, us tough girls had disappeared down the truant-officer-demanding-attendance-at-school cracks.

Nikki was first to go. She didn't attend for the first month of grade ten.

Central Education had always been the threat when we skipped school.

If you can't supply notes covering your absences I'll have to refer this to the people at Central Education, said Miss Lucas, Vice Principal Academic for students whose names begin with O to Z, including S. I'll let this one skipped class go this time, Eve, but only because you do so well in your studies, I really don't want to have to call in Central Education, she said another time.

Central Education worked well in elementary, lost its teeth in junior high and by grade ten, when Nikki skipped four weeks in a row and they called them in, it was all warm fuzzies. Sure, it sounded serious when they arranged her formal hearing. Tamara, Lisa, Chasity and I were all a little impressed and very curious. We waited outside the Central Education building as she was appropriately sanctioned.

I'm sixteen, announced Nikki as she hit the sidewalk.

You're fifteen, said Chasity.

School attendance board and Central Education says I'm sixteen and they're going to pay me to go to college.

Without finishing high school? I was curious and reluctant to say *But you can barely read.*

Yeah, said Nikki. Edquest.

My sister went there, said Chasity. Before she had her second kid. Still wants to go back.

And they're paying you to go? I asked, desperately wanting to be paid to go to college.

Yeah. Because I can't get a job without it and my mum moved away and they say I can't live with my dad.

So, you're living alone? asked Lisa. Sweet.

We all thought it was sweet, but I was content to be one of a group of four, attend school and work at McDonalds a couple of nights a week.

Then Lisa got pregnant and moved in with Dave Enders and his mum and brother and we never saw her again. Not literally. We saw her on the bus when we were waiting on the sidewalk and we saw her on the sidewalk when we were on the bus, but we just never saw each other in the same place long enough to talk.

Finally, Tamara's part time job at Tim Horton's turned into full-time days and she disappeared from school too.

Chasity went to classes, she was studying beauty culture or Cos.

Let me do your hair, Chasity asked.

I don't want it done.

Nails then.

Once a week she painted them a different colour, always trying to foist pearly pink and blush rose on me. I insisted on black and navy. We stayed friends. Best friends. She was good at English. All that reading me and Destiny did must have worn off. We at least had that class together.

While the girls from my neighbourhood changed their lives I stayed in regular school and mostly in class. Mum didn't like homework in the house.

I send you to school so you don't have to learn that shit here, said my mother. Use your time here to do other stuff. She never explained what. Maybe she knew my book learning would amount to nothing.

I was fond of in-class essays and exams because I felt less at a disadvantage. My exam and in-class work kept me afloat academically. It was a large regional school with an International Baccalaureate program. Lucy, who invited me to her birthday party, and Zoe, who I pushed off a chair, were in IB. They weren't antagonistic but definitely unwelcoming when I nodded in the hallway. It occurred to me that I was invisible to them. Didn't bother me.

I still hung out on the edges of the street corners with Chasity closest and Tamara not too far away. We were all bottom feeders and it was good to know in the event of danger there was a group that would not necessarily provide back-up but would at least tell someone I was in danger. Maybe.

So when the letter showed up that Stephanie summer I was unworried.

My world had settled. I read. I wrote. I made lunch. I tidied and cleaned… and then I read and wrote and read some more. I bought the groceries on my way to her house, or I took time in the middle of the day to shop at Bud's IGA. It was an old fashioned grocery store that smelled of cereal and baking and a man in a white coat with a bald head fringed at the neck sliced exotic cheeses. I saw no end to the idyll.

But school intervened.


I got a letter, I said as I put the groceries away in Stephanie's kitchen. Look blue cheese and pears.

Together? Stephanie made a face. She wasn't big on having different foods touch but I was educating her.

In grilled sandwiches. With cheddar. It was in a magazine at the drug store.

Let me see the magazine.

I memorised it.

What sort of letter?

From school.

An expulsion? Stephanie sounded excited. I figured she'd never known anyone who'd been expelled.

They want me to go in and discuss next year. If I don't show up to the appointment, or contact the school to reschedule, my registration is automatically terminated.

Terminated? echoed Stephanie. Interesting choice of word. We need to prepare for this.

As long as I show up it'll be okay.

No, said Stephanie. You need a plan. You must show them you've changed.

I haven't changed.

Tell them you'll work hard, get into university. Say 'this is my year'.

Right, I said and gently squeezed the pears.

Scream at them…

I don't think that will help.

You interrupted, said Stephanie. I wasn't finished. Scream at them that you have converted…

Converted to what? This pear is perfect for sandwiches.

Interrupting again, said Stephanie. They need to know you're a new woman.

I'm seventeen.

Like when a prodigal child returns to the bosom of their family.

School is not my family, I said. And then it occurred to me that possibly it was and maybe I wanted back in.

Let's find you something new to wear, said Stephanie.

If only she'd take me shopping, I thought, as I followed Stephanie up the stairs. To a music store with band T-shirts. I could ace anything with a picture of Curt Cobain on my fronts. Little black dress and stilettos? Not so much.

I watched Stephanie rake through the closet, shifting clothes from right to left with a speed I'd never seen before.

Hey! I said. You're making creases! I had became proficient at ironing. B+. *Eve applies herself effectively and has learned the basic concepts.*

This, said Stephanie and pulled out a knitted suit in raspberry sherbet pink.

No fucking way.

Stephanie pulled out a black dress, I shook my head.

A brown crochet dress that came to the floor.

No.

Bell bottoms in purple.

You're kidding?

Yeah, said Stephanie and set them aside. For me, she said.

It continued.

A pinstripe suit. A tweed suit. Another tweed suit. A leather suit which would have been okay if the skirt hadn't come below the knee. A gauzy skirt that came to the floor. My head was dizzy from shaking.

It's like history, I said.

Isn't it? What do you think? Stephanie held up a lavender coloured suit.

Nope

Stephanie pulled out more clothes.

Maybe I should make lunch.

You have to try something on first.

I looked at the hippy relics and women's clothes in old men's fabrics and sighed. She was my boss and I was hungry. I took a pin stripe suit skirt and a white shirt and headed to the toilet. No way I was changing in front of Stephanie. No way Stephanie wanted to see me in underwear. I peeled out of my jeans and T-shirt and pulled up the skirt and struggled my arms into the shirt. The buttons took a while, I'm not used to buttons on shirts. I crossed the landing back to the room.

What? I asked. What? Don't look at me like that.

Stephanie held out the jacket.

No, I said.

Look, said Stephanie, pointing at the mirror.

I looked.

Today. I tread cautious against ice and pitfall. I enter the market. Smells of damp fabric, seasonal spices and chocolate. The air buzzes with greetings and the hearty sound of fiddle music. The building is full, there is steam and people eat and smile and drink as they shop. Everyone is dressed in holiday shopping finery, thick and bright against the cold. I look again and not everyone is wearing red but at first glance… It is Solstice.

I see food everywhere. I see Augustus, the small time market garden man. All organic, unglamorous vegetables in boxes on a low table. Generous prices, hardy rations. I buy a squash and turnip and beets, well preserved from late summer.

I smell chocolate. I see spoons dipped in chocolate, wrapped in cling film, tied with ribbon, labelled stocking stuffers; waste of money Mum would have said. The line for chocolate spoons loops into my column of slow moving foot traffic. A cake stand of truffles, decorated in red and green, sugar sickly sweet. I carry on, my mother's daughter, bury myself in the holiday confident crowd, greetings, smiles, warm spice in my nose. The smiling woman selling cinnamon buns catches my eye. She knows me, she knows my weakness. I buy a box. We trade smiles.

I see her in the crowd. I stand in place. A man with a bunch of huge and silver painted tree branches in a red plant pot turns and spikes me, thorns and twigs catch in my hat. We smile, me and the man.

I duck behind a square brick column. My heart races. I breathe, I avoid eye contact, burrow back into the crowd, collar up, chin down. I sense her scanning the crowd. She is early, I will be punctual.

I showed up for my interview in a pin stripe miniskirt, white shirt, high top runners and a jean jacket. I'd never worn a skirt before and felt semi-naked. No one at school ever saw my legs. I skipped Phys. Ed. or got sidelined for not wearing gym clothes. It was like a perpetual dare to never be seen without jeans. Even in summer I only wore cut offs at home and hanging out.

I filled out a pre-registration form and my class choices.

Truancy, said Miss Lucas, the Vice Principal for students whose last names begin with letters between O and Z, including S. I waited for her to say more. She didn't. I stared at her bleak and weighty office, giant metal furniture and science books in even rows. Were science books always made the same size to fit together neatly? Nature grew on her window sill, ill at ease and doomed, a glass bowl of lettuce and a jar of bean sprouts. She had a Newton's cradle that I itched to touch, and a model of the universe. And you want to register in academic courses? said Miss Lucas.

Yes, I said, though I wasn't sure it was a question. My right foot was propped on my longboard. I started to move it, back and forward. Silent, soothing.

Don't, said Miss Lucas. If you ride that in here I'll have to confiscate it. You can't register in academic courses if you didn't complete grade eleven. Academic prerequisites. You missed the exams.

Can I write them now?

No.

Why not?

It would mock our system. Someone writing exams when they hadn't attended the classes.

I didn't miss that many.

I have your attendance report in front of me.

Trapped.

I wore a dress and everything, I said. Forcing both feet to stay on the floor.

Skirt, Miss Sullivan.

Suit skirt. Pinstripe.

Is that a fact?

Like bankers wear.

Are you bound and determined to have the last word, Miss Sullivan?

Yes.

Miss Lucas stared at all the information written about me. Stephanie had suggested I offer to do a trial period.

Can't I do a trial?

A trial?

A trial. Not that sort. You know…

No, I don't.

Show you I can do the work, a trial period.

Can you do a trial? I am sure you could do a trial period, yes. May you? Absolutely not. If I allowed you and it didn't work out, then what? It would be too late to register in the other classes.

Is there anything I can do to make it up?

Make it up? This is not a playground squabble over a skipping rope, Miss Sullivan.

She knew! She didn't know. Her eyes weren't telling me. I had been a kid. A little kid. It was ancient history.


I was a good skipper when I was a little kid.

'Down to Mississippi, if you miss a beat you're out.'

I even had a skipping rope.

'Cinderella dressed in yella

'Went upstairs to kiss her fella…'

It wasn't really a skipping rope, not a string rope with shiny painted handles.

'Larry and Lucy

'Sitting in a tree…'

My skip rope was a linen line. A plastic rope, long and perfect for communal games of skipping. One girl at each end turning and the rest jumping in and out chanting and doing as expected.

'I'd like coffee
'I'd like tea
'I'd like Lucy
'To skip with me.'

And count how many times you could skip the rope with two of you.

By the time I found the skipping rope I already knew I pissed people off. I couldn't explain but I knew, no... I sensed that I had to work harder to do things with friends.

Can I play? I had to ask. In the playground. No-one came up and invited me except, occasionally, Lucy. I had to force myself onto groups of girls.

Sorry, we need even teams, said Amelia. Lucy looked at me with big eyes. I willed her to say she wouldn't play either. She didn't. I believed Amelia but it happened again.

Sorry, we've started.
Don't want an uneven number.
Too late.
Sorry
No.
No!

I found the skipping rope behind the apartment building. It was muddy and frayed at one end. The frayed end was meant to go into a pulley so you could move washing along a line without walking from one spot to another. I understood its value immediately. I found an elderly pair of kitchen shears in the junk draw and snipped the ends. Mum was at work so I was able to wash it in the bath tub.

What's all this mud in the bath tub? asked Mum.

No idea.

Don't lie to me! You start the mac an' cheese. I need a bath. Look at this mess. I don't like to think about what you get up to when I'm not here. It's filthy, disgusting, if I can't trust you, Eve…

I boiled the water and searched for wieners in the fridge.

Next day at school Lucy and I started a jump rope game and soon it was all the rage. Jump rope everywhere. Ours was most popular, people thought it was Lucy's.


When I got to the playground, the game had started. When there was a lull I'd jump in between the rope.

'Teddy Bear Teddy Bear

'Turn around

'Teddy Bear Teddy Bear

'Touch the ground.'

Teddy Bear was my favourite. I jumped up high and touched the sky.

Who said you could play? asked Amelia.

I opened my mouth to tell her it was my rope.

I did, said Lucy.

I looked at Lucy and no words came out. I rolled my eyes and kept on playing. Next day I did the same and everyone assumed Lucy had invited me.

Then Max showed up. Short for Maxine, new to the school.

Who said you could play? asked Max. What confidence, first week at school and already asking. Lucy said nothing.

It's my rope.

Let's play freeze tag! said Max. Not it!

The enders pulled the rope and tripped me. Then they let go. Tossed the ends on the ground, lifeless head and tail, beginning to fray. Like the empty skin of a snake.

I picked my rope up by its snake tail and wound. Lucy stared at me. Like I was stupid.

You shouldn't have said that, said Lucy.

It is my rope, I said.
You coming? yelled Max. Lucy!
Lucy turned and I grabbed her arm.
Let me go, said Lucy.
I want to play.
You can't.
You'd rather play with them?
Yes.
Not with me?
Never.
I want to play too. I shook her arm.
Don't do that, said Lucy. Stop! You lied!
I didn't.

You said your mum worked at the university. She's nothing but a cleaner! My Mum told me so.

When I slapped her the whole playground stopped playing. It was like everyone saw. Lucy looked like she was going to cry.

The entire school sided with Lucy. Little girls clustered around her whenever I was close, providing a wall of small girl flesh to ensure I didn't attack. The teachers *tsk-tsked* and the crossing guard pushed his annoying Stop sign at me, almost touching my face.

You wait, he said. His eyes followed me all the way to the other side of the road. Nasty, nasty, nasty, he mumbled under his breath.

Fuck you, I said when I got to the other side. I already had a note in my pocket. A summons for Mum to meet with the principal and myself before school the next day.


… and then she slapped Lucy, said the principal.

The principal and my mother looked at me.

That Lucy whose birthday party you went to? asked my mother.

I nodded and my mother sniffed.

What do you think you should do to make this right? asked the principal.

I could write a letter, apologising, I said.

I hardly think so, said the principal.

Isn't that your job to figure out a punishment? said Mum. Aren't you getting paid for that stuff? She's ten. Why are you asking her?

The principal was taken aback.

What's wrong with a letter, anyways? asked Mum. I think it's a lovely idea.

After we left the office I walked with Mum to the school doors and she left for work. I was meant to go to my classroom but wanted to postpone the moment.

Hey, said Mum, taking the revolving doors round one more time and stopping in front of me. I looked up, expecting trouble.

She's a little snot, that Lucy. Next time make sure you don't get caught.

I stood alone. There wouldn't be a next time, not with Lucy. And try as I could, I couldn't stop getting caught.


Look Miss Lucas, I said, we both know that I don't need to go to class for those courses. I could write the exams now. I need to be in the academic classes, I said and waited to be thrown out of the office. Unceremoniously. On my tail bone.

And the Vice Principal for students from O to Z, including those whose names began with S, peered at me for a long and uncomfortable moment. Time stretched. It was like playing chicken without a train.

Did you read anything last week, this summer?

Yes, I answered.

Tell me. Titles.

*The Stone Angel*, *The Yellow Wallpaper*, and some poetry.

What sort of poetry?

Long ones.

This is not the time to be flippant, Miss Sullivan.

Her eyes scorched my skin.

T.S. Eliot, Anne Waldeman, Ntozake Shange, I said.

Okay, Miss Sullivan. Here's paper and pencil and exam booklet. Follow me.

Miss Lucas took me to a small room off the office where people who had missed exams wrote to get caught-up and people with in-school suspensions (none today because it was summer) did their school work.

Read the extract, answer the question, said Miss Lucas. If it's any good we'll talk trial period.

It was the first part of the grade twelve final exam paper.

*Read the extract from the short story, 'The Yellow Wallpaper', by Charlotte Perkins Gilman, and respond to the following question:*

*In the extract the author is trapped in a bedroom and trapped in her mind. Using the extract as a starting point write about societal expectations and how they can compromise one. Respond in prose—essay form or fiction, but not poetry.*

I sat in the small room and stared at the walls.

Then I read the extract and started to write:

*'My mother and I were poor milkmaids…'*

Today.

She was my friend. Lucy was my friend until she wasn't. Chasity was my friend until she stopped. Just like that. Done.

She preens. Unfair. Not preens. She is dressed in fondant colours. A beige woolness with hints of pink. She stands tall and poised. Shorter than me but looks taller with her take-on-the-world assurance. I am bold and fearless but lack creamy confidence. I breathe deep. I prepare. How many hours awake and still not ready?

Chasity heads for the coffee area. A loft of tables where shoppers eat lunch and watch the crowd, dressed in Saturday morning Christmas run up finery. I have never been a celebrator. We're not the celebrating sort, said Mum. We ate pizza—good pizza—for Christmas dinner. Once she cooked chicken.

Tonight I will make a feast for Solstice. Vinegar and Oils. Lime balsamic, please.

Her face. We made an appointment, it is of consequence, more mine than hers. Run, run, whispers another Eve, run to the hills. No!

Chasity climbs the stairs to the sitting loft, heels on her boots clack clack on the steps. Mug in one hand, plate in the other. A perky muffin balances precarious on the bobbing plate.

I am on the Dawn Treader heading into the wind. Or against the wind or beside the wind. I know little of ships. But balance is central to ships, if unbalanced they surely sink. I have seen headlines of over crowded unbalanced ferries sinking. It takes care and balance and endless shifts of thought, of action, of hopes, of interaction, of food, of light, of day, of sleep, endless interactions to keep afloat. If she claws her way in with outrageous apology and wild ideas I might capsize. I climb the stairs to the loft.

We sit across the table from each other and I smell the coffee with its milk which offends and alters the spice of the bean. The muffin, still on its plate, has an orange brown sheen, must be carrot, I think, and there are zesty fragrances. And in the background damp wool and cinnamon. A well used notebook and books with papers stuck in and falling out on the table beside the muffin. Mollifying me? I read titles unfamiliar and authors all unknown, *Monkey Beach*, *Annie John*, *The Snow Line*. I am curious.

The woman's voice in contemporary literature, says Chasity.

I know none of them. My reading is dusty and belongs in the past. I memorise the titles.

We look at each other. She places her hand on mine. I look at her flesh, a familiar touch through the years, the touch of childhood, the touch of one friend pulling the other into trouble, out of trouble, one way or another. I am not ready for conversation. She leaves her hand on mine. It has pearly pink nails. Mesmerising. Delicate shaped. She smells of summer flowers, lavender, no lilacs. I think of old women sewing samplers, Aa, Bb, Cc, flowers on the border, outdated smell. Up close, her coat is worn, her face is somehow pink, still pink, always was pink, as a child and teen. Her hand, soft on mine, fights to communicate. I am here to apologise says the hand. I want to be your friend, says the hand.

*Mexican Gothic*, *The Hero's Walk*.

Homework, says Chasity.

I want to apologise, says Chasity.

I should have believed you, says Chasity.

Yes, I answer. You should have believed me.

Will you accept my apology?

Is that ink on your finger? I ask.

Yes.

The world around us sparks with winter celebration.

Will you accept my apology?

You have books, I said.

For school.

My apology?

Yes, I answered. Air swells inside me, the pleasure of misjudgement rectified. My heart bounces. I smile.

# The Cleaning Women's Mafia

# Hazel

I don't pretend to be easy humoured, but I am fair, practical, down to earth.

I am the woman I carry on the surface of my skin, no more. This husk bores down to my root, no cloak and no fancy charade. An ugly woman on bad days and not much to look at on good. My face a mess of bulges—forehead, cheeks, chin and nose, spreading at ugly will in all directions—fenced in by hanging skin as wrinkled as overused sheets. My lips a moving line, darting down and out but rarely up. What's there to smile about?

I know what they call me, I know they gossip behind my back. Cleaning Woman's Mafia. Guess that makes me the Don, or maybe the Donna. Maybe I'm the godmother without the god or mother bits.

I expect hard work and dedication. Floors that gleam and windows sparkling like cut crystal, Bedford University at the top of the Premier League in the academic cleaning trials. No time for the lazy. Makes my skin crawl, those who won't get down on hands and knees to polish a floor or skitter along with a cloth on a broom, using a squeegee on windows. Slack workers. I'll tell them once, use vinegar and water for the windows. And I tell them twice—if there's a hint of promise—but I tell no one three times.

And whatever anyone says, I don't play favourites. Those who work hard and clean with skill, those I treat fair and with respect. The rest quit or transfer out. There's no inner circle. There's those who survive and those who die trying.

# Ursula

Hazel saved me. I was so green when I started the job. And excited. Union job, decent wage, some healthcare. I thought I'd got it made.

'First thing you've got to know,' said Hazel, 'is they treat you like shit.'

Everyone had been so nice from job application to uniform to orientation. I looked at her close, thought maybe she was one of those bossy complaining woman.

'Not shit like kicking you when you're down, shit like not seeing you.'

'Right.' I was already confused.

'It's your first day so I'm not going to give you too much to think about. Two things. And one of them's a question.'

I was standing to attention. Two things. I had to get this right.

'First is class change.'

'Class change,' I repeated.

'There's a buzzer. Right through the building. A cleaner can get killed during class change, if she's not careful.'

She had to be exaggerating but I was curious.

'Ten minutes to the hour, Monday, Wednesday, and Friday, because classes are fifty minutes long. On Tuesday and Thursday, classes are eighty minutes, starting at 8.00 a.m. and with a ten minute break in between. So the class change is 9.20, then 10.50. You do the math.'

'Should I be writing this down?'

'If you must. Be aware of the time—constantly. If you're on your hands and knees when class change happens you're a goner. Fifty thousand students plus are registered in this university and all of them leave one class and race to the next at the same time. They fill these halls and they are biologically programmed not to see cleaners. They'll knock your bucket over, they'll knock you over, if you're flat on the ground they'll trample you. And not a malicious bone in their bodies. If they're wandering down the hallways with nowhere to be and they see you, some of them will say good morning, smile, even—on very rare occasions—ask how you are. But class change, best place to be is flattened against the wall, bucket between your legs, mop straight up. Go on try it.'

I shifted my bucket and leaned against the wall, hanging on to my mop.

'Not bad,' said Hazel. 'You've got the makings of a good cleaner. Other thing, do you read?'

'Read?' I thought it must be a trick question. I was still flattened against the wall with my pail between my legs and clutching my mop. I thought hard, what else could read mean?

'You know, books.'

'I can read.'

'I know you can read. How could you fill out your application if you couldn't? But do you read? That's what I'm asking and you don't need to answer. I can see you don't, not really. Recipes? Magazines at the grocery check-out?'

I nodded.

And Hazel paused. For me to think about my magazine buying?

# Hilda

I thought she was an angel.

Never imagined I'd be hired, not a job like this. I don't expect much. Bad posture, poor complexion, over fifty, body like a sack of potatoes and clueless with clothes. I was used to being overlooked, not getting the job, not getting the apartment, not finishing school, never having a boyfriend. Then I got the job.

'I want her,' said Hazel, 'I want Hilda. On my crew.' That's what they told me. When I signed the contract. 'Head cleaner picked you, insisted, don't let her down.'

She was a wonderful boss, Hazel. Treated people fair, for the most part. Authoritarian when it came to literature and cleaning but always fair. Of course, there were always critics. Came with the territory, doing your best for people, caring. I believe she meant it. Every last ounce of her was wonderful. Authentic.

# Janet

I saw right through her, all the way to the other side, and I was unwilling to be her acolyte. But I wanted in. Her team were professional, proud of their work, and they had an inner glow. I wanted that glow. I knew her game, she chose those with nothing to lose, no ambition, no expectation and she moulded them into something more, something quiet and colossal at the same time, like a daring landscape. I wanted in.

I watched and evolved. Developed a stoop, a tic in the eye, the right eye, deliberate, walleyed, ticking over in random directions. It was resurrected from childhood. I'd developed it in school to irritate teachers once staring them down no longer worked. It was my party piece.

'I want Janet on my team,' she said.

I didn't smile, I didn't light up, I squinted upwards from my curved back and fluttered the eyeball this way and that and nodded. I was in, part of the inner circle. I would get that inward glow.

# Talking about books

'It seems to me,' said Hazel, 'that an increasing number of novels start with someone in bed.'

'I can't say I've noticed,' said Janet.

'Look closer,' said Hazel. 'Of course, I'm not talking about sentimental literature.'

'I suppose it makes them more vulnerable,' said Hilda. 'I think we all appreciate vulnerability in others. It bolsters our tolerance for the protagonist.'

'Bolsters our tolerance,' said Janet. 'I like that.'

'Instant sympathy,' said Ursula.

'Maybe it's just me.' said Hazel, 'but it's like it's there every time I open a book.'

'Unless of course the protagonist is a cockroach or a former cockroach. In those situations I think I'm expecting a certain cleverness to engage me,' said Hilda.

'You've noticed it too,' said Hazel.

'*Saturday*, *The Metamorphosis*, *Landing*, *Room*,' said Hilda.

'We appreciate their vulnerability, share it,' says Hazel.

'It's an opening deceit. An attempt to rein us in,' said Janet.

'I think,' said Hazel, 'that it's effective. If I were a student I'd write about it. I'd read all these books that have characters waking up in beds in the opening pages and I'd imagine what they'd be like if they weren't in bed. How would the story change? What is the importance of what's happening in those first pages?'

# Hazel

I cracked open a spine and it all spilled out, the ideas, the people, the places, truths, lies, arguments. The pleasure and power in understanding, a greater authority, a shining understanding of these locked away ideas, buried in bookcases that were no longer dusty because I was a good cleaner and my team were good cleaners. I ensured everything sparkled. I was worth my pay cheque, I was in the union, I was on fire, I was unstoppable, I was a reading machine, I was ahead of myself, I was in foreign territory, I was on rocky ground, I was a fish out of water.

# Ursula

'It's my job,' said Hazel, 'to make you into a reader. A real reader. It's the only thing that makes this job bearable. You'll thank me for it.'

A week into the job Hazel started me with *The Fire-Dwellers*.

'Looks like a romance,' I said.

'It is and it isn't. Read it and then we'll talk about it.'

I was confused. It was like she was giving me homework. I was standing there in the hall, end of my first week, nimble, knowing I'd impressed Hazel with the speed I could dodge the class change stampede. And she was giving me a book.

'At home, do I read it at home?'

'Never,' said Hazel, which was a good job because Frank would have only ridiculed me if I'd read at home. Jealous, I suppose. He wasn't much of a reader, lacked patience and vocabulary. 'This book is work, the most pleasurable work you'll ever have. But exacting. Always think about what you're reading. And read it here. On break. As you get familiar, you'll push the break a little at each end. Find an empty office and read there.'

'There's empty offices?'

'Offices where the occupants are out. In class. In libraries. Go in ostensibly to clean, then sit down and read. Have the door closed and an ear ready, close the book and jump into cleaning mode as soon as someone puts their hand on the door handle, but read. And if you get caught reading say, I am so sorry, it was my break time and I couldn't make it all the way to the coffee room and back, not with a sit down in the middle, so I just thought I'd read here. I am sorry. And they'll be so shocked you're reading a real book they'll smile and think what an enlightened place this is, cleaning ladies that read literature.'

And Hazel was right. When I got so deep in a book that I was walking its pages, mixing with the characters and didn't notice the door open… when that someone came in, I jumped and apologised, and they gave me these benevolent smiles and indulged my reading like I was an urchin child acting with impeccable manners.

I asked her once how she got started. Reading.

'Accident really, I was in an office and it was break time and I knew I'd never make it to the cleaners' lounge and back with time for a sit down. So, I sat in a chair and there was a book on the table. Short Stories. *Lives of Girls and Women* it was called. That's me, I thought. I was a girl, now I'm a woman. And I looked inside. I wasn't expecting anything. Well. I was, I was expecting crap. But it was like stepping into a parallel universe that gave me permission to think about all these things I hadn't known I wanted to think about. It gave my world colour and dimension. Sounds phoney but it's true. I became a bigger person.'

I wanted to joke with her. Say that was the chocolate biscuits. But I couldn't because she was right.

# Janet

I resented the books, at first. I didn't want to read. I'd got this far in life without it.

'What are you reading?' asked Hazel.

'Haven't decided,' I'd say.

'You're a cleaner in a university,' she'd say. 'Be literate.'

Not likely, I thought. You're not the boss of my mind and I'd drop the overalls to show a shadow of my real self, a tad straighter, more presentable.

'What are you reading?' asked Hazel.

I'd carry books around to deflect, a heavy hardback under my arm so she'd definitely notice.

'What you reading there?' she'd ask.

I wouldn't even know the name. I flashed the book at her and she'd read.

'How is it?' she'd ask.

'I haven't started yet.'

'Read something,' she'd say. 'And don't haul them out of the office.'

All the rules I didn't know.

'Read something. What are you reading?'

I didn't want to but I capitulated. I was on Hazel's team. She wasn't my boss but I was on the team, not part of it. Not yet.

'*Rumblefish*.' There was a picture of Mickey Rourke on the cover and I liked Mickey Rourke. I liked his voice. I read the book.

'Young Adult,' said Hazel.

'It's special,' I said.

'What's so special about it?'

A challenge, I thought. The way he looks out from the cover, I thought, the person he was in the movie, *Diner*.

'I like how he lives on his own terms,' I said,

'Motorcycle Boy, outside society. You start to think he's a god and then you realise he never had a chance.'

Hazel sniffed in a different sort of way.

# Hilda

I became a reader. At my age. I flourished.

But first… Hazel. My gratitude turned into respect, into idolisation, into something closing in on obsession. She was my god. I'd walk down an unknown street, pause look around and think why am I here. Is this some strange blackout illness where I forget what I'm doing and come to in another place? A seizure? Sleepwalking? And then I'd see Hazel. Up ahead. I'd freeze. What if she sees me? What am I doing? Is there something wrong with me? I'd stand absolutely still. I'd turn. I'd go home. I'd sit, shaking or staring into space, scared to breathe, to eat or drink. A near miss. Another near miss. I grew the habit of heading straight home after work, I'd shut the door, stay inside, no temptation.

The reading got me. I'd wanted to please, to please Hazel.

# More Talking About Books

'What Shakespeare are you reading in Miranda E.'s room?' asked Hazel.

'I'm re-reading *Romeo and Juliet*,' said Ursula. 'You need to look at the schedule, get me re-assigned to the modern lit. hallway, I'm always getting the Shakespeareans. It's like someone's got it in for me. I wouldn't mind a little mid-century beatnik. A few less metaphors and similes. Or maybe some Victorian romance.'

'I'm in Shakespeare too. *King Lear*,' said Janet.

'Is that the one with the eyes?' asked Hilda.

'It is,' said Hazel.

'Don't tell me, you'll spoil the ending for me, let me read it myself.'

'I don't like the eyes in that one, not at all,' said Hilda.

'It's not about eyes,' said Hazel.

'It is. The eyes are buried all the way to the core. Only the blind man sees. It's a brutal world, they're a symbol of the brutality, it's about chaos.'

'Stop her,' said Janet.

'Me, I'm back to Haruki Mirakami,' said Hazel.

'Seriously? Not the one with the bird?' asked Hilda.

'A bit too post modern for me,' said Ursula.

'All that desire,' said Janet.

'You know, I read the first sixty or seventy pages and just couldn't get any further, but it haunted me. Loss and desire. That young man searching for his cat. And you just know there's something going on with his wife.'

'Not like you to give up on a book,' said Janet.

'I didn't. I took a rest. And when I went back to it—now this is interesting so listen up—I still remembered the details from those first pages. Every little bit. And there was me on the edge of my seat, worried he was going to get up to something inappropriate with the young neighbour and suddenly he's meeting this old guy from the Second World War and I'm learning stuff about Japan I never knew and then he's down a well and it's just riveting.'

'I'm re-reading *Ulysses*,' said Janet.

'*King Lear* and *Ulysses*?' said Ursula.

'After all you went through the first time?' asked Hilda.

'Others don't do it for me, not in the same way. Well you all know I really enjoyed the *Odyssey* and the first time I opened *Ulysses* I had a hunch. I thought to myself this is the same story. I did.'

'You just knew that because you read the back cover,' said Ursula.

'Or analysis,' said Hazel.

'Why would I want to read the analysis before the book? I wanted to let his words sink in, you know. He does a very good job with all the little things. The details. It's like you're there. Sometimes, well I can just smell the insides of that book world. I didn't read a word of commentary, not even a review, until after I finished. And I just thought, to do it justice, this time I'd read it with the *Odyssey* lingering in the back of my mind, so to speak. And I'm taking notes.'

# Not Talking About Books

'I was languishing, ladies,' said Hazel. 'Only word for it. I'd got a nice pot of Earl Grey on the desk, feet up, plate of cookies. I just found them there. On the desk. Homemade by Frederica.'

'Frederica,' said Ursula, 'she makes good baking.'

'Her cookies are legendary,' said Janet.

'Legendary,' said Ursula. 'Every time she sees me she gives me a little bag of cookies and at Christmas time, when she gives me the Big Tip, cookies too.'

The women all smile at the words Big Tip. Each smile a silent thank you. Hazel established the system of Big Tips at Christmas several years ago. There are also

Big Tips at the end of every semester and baked goods and small treats throughout the academic year. Hazel developed the system slowly and without malice or greed.

'So there I was, feet up,' said Hazel, 'enjoying my break. The break I'm entitled to. The break that it says I'm entitled to in the contract.'

'The contract,' said Hilda holding up her tea cup.

'The contract!' They all drank.

The tea cups were grand. The saucers black and white stripes with gold scrolling and in the centre pink and blue roses, the cups were plain white on the outside but inside the same black and white and gold and roses. Hazel kept them in her locker and only pulled them out on special occasions. The signing of a new contract, when they'd hunker down in an unused office or classroom, was always a fancy cup and saucer occasion.

'And in comes Lois, Frederica's replacement,' said Hazel.

'I'll miss Frederica,' said Hilda.

'Won't we all, said Janet. 'The cookies, the cookies.'

'Anyways,' said Hazel, 'she comes in, this Lois and I say 'I am so sorry', you know, cowering a touch, making myself look smaller than I am. 'My break is so short I don't have time to make it to the cleaner's lounge. And Frederica always said be my guest.' 'No worries', said Lois—I think she might be Australian, said it with an accent. Did no worries mean I could stay? Keep having tea there. I figured it did. I swooped in. 'I cleared it with the head of janitorial,' I said, 'using an office for my break if I was stranded here. Or any of my cleaners.' 'Please,' said Lois, 'make yourself welcome."

'Lovely,' said Hilda.

'So, I had another cookie.'

'And why shouldn't you?' said Janet. 'If there's cookies on the desk, why not assume they're for us?'

'I figured a little going away present from Frederica since she knows I'm going to have to search out another empty space for the next tea break.'

Hilda, leaned in close and whispered, eyes checking this way and that, over both shoulders and under the table if you'd have let her. 'Did you ask her—the new one—about the Big Tips?'

Ursula and Janet leaned in too.

'No, I didn't ask her about the Big Tips, I don't ask anyone about the Big Tips. I tell them. And I'll tell this Lois at a later date. She needs to get used to us first and then she needs to get a little curious and then she needs to ask if there's something she can do for us—given how supportive we are—and then I'll casually mention that some people see fit to give us Big Tips on auspicious occasions. But it's not necessary, I'll say, it makes no different. It's just that some people are generous and like to treat us. Other people just can't afford it. I expect when she broaches the subject and I explain that she'll actually think it's her idea.'

'Excellent,' said Hilda.

'Copy for everyone. The contract Lois signed saying we can all take tea in her office. I think that's the entire English department sewn up. We can have our breaks wherever we are when the time comes. What's theirs is ours and what's ours is theirs.'

'Lovely bunch of young women in the English department this year,' said Janet. 'Pity they're always leaving after a year or two.'

'But more come,' said Ursula.

'Means your work with the contracts is never done,' said Janet.

'True,' said Hazel.

'So generous of you,' said Janet.

'Right, said Hazel. 'So, how is everyone? Read anything interesting lately?'

# Ursula

I was different from the others in that I had Frank. No kids and no idea why. Never stopped trying, just time caught up with us. Now it's long gone, the opportunity.

Work was work and Frank was home. I'd close the door when I got home. No books, no work, just Frank and me and a few magazines with quizzes and recipes. Gardening for Frank in summer, work and snow clearing in winter. A car held together with wishes and string. We'd watch television, sometimes go to a movie on a Friday, or a meal out on weekends. My life. Separate from books, separate from theirs. Hazel had her kid and Janet had her looks which she cultivated, and the men she hooked in with them though nothing ever stuck. Less men now she's older. Doesn't realise she's fading, thinks she's fighting it tooth and nail, but she isn't—some days she looks no different under the coveralls than on top. And Hilda. Lovely woman. Keeps herself to herself. Says little. A widow someone said once. I've heard divorced too. Lives in a tiny house I heard.

# Janet

The reading got me. It dragged me in kicking and screaming. In the evening I'd stay in with a book. Don't take it home with you, said Hazel, but I couldn't stop myself. It was an addiction. I should have listened. You don't want to have a nose in your book all the time, she said, like she was giving me permission to still be myself when I wasn't working. You'll get round shouldered, she said. She knew where my unshelled centre was, she aimed for that inner vulnerability.

The reading leaked out, an all-over mess. Sometimes I was reading three or four books at once. I'd get so filled up with joy and wonder that I'd have to put the book down, but then I wasn't reading so I'd pick up another. I was terrified they'd bleed together. I made lists. Lists of each book I finished and when. I hopped from one world to the next. It was wonderful, I had one book by my bed and another in the kitchen; I put one down to pick up another. I was trapped at home with the books—old friends went dancing, to movies, men from my past asked me out for drinks, but I stayed home. Hazel knew. You have to stop taking them home, she'd say. I will, I said; I can't, I thought. Stop altogether, she said, or ease off gently… your choice. I ignored her, kept on reading at home. I assumed she was worried I'd out read her. I didn't care what she thought, I had my inner light.

I couldn't let the others know I was unravelling at the reading edge. So I kept up the charade of the glam me, but my heart was absent. I'd smile through lipstick and heels and low cut necklines but all I cared about was the books.

# Hilda

It was like I had friends. All of a sudden. Me, Hilda, with friends. Tea, cookies, bookish conversation, who's reading what, talking about stories, polite inquiries into others' lives. Asking after Frank—Ursula was quick to update us, he's set out the tomatoes, working overtime, his hours are cut back, anyone want some zucchinis? the crop this year was enormous. Asking after Eve—Hazel always reticent but proud, she's doing well at school, we moved to a bigger place, she's growing and needs more space, she's changed schools, so many friends. Asking Janet about her social life—I went for a drink, I stayed in, I passed on a movie, I spent Saturday shopping.

## Talking About Books Again

'Who was your first?' asked Janet.

'I beg your pardon?' said Ursula.

'For me it was *Rumblefish*.'

'Young adult,' said Hazel.

'Okay, then it was *The Great Gatsby*, first adult! I picked it up all casual. Never expected to like it. It wasn't about a famous singer or rock group, it wasn't a romance, not like I would want a romance to be anyway, but it had me from the beginning. Unfair. It made me think. It made me think about being a cleaner and getting to read these books and it made me wonder about what life would be like without the cleaning bit. No empathy though. I was still outside the pages, know what I mean?'

'If we're talking novels, I suppose it was *On the Road*,' said Hazel. 'It was the energy, all these adventures happening one on top of another. It was his, he owned those pages, they were his life but he gave those words to me in such a way that that life became mine. He's got the language, Kerouac has.'

'Had,' said Janet.

'Uses his words like they're musical instruments.'

'Did you want to marry him?' asked Ursula.

'No, I wanted to meet him as a cleaner on one of his busses or in a motel and have a fling in the back seat or a broom closet or maybe in the fancy honeymoon suite. But I didn't want a man like that. I wanted a generous helping of his energy and to leave the rest. Let it simmer away and change my life. I think he would have wanted to be just like us.'

'Jack Kerouac? Like us?' asked Janet.

'Not giving in to societal expectations… yearning for the life of the common man. He'd approve of us, enjoying the stories, snitching the stories, reading them all cavalier on coffee breaks and in other people's offices, chewing on their cookies. We're no different from Neil Cassidy as brakeman.'

''Cept he wrote too,' said Hilda.

'They should warn us when we start this job,' said Janet. 'That there are books and once we open those books we'll be done for.

'Mine was *As I Lay Dying*,' said Hilda. 'All those voices, I couldn't keep track, not at first, but I was there, right there, at the heart of it. These were my people, I thought. And this can't be university, I thought that too. It was sad and amazing and it was life and death and it was like I was gaining entry to something, to life I suppose, a secret kingdom…'

'Right,' said Janet. 'How about you, Ursula?'

'*Brideshead Revisited.*'

'What about *The Fire Dwellers*?' said Hazel.

'I thought we were talking male novelists,' said Ursula.

'I think you misinterpreted the question,' said Janet.

'*The Fire Dwellers* was unexpected. He wasn't a pilot or a veterinarian or a doctor and she wasn't a nurse or an actor, they were real, flesh and blood, and thinking. I liked how her body and mind reacted to the air around her. How her body reacted to the furniture in her house, to her kids. I tried to talk to Frank about it, but he didn't get it.'

'I get it,' said Hilda.

'We all do,' said Hazel.

# Janet

I remember the day she brought the profs into the Big Tips club. She was magnificent, that day. A goddess among cleaners.

It had been a joke up to then. Or a dream. Something beyond our grasp.

'You need to be careful,' I said. 'We all need to be careful.'

'Congratulate her,' Hilda said, 'don't caution her.'

'The money's welcome,' said Ursula.

'I never asked them,' said Hazel.

'She knows what she'd doing,' said Hilda

'Not what I heard,' I said, soft, swallowing my fear.

'What did you hear?' asked Ursula. Her head like a turtle's, propped on top a fuchsia velour leisure suit.

'Somebody's gossiping?' said Hazel.

'I heard that you had cajoled your way into their hearts with stories of penury,' I said, joking, smiling.

'Never,' said Hazel.

'Hazel's good with people,' said Hilda.

'Tell us again, how they offered the tips,' asked Ursula.

'You don't want to hear it again,' said Hazel.

'We do,' said Ursula.

'We do,' said Hilda.

'I'm all comfortable,' I said, but I wasn't. I wriggled into my skin, trying to get it to fit. My outdoor skin. I was having a quick coffee before going home, the others were all working late shift, just about to start. I thought I was elegant when I peeled off my work clothes, like a creature from a different world, but now my dress was a little too short at the bottom and a little too low at the front.

'I was sitting having coffee,' said Hazel. 'I don't normally go for coffee but Helen—young adult, nothing to get your teeth into but at least you can get to the end of a book in a week—she's been encouraging me to check out these little tins of instant. I was trying an international orange cappuccino.'

'Mmm, Hazelnut,' said Ursula.

'Too many calories,' I said.

'What's that meant to mean?' Ursula asked.

'Velour hides a lot of sins,' I said, mean without meaning it. Out before I could edit it back.

'Velour,' said Ursula, 'is practical and fashionable.'

'I wish I could get away with velour,' Hilda said.

'Some of us,' said Ursula looking right at me, 'could do with a little more velour in their lives.'

'Is there a problem with how I dress?' I asked.

'It's the transformation I love,' said Hilda. 'When you take off your overalls and there's all this sex underneath.'

'You're not helping, Hilda.' said Hazel.

But she was. I turned towards her, like a sunflower to the sun. I smiled.

'I was having a lovely cup of coffee,' said Hazel, 'and I really don't think they're fattening. If anything, they reduce your calorie intake because you don't eat as many cookies.'

'Exactly,' said Ursula.

'Then Helen wafts in. Herself. With the head of department. You know, Dr. Fontaine. 'I am so sorry,' I say. 'I was just leaving. Helen, I hope you don't mind.' 'I wanted you to try the coffee,' said Helen. 'What do you think?' 'Delicious,' I said. 'I wanted to talk to you,' said Dr. Fontaine.'

'Is she related to the dancer?' I asked.

'You always ask that,' said Hazel.

'I'm curious,' I said but I'd asked because I always asked when her name was mentioned and it was part of the me I set against the world. Inside I'd changed but I couldn't let them know.

'No idea,' said Hazel. "I was curious about how the

staff should go about tipping the cleaners,' said. Dr. Fontaine. 'The staff and I would very much like to do our bit. We can't be out tipped by the students, can we?"

"Can't be out tipped by the students',' said Ursula, gloating inside the words. 'I love that bit.'

"It's really not necessary for anyone to tip,' I said. 'Of course, if someone wants to, I don't think there's anything in our contract to refuse.' 'Does an envelope every Friday on the desk work?' asked Dr. Fontaine. 'Absolutely,' I said.'

'Sounds legitimate to me,' said Hilda.

'I heard,' I said, 'that you had Professor Fontaine in a wrestling hold.'

'Where would you hear that?' asked Ursula.

'It's a joke, obviously exaggerated, but I always assume that reality lies somewhere in the middle,' I said.

'And where would somewhere in the middle be?' asked Hazel.

'Oh, you know, gentle persuasion.'

'Don't know what you mean,' said Hazel.

'What's everyone reading?' Hilda asked.

'Not now, Hilda,' I said. Hurt.

'Excuse me,' said Hilda.

'I think Hazel's doing a lovely job,' said Ursula.

'Exactly,' I said. 'All I'm saying is we should be careful.'

'I am careful and I never asked for anything,' said Hazel.

'Of course, she never asks,' said Ursula. 'But we're all glad for the extra aren't we?'

'All hail Hazel,' I said.

'All Hail Hazel,' said Hilda.

'All Hail Hazel,' said Ursula.

# Ursula

Hazel grew moody with the years. First time I noticed it was when I asked for the German dictionary. We were sitting around in an empty office, talking books.

'Has anyone got a German dictionary?' I asked.

'Not on me,' said Hilda.

'Why?' asked Hazel. Brusque, abrupt. Demanding. A different turn to her speech.

'I was having coffee in that Adriana's Office—the one with the Cuisinart coffee maker...'

'And the dictionary?' said Hazel.

'I'm reading *Novel on Yellow Paper* and bits are in German.'

'Girl looking for love,' said Hazel.

'I suppose it is,' I said. 'But I want to understand what it was like then. In the thirties.'

'I know where there's one whose absence won't be noticed, ask me again tomorrow,' said Janet.

'Better buy a cheap dictionary. Don't cross a line and get caught stealing one,' said Hazel.

'I wasn't suggesting anyone steal,' said Janet.

'I keep meticulous files,' said Hazel. 'Everything documented that moves from room to room. No one does anything inappropriate.'

Hazel had always been supportive—hold your bucket this way, here's where you clock in, it's perfectly legitimate to read a book when you're on break. Then this stare. I just needed a German dictionary. Giving me the ninth degree with her eyes. Like I'm undermining her authority, trying to manipulate someone into stealing a dictionary for me...

'Don't bother with the dictionary,' I said. 'I'll get one from the public library.'

Hazel nodded.

# Hazel

I was prepared for Stephanie.

The office wasn't much, the bookshelves empty, the desk cleared except for the obligatory blotter—one in every office as if people still used fountain pens and the metal desks so valuable they needed protection. I hate the blotters. Their plastic backings melt in the heat and stick to the desk. The rooms are over-heated in winter and stifling in summer. I have chipped blotters from desks in all seasons and then scrubbed metal to remove the last scraps of melted plastic. It's time consuming work, messes up the schedule. The scraping rasp of abrasive cleaner on metal sets my nerves on edge. I'm tempted to throw the blotters away but still waters are best not stirred.

By the time Stephanie arrived they had started bag checks before and after shift. Security, it's a university, prime target according to the bosses. Prime target for what? I didn't trust them.

That day I perched on the edge of a chair delicately drinking tea from a small cup and saucer. It was a soulless room when empty. I was like a hospital visitor whose patient had died. A pot of robust Earl Grey sat on a silver tray. There was a second cup of fine china waiting, a sugar basin and milk jug, lemon slices. A plate of chocolate cookies was edged into the emptiness. I sipped my tea and hoped Stephanie wouldn't be late.

I heard a key in the lock. I smiled and turned, watched the knob turn and twist. The person the other side of the door assumed it was locked. It wasn't. It's important to gain the upper hand with every new office resident. There was a time I was soft and welcoming, compliant. And I'd been treated like shit on a shoe.

'Oh,' said Stephanie when she opened the door and saw me.

'Excuse me,' I said, grabbing my cup. 'I didn't expect... the door was open... I didn't mean...' I half stood. 'I'll be done in a minute. Then I'll be out of your way. I'm Hazel.'

'How do you do, Hazel?' Stephanie held out her hand.

'How do you do? You don't want to shake my hand though, my dear. You never know where it's been. I clean toilets.'

'Oh.'

'The young women here before you let us have our breaks here. Out with the old and in with the new. It'll be a nightmare taking my tea breaks after this, I'll just trot over to Central Academic tomorrow. It's good for me, the walk.'

'The people in here before mc let you drink tea here?'

'Lovely young women.'

'Then... I suppose... drink tea here whenever you want.' All magnanimous she was, you could see it took a lot for her to offer and you could see she felt conflicted and at the same time exceptionally proud of herself.

'How kind. Tea?' I asked, holding up the pot. 'It's earl grey. Milk or lemon?'

'Lemon.'

'How lady like,' I said.

We sat and sipped tea. My smile was reluctant, it had done it all before. Come on out smile, I thought. It cringed and I coaxed until it bloomed across my face. Phew.

'Such a lovely room,' I said. 'Window and everything.'

'Don't all the offices have windows?'

'No. You must be very special, my dear. I'll make sure I shine things up extra nice for you. Like a cookie?'

'No, no thank you.'

'Me, I can never resist. Now, were you serious about me having tea in here?'

'Oh yes, of course.'

'Lovely. Aren't you a sweetheart? Now just to formalise things, would you sign right here?'

'Why?' said Stephanie, bewildered.

'See, I don't want someone coming along while you're doing something ever so important in another part of the university and finding me here and when I say you said it was okay with you that I drink my tea here, them questioning my honesty.'

She hesitated.

'All the students have signed at one time or another.'

I edged the paper a touch closer. Her fingers tapped at it. Unsure, but I could be patient. She looked up. I smiled—just—and sipped my tea. Carefully placed my cup on the blotter.

'Of course.' Stephanie signed.

I paused in the doorway. Come on smile, don't desert me now. 'Welcome.'

# Hilda

Hazel had good method, lots of water, then a wrung mop, then a dry mop, then polish on her hands and knees. Her floors shone, you could see your face right down to the fingerprints on your glasses in Hazel Sullivan's floors. I watched as she washed and mopped and mopped again. And I watched as she slipped on her top of the line, gardening knee pads and broke out the polish. She hummed as she worked but the hum was just a touch concerned. She was close to happy.

I wanted to say run, run now, but I couldn't.

The world was closing in. The business of the Big Tips. Especially the Big Tips from the profs. Welcome but out of control. I'd watch her open her locker. She did it slow, like she was expecting it to blow up or maybe harboured a wild animal. She'd peep slowly round the corner. Stilted little movements, small for a large woman. When I watched her clean, it was all elegance and sweeping arm movements, her body like a ballerina's, stretching and dipping with grace. But she'd stare at the envelopes stashed in her locker and shadows would cross her face, her skin would pinch up. Fear, I figured.

# Hazel

Came a point all I wanted to do was read. Things got more lucrative, it was a money roller coaster and all I wanted was to escape into a thick-with-story book. When we met as a group there'd be comments.

'Always got a nose in a book,' said Hilda.

'So engrossed,' said Ursula.

'Always first here, always got her nose in a book,' said Janet.

Their eyes would stray. Into my purse. X-ray vision, their lips moving and no words coming out, like they were counting, totting up the numbers. I'd struggle to stay with the story. My nose in the book, my eyes reaching to my purse. Get it over with, I'd think. Get back in the story. Sooner—never later—I'd reach into my purse, open the envelopes left in the offices and start recording the tips. Then I'd divide them into four, back into envelopes, handed out.

# Ursula

Hazel never played favourites.

'What's everyone reading?' she'd ask.

'D.H. Lawrence' said Janet. 'Skin tingling words! Imagine if your job was just to read him. All day, every day.'

'And analyze and write and teach,' said Hilda. 'I wouldn't trade. Best of both worlds us, that's what I say. We get to read whatever we want and no headaches.'

'In fifteen-minute slices', said Janet. 'Handsome too. That picture on the back of the book.'

'You looking at the pictures not reading the book?' asked Hilda.

'His picture,' said Janet, 'sinks me further into the story, buries me in Nottingham. I don't want to come up for air after my break. I want to stay in that pit with those children, I want to breathe their air.'

'Whose air?' said Hilda. 'The characters in the stories or the students and profs in the university?'

'Both,' said Janet.

'Dissatisfaction,' said Hilda. 'We've got it all. Pick of the stories, good pay, no stress and all the extras. All the little extras we have Hazel to thank for.'

Hazel shifted in her seat. We were sitting in a larger than normal office that day, maybe a professor's, can't remember. Hazel was on a nifty little mid-century modern chair, beautiful lines, all tarted up with a Victorian brocade upholstery. Didn't work for me. Or Hazel's rump. She was uncomfortable with the compliment, with Hilda's intruder eyes. This was Hazel's territory, defending our position.

'It's a system we're all responsible for,' Hazel said.

I was surprised. It wasn't like Hazel to share the glory.

'But you are our leader,' whispered Janet.

'Yes,' boomed Hilda. 'You are our leader. Without you there'd be no big tips. Right ladies?'

'It's a group effort,' Hazel said.

That was my missed opportunity. I should have said something, I should have said yes, should have buoyed up Hazel. I said to Frank when we got home, 'She was uncomfortable, it was like they were attacking her but she's always wanted the responsibility, it's like we're breaking down, as a group, it's like she's distancing herself from the Big Tips.'

'You're imagining it,' said Frank. Then he said, 'Is there anything you should worry about? Watch yourself.'

# Janet

I believe she was meticulous with that money. And absolutely honest. We each got an equal share. Ursula had developed a fondness for tracksuits, Fila track suits. The velour, the velour. Hazel worried. 'People are beginning to think you've come into shares of that company,' she'd say. It was meant to be a joke but I could tell by the wrinkles in her forehead that it bothered her beyond Ursula's lavish spending on leisure wear.

Hilda. Who knew what Hilda did with her money? Who knew what Hilda did with anything? She was a dark donkey, all mystery and tough. But Hazel trusted her, valued her silences and perceptions. We all did.

Herself, Hazel was discrete. Maybe too discrete. It was rumoured she kept her money in an old teapot under the sink. Then there was that kid of hers. Who knew what she did when she wasn't working and reading? Hazel was a bigger mystery than Hilda.

I had started buying books, my own books, I wrote

my name in them, I stacked them in piles on the floor of my apartment, I stopped at little libraries, I considered bookcases in Ikea catalogues, I wandered into the university bookstores and filched them from the class piles, I ordered them by author and then by colour and finally by joy, I treated them like children.

# Hilda

They shouldn't have locked her up. Not even for the little while they did. Why couldn't we read? It was awful standing in that court room, everyone looking at us. Of course, Hazel shielded us, even then. Don't you do anything to my girls, she said. It was all me. The ideas were all mine. But she'd got it wrong. The ideas were all in the books and we weren't meant to read them. We got our work done. Every scrap. There was provision for us to spend extra time in the cleaners' staff room in the event we finished early. So what if we read the books? They belonged to the university, didn't they? Like us. Property. To be used as determined by management.

# Janet

Ultimately, it wasn't the books, it was the tips and the contracts. They bled them altogether.

'I can't believe it,' said Ursula. 'I said to Frank it's not really happening.'

'It's happening,' said Hazel.
It happened.

# The Rest of Part One

Graduate Student Presentation

# A Creative Analysis of
## Charlotte Gilman Perkins' 'The Yellow Wallpaper'

Second year MA candidate, Stephanie Walker, shares her research.

Light refreshments to follow.

November 6th
7.00 pm

LT 17 (Lecture Theatre 17)
Everyone Welcome

Event co-hosted by the Departments of Women's Studies and English

I walked up the broken down stoop come front porch to Stephanie's house, arms aching with groceries, mind bouncing. I should have bought chocolate ice cream not Tiger Tail; five paragraph essay: intro, body one, body two, body three, conclusion; would orange sherbet melt faster than the liquorice in the Tiger Tail? easy to expand a five paragraph to seven to nine and even eleven; was there room in the freezer for the ice cream? school was about to start; Mum would be pissed off if she knew I shopped for Stephanie's lunch; I enjoyed the shopping; shopping wasn't part of the cleaning contract; Mum foisted this on me, why shouldn't I enjoy it? summer was waning, good word waning.

I searched for my keys, one handed, ice cream leaking cold through my T-shirt to my skin. The door opened.

Guess what? said Stephanie. It's a surprise.

She was hopping on one foot.

If it's a surprise and I guess, it won't be a surprise anymore, I said.

I want you to guess. It'll be a surprise until you guess.

We're having ice cream, I said.

No.

Yes, we are, I just bought some. Tiger Tail.

Guess again.

It's the best.

Guess again, guess again.

How old are you?

Twenty-eight. Would you please guess!

You're pregnant.

That's mean.

It's a joke. Sorry, I said. We're going to sit in the garden today?

Tiny bit warm.

We're going to read in the garden today.

Warmer, but colder too.

We're going to read in the house.

Warmer.

Can I put the ice cream in the freezer?

Yes. No. Cold. Guess again.

I walked into the kitchen to put the groceries on the table and it was gone.

Where's the table?

Warmer.

No, I said, where's the table?

Cooling off.

I stashed the ice cream in the freezer, grinned, and looked for the table.

Where will we eat?

We're going to read and eat in the living room, said Stephanie.

What about the mess?

Close your eyes, said Stephanie, and follow my voice.

Seriously?

This way, this way, careful, right a little, forward, straight ahead. Left an inch.

I trod gently behind Stephanie's voice.

Ta dah!

I opened my eyes.

There were two forts in the living room.

One had the red Formica table as its main wall, a pink velvet armchair for another and blankets and table cloths for the roof and other walls. It was beautiful, the reds and pinks whirled together and haunted the table and chair, shimmering in the sunlight.

I peeked inside. A small table, orange tablecloth, a book on top, a small bowl of pink and red ceramic eggs and a lamp shaped like a candelabra only all its crystal bits were red and orange. It glowed pink and red.

I checked out the second fort. A table I hadn't seen before formed one wall, a pink armchair another, with gold, orange, and yellow blankets and tablecloths for the roof and sides. Elephants and camels skipped around the edges of the blankets, the middles were filled in with wild fern leaves and tiny suns, tiny moons.

Like the crusades, I said.

Knights in tents on the battlefield, said Stephanie.

Where did that table come from?

Basement. They're for reading in, the forts.

How did you get the walls to stay up?

Linen lines. Two.

Cool.

Which one do you want to read in?

Wait! I dashed to the kitchen and returned with apples, a pile for each fort.

Perfect, said Stephanie.

We'll have to eat lunch and ice cream outside so we don't make a mess, but we can eat apples in the forts, I said.

Which do you want?

I like them both.

Pink's my favourite, said Stephanie.

I'll go orange. Do I pick a book?

After you read my absolute favourite story, said Stephanie. I left paper and pencils. In case you want to make notes.

I settled down on my tummy on the cushions, crunched apples, and read. 'The Yellow Wallpaper' by Charlotte Gilman Perkins. An old friend. Stephanie foisted it on me regularly; a saviour, it had secured my return to school; with each reading I edged further into the story. I was inside the yellow wallpaper. I was sizing up the ancient house, I was a doctor unlocking a baby mother's mind, I was the baby shrieking for consideration—well, maybe not a limited vocabulary baby. I doodled across the top of the page, then started to write, revisiting my answer to the grade 12 exam.

Dear Editors,

I beg to disagree with guest editor, Lucia Tavares.

Expulsion from high school—the inability to complete the necessary prerequisites for any formal training, exclusion from employment, the stress and slur of the penalty—this is a life changing event.

A Permanent Expulsion Order prevents this young woman from fulfilling her potential in any way. This was an extreme and inappropriate punishment.

My understanding is that there was no inquiry into the accusations. The young woman's guilt was assumed, and she was allowed no opportunity to defend herself.

I suggest a full inquiry be conducted into this situation.

Sincerely,

Tanys Lystrom
Social Work,
Year 4



At school all the teachers claimed some small credit for my rehabilitation.

Such a change, said Mr. Costa, from careless

disrupter to budding mathematician.

You're fulfilling your potential nicely, said Ms Chernyshevsky, the Careers Counsellor as well as the keeper of students' minds and souls. Now take this pamphlet on university. You'll have to pick up a language, of course.

I'm not going to university, except as a cleaner, I said.

Ms Chernyshevsky laughed as if I'd told her the best joke ever.

I was on track to graduate and graduate well. And suddenly reluctant to leave school.

Two months into the semester, in early November, I had a moment of perfect happiness. I supposed it started with not eating Honey Nut Cheerios for breakfast. I was dressed for school and drinking black coffee at the red Formica table.

Can't get used to you dressed in her clothes, said Mum.

They're my clothes now.

Mum sniffed.

Can't get used to you being up this early, said Mum.

I got up all summer, just not this early.

There's Honey Nut Cheerios.

I don't want Honey Nut Cheerios.

Pity. They were on sale and I don't like 'em much, said Mum.

Me neither.

Granola bar?

I'll take one with me.

Good. Mum nodded, motherly duty done for the day, motherly instincts well flexed, nothing auspicious, a regular mother-daughter exchange.

I stepped into a bright fall day, warm and cosy in my battered leather jacket (Value Village, twenty bucks) on top of a white shirt and short tartan pleated skirt. My legs, shielded by red tights, disappeared into a pair of knock off, yellow, barely worn by the previous owner, Doc

Martens.

The world prickled at my skin. Possibility, with all its unknown hopes and complexities, lay in wait. Just around the corner. Last night I had made peace with a giant from my past. I'd worked a casual shift at MacDonald's, serving coffee and muffins and crisped grease through the take-out window. First McDonalds shift since before my Stephanie summer. I never expected to return to MacDonald's but Lisa was desperate. A phone call out of nowhere, a sick baby, alone, panicked she'd lose her job, desperate for someone, anyone, even me, to cover her shift. The boss looked flabbergasted when I walked in but needed a body at the take-out window. I was still technically an employee—this could be done. Then my eyes crossed and sunk into my skull. There was a new boss and the new boss was Deirdre.

I know you from junior high, said Deirdre. And smiled.

I was instantly wary.

I recognised the name when Lisa said you were covering her shift but I didn't realise it was you.

Old habits kicked in and working the take-out window was near meditative. I smiled my way through the orders, almost relaxed.

Have break with me, said Deirdre.

I drank coffee and Deirdre ate burgers. Two, patties thick with toppings.

How're'ya' doin'? she asked, mopping up meat juice with a napkin. A single globule of grease flickered on the plate.

I was shocked by how much smaller Deirdre was in maturity. Her black hair was dyed still blacker and her eyes were a strange but haunting green. She had a huge smile I had never seen before. She looked mythical.

Deirdre of the sorrows, I said.

What did you say?

Your namesake, Deirdre of the sorrows. A beautiful myth.

Still in school? accused Deirdre.

Her father was a story teller and he was told by a Druid fortune teller that she would be the most beautiful woman in the kingdom.

Her name was Deirdre?

Yup. He decided to kill her.

That is so not right.

Didn't happen. The King of Ulster stole her away and gave her to an old woman to bring up. He planned to marry her himself when she was old enough.

How old was this guy?

One night Deirdre dreamed of the man she'd marry. His hair was black as a magic cat, his face as white as snow but with cherry pink cheeks.

Black hair and white face are okay but I could do without the red cheeks.

The old woman identified the man of Deirdre's dreams, they met and married and moved to Scotland from Ireland.

You never said they were in Ireland, said Deirdre.

It's an Irish myth.

But now we're in Scotland. Am I happy?

Absolutely, you have two beautiful boys, strong and brave.

And I live happily ever after?

No, you are lured back to Ireland. A trick.

Do they kill me?

You survive but your husband is killed.

I marry the old king.

Yes. But you are unhappy and refuse to love him.

Good on me.

The king asks you the name of the man you despise the most and you name the man who killed your husband. He then gives you to him to be his wife.

That's wrong!

You leap out of the chariot taking you to your next wedding and dash yourself to death against the rocks.

Break's over. You on the take-out window?

Yep.

Right now the name's Deedee but when I'm old…. maybe Deirdre will work.

> Dear Guest Editor, Lucia Tavares, et al,
>
> I have read with interest your concerns surrounding the attempted appropriation of Stephanie B.'s work.
>
> I agree that academic integrity should always be beyond reproach.
>
> I do, however have some concerns. The accused was briefly a student of mine. Contrary to statements made in the editorial, I found her to be articulate, well read, mature and with unlimited academic potential. Her in class essays, essays that could be written by no one other than herself, were easily of senior undergraduate level and possibly beyond.
>
> My understanding is that the accused believed she contributed short creative responses after reading a short story. Has it been proven, without a doubt, that she

could not have written these
responses?

Sincerely,

Veronica Starling
B.Ed. (1989)
Bedford High School

That perfect day morning the air vibrated with possibility. Two days ago it had been heavy with premature winter, now it billowed against me, full of optimism, autumnal reprieve. I was full of gracious amity. Grown up; last night the ill will of teenage hostility evaporated. Deirdre was an almost friend, a small rift mended.

I was suddenly full of Naomi. After shift I read *Obasan* by Joy Kogawa. Tears prickled my morning eyes as I remembered the sadness of the story. The book reading was homework and I wanted more stories of the same and would check the school library for a sequel and other books by J.K. Today I would write an excellent response to the book, I would write for justice.

I ordered my response in my head. Vancouver at the outbreak of the Second World War, Naomi's confidence and optimism, her belief in her own potential. And then the horror and Naomi's life tumbled down. Layer on layer on layer of horror. Naomi in a camp. I'd call my essay 'The Trust that Leads to Horror'. I'd summarise the curiosity and joy she felt at the beginning of the story. (One sentence, two max. Don't get caught in the summarising trap, Eve.) I'd move on to the terror and the question of why it happened. I thought through the various levels of guilt I'd experienced reading the book, I sifted through examples and ideas. I had control of my day, I would write an excellent essay and when it was returned I'd feel good. All anticipation was positive. And my boots looked new.

I turned onto a street with almost bare sidewalks. In the distance a small shaded section of street with ice. Warning! Fake Doc Martens don't do traction! I watched carefully as the ice closed in, stepped with caution. The ice snapped and crackled under foot. My boots had thick soles. Water gushed up as the ice shattered. My feet stayed dry. Not that a drenched foot would have bothered me. I stepped again. The ice splintered and chimed, splashes of leftover snow disappeared under my boots. I laughed. I stomped my way from one end of the ice to the other, sprays of melted snow shining up my yellow boots, my laugh louder and louder. I was the first person to walk on that stretch of ice, I had a granola bar in my pocket, I'd read a book that touched me all the way to the soles of my feet, right to my apple core, I was tempted into life, into optimism. The world tinkled with joy, ideas everywhere. I stamped some more and the heartening ice crackles shot through my brain and heart. Anything and everything was possible. I laughed louder. I stood in the middle of the street, my face lifted to the thin sun, and laughed some more. I was caught between summer and winter, between ice and snow, desire and circumstance, hope and destiny. My world was exactly as it should be.

Dear Miss Starling,

We applaud your loyalty to your young student.

> As fellow travellers on the
> instructional road dedicated to
> literature we understand both
> your commitment and opinion and
> are impressed by your confidence in
> judging the essay.
>
> We are curious as to your method.
> What rubric were you using?
>
> The Graduate Students English
> Association
> Bedford University

Your Stephanie's giving a talk at the university, said Mum.

She's not my Stephanie, I said.

You should go, said Mum. Moral support. And it'll get you used to the university.

I never said I was applying to the university.

I put your application in. My boss says you're a shoe in. Union membership and full benefits.

*The Voices of The Invisible in Charlotte Perkins Gilman's 'The Yellow Wallpaper'*

BS, Before Stephanie, I'd have lurked in the doorway of the university, debated on whether I wanted to go in, remembered the place from childhood, remembered Zoe's mother, if I'd had the courage to go in and walk down the hall, I'd have mocked the quiet confidence and gentle jokes of the inhabitants, then I'd have run for it.

AS, After Stephanie, I walked down the hall impressed by the cleanliness—who wouldn't be?—and turned into Lecture Theatre 17.

Hullo dear, said the ancient woman at the door. Her name was Winnifred and she wore a magnificent red felt hat, with fruit attached. She was a volunteer. It said so on the button that peaked out from beneath a bunch of cherries.

Have a name tag, said Winnifred.

Thank you.

Marker?

Yes please. 'Eve', I wrote my name on the shiny square. The paper squealed and Winnifred grimaced.

Sorry, I whispered.

Not your fault. Nice name, said Winnifred.

Thank you.

Would you like to sign the guest book?

The guest book was a stack of photocopied sheets stapled together. I wrote my name and address and phone number.

A lot of people wanted to hear Stephanie. I sat in an almost empty row and counted. Thirty-seven and still arriving. Behind me, a jumble of voices.

*She won't show up.*
*She's already here.*
*Going to be a car wreck.*
*I bet she doesn't.*
*Bet what?*
*Beer in the Library Bar.*
*Should never have let her in.*
*Grandparents…*
*Rumours.*
*… donated.*
*Rumour, rumour.*
Whispers and shuffles.

I should have brought a book. Or homework.

When Stephanie walked onstage the voices behind

me catcalled and whistled and Winnifred appeared at the end of their row and shushed them. Instant silence. I was impressed by Winnifred's authority.

Applause, a man at the microphone, introductions, then Stephanie at the microphone, quiet enough to hear her breathing—I gave a little wave, too low down to be seen, an invisible gesture of solidarity—her finger tapped the microphone with an echoing metal knock.

I half expected Stephanie to bolt. The papers in her hand shook, she looked across the hall and sucked her breath in. I held mine too. Then Stephanie read.

Hmm, said someone in the row behind.

The words came low and slow and halting. I listened.

You owe me a beer, said a voice from behind.

I recognised the words. Stephanie paused to swallow and I knew. I understood. My body froze into underdrive. This must be apoplexy, I thought. I wanted to run and run and hide in a small hole and never come out. On the outside I was a statue sitting on an uncomfortable chair in a hall with thirty-seven other people and Winnifred plus assorted latecomers. All my motors spun their cogs in double and triple time. My blood pushed and drained and bulldozed its way through my veins, looking to burst free. I registered every inch of every blood pump at the same time. And then I wanted to roar and I wanted to scream and I needed to be seen.

This stuff is okay, original, said a voice behind.

I stood.

I take it all back, said another voice, beers are on me.

I wrote that, I said.

Sit down, said a voice.

Snorting from behind.

I wrote that, I bellowed. There was silence. Eyes latched onto my skin, embarrassed eyes, staring and then looking away. More snorting, half strangled snorting, a smothering of snorts.

I turned.

I wrote that!

The row of assorted young women, a show of black fabric and bright colours, lowered their eyes to stare at their sandals and cowboy boots. Snort away, I thought, as my eyes froze on my wrist, the veins under the skin moved up and down, and in and out, a thousand moving blood bulges. Squeezing, squashing, an animal inside my veins, spiralling its way through my body. Searching for escape. Nausea inched its way from my stomach to every body corner and burrow, to my toes, to my fingers, to my knees, to my elbows.

Stephanie was never my friend!

Dear, said Winnifred, the cherries and a pineapple bobbing up and down in excited alertness.

Sit down, dear, the people behind you can't see.

That's mine, I said. I wrote that.

Come along with me dear, said Winnifred.

Stephanie read on. I turned to the words, my words. I searched for an attack but found none.

My head was only nausea. My belly was nauseous. My arms and legs were squeamishly limp.


I gulped air, I choked on the air, I needed more than would fit in my mouth. I needed every inch, every cubic inch in the room—that would silence her. And suddenly in the midst of my body's rebellion, time slowed down and I wondered, how do you measure air?

Eve, whispered Winnifred. Can you hear me, Eve? How many fingers am I holding up?

I wanted Stephanie to see me. I waved my arms in the air.

Stephanie, it's me, I said.

Everyone in front turned to look. Behind me, more giggles, tottering and gurgling, like some sort of giggling baby learning to walk, bursts of giggle accomplishment faltering, stumbling, half swallowed titters. Why didn't

Winnifred turn on them?

I needed all the air to keep the blood moving, to stop the veins expanding and bursting. And then the noise. Louder and louder and louder. Like banging on a door knocker. Like knocking inside a dream. Like a hammering machine, cracking the crust of the earth. I needed earplugs. I wanted to look around and figure out where the sound was coming from. Unnecessary. The sound was coming from inside me.

Stephanie heard. Stephanie saw me and stopped reading.

Sit down.

I can't see.

Sit down!

Hey! Security.

Eve, whispered Winnifred. Half bent over, the old woman walked through the row of chairs towards me, slowly. I sidled away.

Stephanie stared.

Could we get security please? This young woman's causing a disturbance, said Stephanie into the microphone. Would you please leave?

Eve, whispered Winnifred, closer and closer.

The miniature orange pineapple bobbed against the cherries. The pineapple dipped towards me and I moved away. Then Winnifred's magnificent felt hat fell off. I wanted to pick it up but couldn't be kind.

I stood in fury and the voices rustled and shuffled their feet and cackled. Hands reached for me, kindness won out and I picked up the hat and gave it to Winnifred.

Thank you, dear. Now... I turned and ran into the arms of a security guard who dragged me to the door.

Let go of me!

Ssh!

Let go!

Indoor voices, dear, said Winnifred.

## DISTURBANCE AT ACADEMIC SOIREE

Last Monday, November 6, a seventeen year old female interrupted the presentation of research by MA candidate, Stephanie Blake. The young woman claimed the research was hers and refused to be silent. Louise Halton, office mate of Stephanie Blake and fellow MA candidate described the incident. 'She screeched and screeched, no one could hear Stephanie, and she claimed the scholarship was hers. Obviously false.'

'Such blatant plagiarism cannot be tolerated,' said the Chair of the English Department.

'The student is no longer attending school and proceedings for a full expulsion from the system are in progress,' according to Mark Sergeant, spokesperson for the Bedford School Board.

'She really believed she'd written it herself,' said volunteer, Winnifred Hope, herself an MA in English Literature (1948). 'She was distraught, you had to feel for her, a bit of a street urchin if you know what I mean,' continued Miss Hope.

'The research itself was interesting,' said Kristen Stoop, PhD and supervisor of Ms Blake's research. 'Quite unlike anything she'd done before, creative, rather primitive stories and a fascinating exploration of one of the texts studied.' When

> asked if she had seen the work before, Kirsten Stoop, responded in the negative. 'Oh, no. That's what the evening is all about, a first unveiling of the preliminary research.'
>
> The young woman was escorted off campus by security. Charges are pending.

Next morning I hammered on the staff room door.

Yes, said Ms. Chernyshevsky. I hadn't expected to see her in the staff room. She was always so separate.

Can I talk to Miss Starling?

She's not here.

My back up plan was Miss Lucas. I ran down the hallway to the office of the Academic Vice Principal for students with last names beginning with letters between O and Z, including S.

Can I talk to Miss Lucas? Please.

Er… said Mr C., the receptionist.

I was shocked. Normally the short and balding gentleman that guarded Miss Lucas's door was quick to find the perfect words to ward off or warmly greet students.

I stared at Mr. C. and Mr. C. stared back.

One moment, said Mr. C.

Mr. C. tapped on Miss Lucas's door and then stuck his head inside, the opening no wider than Mr. C's neck. He whispered but I heard my name. Mr. C. straightened himself—it was a bit like watching a rumpled tablecloth being ironed—opened the door wide enough not to decapitate himself and beckoned me through.

Well, Miss Sullivan, said Miss Lucas, what have you got to say for yourself?

Miss Starling!

Eve, said Miss Starling.

I hadn't expected my English teacher to be visiting with Miss Lucas. Maybe staff were also assigned Vice Principals according to the first letter of their last name.

I wanted to talk to Miss Starling, said Miss Lucas. And we both want to talk to you.

Someone at the university took my stories, I said, a touch too loud. I expected comfort, commiserations.

No need to shout, said Miss Lucas.

I expected them to be horrified, I expected them to forgive shouting, I expected a plan to action. Miss Lucas and Miss Starling looked at each other and each raised an eyebrow. Like a secret society. I remained cautiously optimistic.

I cleaned for her but she made me read and write things… all this summer she gave me books to read and told me to write and I went to her talk at the university and she was reading my words, I said.

Sit down, Eve, said Miss Lucas.

Miss Lucas nodded at Miss Starling and Miss Starling cleared her throat. Her throat clear reminded me of a sad bird chirp. Trapped in Miss Lucas's gloomy office, Miss Starling resembled a bird. Heavy dark grey metal furniture like all the other Vice Principals (A-H, G-N, Applied Trades, and Resource Room), heavier than the teachers had in their rooms but still metal. Only the Principal had wooden furniture. There were books in Miss Lucas's office, all science, and on the windowsill an empty glass container. In the summer I'd seen lettuces growing in the container. Miss Starling cleared her throat some more.

Have you ever noticed Eve, if you read something

enough times it seems like you've written it yourself?

No.

Miss Starling's eyes flickered around the room, like she was searching for a way out. Well, said Miss Starling, how about you write something and then realise you're writing down what you had just read?

No.

The university called and has lodged a complaint, said Miss Lucas. They are considering charges against you and threaten to implicate the school. You'll be expelled of course. With your record you barely need this incident.

She stood up in front of thirty-seven people and read things I wrote and said they were hers, I said.

They also said you created a disturbance and had to be escorted out of the building, said Miss Lucas.

You don't understand.

Yes, I do. Don't we Miss Starling? Miss Lucas snarled at Miss Starling. Miss Starling fluttered and chirped.

The university has been very clear, said Miss Lucas. Even the essay you wrote for me was… filched.

But you saw me write it.

I wasn't in the room, said Miss Lucas.

How could I have known I'd have to answer that question? I turned to Miss Starling. My essays, you said they're good.

They are, they were, said Miss Starling.

What she read was good. Besides, this is not about essays, said Miss Lucas.

You're over extended, you're pushing yourself too hard, said Miss Starling.

This is far more serious than a few essays, said Miss Lucas. The university is involved.

Do I get an appeal?

An appeal? asked Miss Lucas.

Someone who got terminated told me they could

appeal… to someone.

And did they? asked Miss Lucas.

No.

They were very wise, weren't they? said Miss Lucas. I suggest you are also wise and leave now. A smart girl like you, always making excuses and looking for the easy way, pity you had to cheat and implicate the university. I suggest you go now.

I left.

**Expulsion hearing for Eve Sullivan.**
**Bedford Public School Board.**
**(Summary)**

Given that,

Miss Eve Sullivan has been able to supply no satisfactory explanation for her behaviour.

Miss Eve Sullivan has refused all requests to seek psychiatric support.

Miss Eve Sullivan refuses to accept that the writing in question is not hers.

Miss Eve Sullivan is expelled from the system.

November 28, 1994

I lay on a table in the mall food court and stared at the ceiling. The food court was in the basement and the ceiling three floors up, the roof a mix of girders and glass and through the glass clouds puffed up the sky as if it were an ordinary day. A bird, inside, flew towards the sky, swatted back by the cat paw panes of glass.

I searched for a book to hide in. Miss Starling had assigned *As I Walked Out One Midsummer Morning* as a free reading project book. Made no sense, assigned free reading, but Miss Staling said it was free because I didn't need to write about it on final exams. The guy telling the story had woken up one morning and walked out of his house and carried on. He'd gone from the country in England to London to Spain. He'd just picked up his violin and walked out of his life and into another one. I struggled to get into the book but it wouldn't have me. It booted me out again and again. I wasn't a boy, I didn't have a violin.

I followed the bird with my eye and forced my thoughts into a night-time self, rolled up in a country ditch and then a boot bumped onto the table right by my head and for a moment I thought the boot belonged to a farmer, but it was Chasity.

New Doc Martens? I asked.

How could you? said Chasity.

Very authentic, real thing?

You cheated! said Chasity.

What?

It's all over school. You cheated.

I didn't.

The countryside was gone.

I trusted you, Eve. You made me want to stay in school because… because you were so good at it. But you're a dirty fucking cheat.

You know I can do school.

I don't! Not any more. You lied and you cheated and you copied and you've never been anything but a liar and

a cheat. You betrayed me!
Boys, I said.
I needed Chasity be quiet, to go, to leave me alone. I was the one betrayed.
I am so hurt, said Chasity. You know my life is collapsing, right? I might as well go and work in McDonald's for all I'll ever be a manicurist or hairdresser.
Prince Masterson and his bros, sitting on tables, whispering about lifting pop and chips from Dollarama, stealing a twenty-six from the liquor store. Him and one of the boys would play fight and when the liquor store clerk tried to break it up someone else would steal a bottle.
Boys I said again. Look at the boys, I thought, be distracted.
That's how you got back into school? Stealing her story?
No. It's not true.
I think it is.
Cat fight, said Prince Masterson and strutted over with a bounce and sway which looked ridiculous.
Chasity and I were eye balling each other big time. Prince folded his arms and angled his body, watching like he was in the movie theatre.
What's up? said Prince. You're giving me that green light loving look.
I am not.
Take her, said Chasity.
Prince peered at me like I was an exhibit in a museum with tiny print.
You know she's a phoney, said Chasity. She cheats.
Cool, said Prince.
Jeez, said Chasity, I'm outta here. And clopped off in her Doc Martens
What the fuck, I thought, life is shit. Wake up and smell your future dying in a mall parking lot why don't you.

Dear Miss Starling,

It has come to our attention that you have openly supported Eve Sullivan, a student expelled from the Bedford School System. (BSS)

This support places you in serious opposition to the goals and philosophy of BSS.

We request that you desist from this support.

This letter is a formal sanction and will be attached to your permanent record.

Sincerely,
Dr Gladys Smithers
President,
Bedford School Board


Your poor mother, said Aunt Lilac, her almost purple suit sucking in all the light from the kitchen window. It shimmered ever so slightly and matched her almost purple but paler nails. The light pooled around my aunt's head, trapped in her puffy hair. She dabbed a floral handkerchief, against her eyes. It was made of real fabric and matched her blouse, both had tiny yellow flowers on a purple background. The floral fabric and my aunt's eyes both looked dry. I concentrated on Lilac's straight, and too small, nose. It reminded me of my own.

Whenever you want a makeover, said Cousin Iris. Come and see me. I see you in a shaft of sunlight all purples and shades of blue.

I looked at my aunt's light gobbling outfit.

I could do wonders with your cheekbones, said Cousin Iris. And being family, I won't expect a tip.

I grimaced and Cousin Iris thought I was smiling.

You are so brave, said Iris. I'll even give you my discount on the make-up. I get such a good commission I can easily share.

Iris grasped at my hand and patted it.

Did someone say commission? asked Jason, Iris's brother, my other cousin. My next promotion—and its coming soon—I get to sell the mid-size almost luxury models. The commissions and bonuses are going to roll in.

I wondered who my father was. Maybe he had a family.

The washing machine, said Uncle Sid, is a measure of our cultural progress. First one I sold had one speed and two temperatures. Can you believe it? Now you need a degree in computers to sell them.

You have a degree in computers? I asked.

No. I'm grandfathered in, learnt on the job, I know it all. I'm the best. I always say you can judge a family by its appliances, small and large.

I shuffled my lips into a smile, it was like shifting heavy appliances.

One day you'll want your own washer dryer in your apartment and when that day comes, when you're in the market, you come and see your Uncle Sid, and we'll see what I can do for you. Same goes for small appliances, said Uncle Sid.

I tried to move my lips again but they had had enough.

And when you marry—you're not married are you? asked Sid.

No.

Engaged?

No.

Going steady?

No.

Good. Then you're not connected to a gift registry. When you are, any one of those, when you're ready to register for your small appliance gift registry you remember your Uncle Sid and if you take care of me, Uncle Sid is going to take care of you. Understand?

Yes, I said.

You can use my name in any Hudson Bay Household Appliance Department, large or small, said Uncle Sid.

He tapped his nose with a manicured fingertip.

I had thought Mum was shunned by her family. I'd felt guilty, assumed it was my fault.

You'll have to come and stay with us, said Aunt Lilac.

Goody, said Cousin Iris and clapped her hands.

Why? I asked.

You're family, said Aunt Lilac.

You can't stay here alone, said Uncle Sid.

Eew, said Lilac. Scary.

Eve's coming to stay with us, said Aunt Lilac to Jason. Until she gets settled, until she's a little older.

Can you drive? asked her cousin.

I shook my head.

Pity, said Jason.

You still in high school? asked Uncle Sid.

Sid! said Aunt Lilac. I told you not to mention that, Sid. She's been e-x-p-e-l-l-e-d.

She turned to me like I hadn't heard. Still time, isn't there, Eve? We could get you registered in our local school. You're not twenty yet, right? School's still free until you're twenty, said Aunt Lilac.

I'd like to stay here tonight, I said.

I don't think so, said Aunt Lilac. Not alone.

If she wants, Lilac. She's twenty, said Sid.

Not yet, Sid, not yet, she isn't. You stay with her, Iris.

I don't want to stay here. What if it's haunted. And all my stuff is in my bedroom.

It's okay. I stayed alone when Mum was in the hospital, before she died.

All four of them looked at me in shock. I'd said the D-word.

Like I said, she's old enough, said Uncle Sid.

Dear Miss Lucas,

You are obviously aware that the authenticity of Stephanie Blake's authorship of her research has been questioned.

While I commend your suggestion that Eve Sullivan be assumed the author these are early days and I think we should await confirmed proof of authorship.

In response to your question, no, I do not think now is the time to walk back our decision on the expulsion and re-instate Eve Sullivan in high school.

Sincerely,
Bert Swift,

Assistant Superintendent,
Department of Student Deletions,
Bedford School Board

I wrote down my memories on imaginary papers and folded them into paper cranes in my brain. Lilac and Sid and Iris and Jason, a string of mind's eye words, the paper folded and folded again and again and again until it could fly like a bird, until it was a bird. Then I launched them with an inward breath.

A hawk and Ron and the blue car and Don. Write and fold, painful and sweet, memory after memory, write and fold, imagination overdrive, then they were gone.

Each memory, better than origami. Miss Lucas, Miss Starling, Stephanie, Chasity, Lisa, Nikki, Tamara, everything. All stories shed.

I was Pony Boy and Johnny heading out of town. Three of us together and then I realised no more stories meant no more stories. I packaged my books into paper cranes, imaginary paper cranes, like the ones in Destiny's apartment, until my mind's fingers were numb with folding. Another and another and another. Every book and story, every excerpt and poem, everything gone.

My mind was empty. No more stories, all taken away. Gone, gone.

I was headed to the mountains.

# Ten Years in the Mountains

'You're in luck, we just had a cancellation. One night or two?'
'Two.'
'Just passing through?'
'Looking for work.'
The woman hunches over registration, her skin glows green, a single light bulb hums and bounces off whitey green walls.
'Address?'
'Here.'
'No address somewheres else?'
'No. I'm moving here.'
'Gimme a sec.'
She scurries away, slight furry woman, soft hairs cover the backs of her hands, sides of her face, below the ears, ageless. Darts back.
'You know we're the YWCA, right?'
'Yeah.'
'I can put you in weekly. Not long term but a bigger room, upstairs, less money. Cheapest you'll find in Bluff Ridge. Ninety bucks, weekly rate. Decide every Friday if you want to stay or give one week's notice.'
Single bed, small window, desk, chair, lamp, closet. Itty, bitty, small. Window with bars looking onto rat hole garbage yard, cat skulking through. Why'd anyone want to jump down there?
'Change of sheets every Wednesdays, leave them outside in the dirty laundry bag. Bag's replaced by clean ones in a clean laundry bag. Here's the key.'

Eyes closed.

Sleep tugs at rag doll body.

Lush, reedy, sleep. Rainforest green sleep. Relentless sleep. Wholesome. Welcome. Dragged down by roots deep into the ground, moist, mulched, sucked down. Legs leaden. Ground shifts, closer, closer, tightening, imprisoning, sleep.

Soft, soft, gentle easing, softening grasp.

Bird sound. Whistle. Tap. Whistle, tap. Exotic woodpecker.

Muddle of leaves and branches and twine-ey shoots, wrap legs, slap back into face.

Translucent green. Pale, rolling, like an apple. Rotten. Faster, faster, through the forest rain, wet heat, skin bulging, skin dimpled, skin rotten.

Eyes open. Heart beat. Footsteps. Eyes open, out of bed, into bathroom, out of building, search for job. Don't move. Can't move. Eyes closed. Smell apple, smell dream. Legs like lead.

Sleep. Bitter sleep. Sour green. Bitter green. Noise, mechanical noise, tree felling, machinery, chain saw chain sawing. Cold sleep.

Eyes open. Garbage truck in the garbage yard beneath barred window. Footsteps, cough, chatter, late like a story book rabbit. No. No rabbit. No storybook.

Silence. Walls drift away. Soup smell, packet soup. No hunger. Pad, pad, pad, down the empty hall to the bathroom. Clean teeth. Pee. Wash hands. Pad, pad, pad, back to bed. Sleep a day.

Eyes closed. Deep sleep. Dreamless sleep, please dreamless. Voicing sleep, voices.

How could you do this to me?

We take cheating very seriously.

Mention my name in any Hudson's Bay.

Voices. End of day voices.

Whiff of food.

Not hungry, only sleepy.

Eyes closed.
Sleep.
Running.
Eyes open. Must wash, eat, search for work. Wash, eat, search for work.
Eyes closed. Sleep. Footsteps leave. More footsteps. Leave. No more hunger, no more thirst. Eyes closed. Sleep.
Another night.
Eyes open.
Cannot live on toothpaste alone. Tug legs from jagged forest-green trap and sit. Head light, like a dandelion clock, like a woozy dandelion clock.


Help wanted. Bartender. Crown Hotel. Experience needed.
Wait Staff, midnight shift, Mountain Truck & Grill. No exp. necessary. Must have own vehicle.
Wait Staff, A Step Above, Silver Service. Experience absolutely necessary.
Bus people needed. Lollipop Diner. Under eighteen only.
Cecil's Donut Shop. Counter Help. Good tips. Room for advancement. No experience necessary.
Fudge Maker. Graeme's Fudge Factory.


Fudge Factory. Air weighted with vanilla and chocolate. Inhale sweetness. Hair in bandana, Fu Manchu moustache, Graeme. Cleanest, palest, boniest finger prodding at application form.
'You got experience?'
'McDonald's.'
'Anything else?'
'Cleaning.'
'Sorry.'

Cecil's Donut Shop. Bald head, hairy belly slipping out his pants, Cecil. Yanks head through apron straps, hangs down to his knees, belly disappears, smells of cinnamon and bitter man perfume.

Fat and hairy fingers tap the counter.

'You never worked donuts?'

'Ad said no experience necessary.'

'Doesn't mean it's ideal, does it?'

'I've eaten them.'

He scratches his chin with a raspy stubble scrape.

'Minimum wage plus tips—five to ten bucks a day. 7.a.m.–1.30. Payday's Monday. Name's Cecil.'


Home.

Turn right, Vending Machine Room at the end of the hallway. Table and three chairs, fridge, stove, cupboard, and sink. Almost a kitchen. With vending machines.

Turn left, end of the hallway, communal washroom. Two showers, three toilets, three sinks, orange metal doors, brown walls.


'Two maple glazed.'

Lean into donuts, bakery tissue in hand.

'Those aren't maple glazed, they're maple long johns. I said maple glazed.'

Cecil checks the till. All money present.

'I know my float, I can tell by looking if the money's all there.'

'What's the difference between maple glazed and maple long johns?'

'Nothing. Customers like variety, too much variety costs money. Shape's different.'

Stare out the window.

'List your eats on this here paper. I deduct fifty

percent per donut from your paycheque.'

'Two cherry glazed, one Boston cream and a cruller.'

Cecil checks the till.

'Half a dozen Old Fashioneds.'

Cecil casually wanders out of the kitchen. Checks the till.

'A sugar donut with strawberry filling.'

Cecil opens the till, fondles the money.

'A couple of maple glazed.'

Cecil shifts trays of donuts into delivery van out back.

'One chocolate dip.'

'One maple.'

'Do you sell bran muffins?'

'Just donuts.'

Cecil stands in the kitchen doorway, his eyes twitch on the till.

There are no tips.


Eyes closed.

Scurrying sleep. Mouth all bitter sugar. Almost awake, teeth wince and cringe. Yank downward, crawl upward, see air, almost, almost, awake.

Startle. Awake. Late.

Day off.

Eyes open.


Vending Machine Room.

Stove, ancient stove, gas flame, drawer beneath, frying pan, cabinet, chipped bowl, another chipped bowl, unchipped bowl, plate, drawer, rummage, rummage, fork, wash, wash.

Fridge, eggs, bought from the store beside the donut shop.

Crack an egg, crack another, whisk, whisk.

Eggs scramble on the stove.
Soft footsteps.
Scramble, scramble.
A throat clears.
'Smells like eggs,' says a voice.
'Scrambled eggs.'
'I'm Debbie.'
'Hi Debbie.'
'Are you going to eat those here?'
'Anywhere else to eat them?'
'Your room.'

EATING IN ROOMS IS STRICTLY FORBIDDEN

'Nobody pays attention to that,' says Debbie.
Sit at table, eat eggs. Debbie sits at the table, stares at eggs.
'Would you like some eggs?'
'No, I had fudge for breakfast. I work at the fudge shop.'
'Applied there, didn't get hired.'
'Eggs kinda make me nauseous,' says Debbie.


Morning.
Cecil checks the till.
'You writing down every donut you eat?'
'I don't eat donuts.'
Donut shop air. Heavy, stink of scorched sugar. Donut sweat hovers in armpits—stale vanilla—fights with natural lavender deodorant. Sickling sugar, unnatural maple, almost chocolate. Donut crumbs pool on clothing—brush, brush—like pilled wool. Loose but static.
Cecil checks the cash register, looks out the door at the empty parking lot, turns the open sign to closed.
Hooray!
There are no tips.

'What do you do with the donuts you don't sell?'
'Throw 'em out,' says Cecil.
'You could donate them.'
'Do I look like a man who donates?'
'My school got donuts donated.'
'Take whatever you want, just add them to your eats list.'


Bluff Falls.
Deer in the streets, chomping on gardens, antlers rattle and wobble.


HELP WANTED
The Back Street Ukrainian Restaurant. Lazy neon.
'I am Miriam,' said the woman. 'And I need a waitress. You have experience?'
'No.'
'Good, I'll train you. You look very honest. Can you start tomorrow, noon?'


'Cecil?'
'I've got to go out.'
Offer envelope.
'What's this?'
'Quitting notice.'
He reads slowly.
'You're leaving me in the lurch.'
He reads, cautious of the words.
'And you'll still work mornings? 7.00–11.00? Well doesn't that suit. You! Haven't given it a chance, have you?'
'You said there'd be tips.'
'Not my fault.'
'What about the morning? Until you get someone?'

'Back in twenty,' says Cecil and clears the till of all banknotes.
Minutes, hours, days, weeks, months, years?
Cannot wait twenty years. Heart topples.
'Two dozen, mixed.'
Cecil walks in.


'You can work the cash,' says Miriam. 'All the money goes in the till. At the end of the day, I take out my float and the total amount on the cash register slip. Everything else is yours. Make sure you ring things in accurately. If you make errors, you can stay afterwards to check things out. You are in charge of the front.'


Mavis—wispy permed hair, watery grey eyes that look like they're solving a puzzle just behind the horizon, smudged lipstick, faced lined and dry like a riverbed—walks down the YWCA hallway, trying her key in each door until it fits.


'People don't need a fancy name, people need to know what I cook,' says Miriam.
She has a point.
'I am forth generation Canadian,' says Miriam. 'My great, great, great, great, grandfather worked on the railroad.'


Mavis is unsettling.
'I see you've met Mavis,' said Amelia (furry hands, skin grows green in artificial light). 'We take group responsibility—if you see Mavis making a break for it, haul her back in.'

'Physically?'
'If necessary.'


Blonde hair, green eyes, and dimples.
'This is Cassie,' says Cecil.
Cassie waves, mouth full of donut. She's eating a traditional sugared jam.
'You can go now,' says Cecil.


Miriam serves takeout. Four tables in the restaurant. Only four. Three dollars and sixty-seven cents in tips.
'I'm sorry. I trained as an accountant but food is my passion, take-out's my bread and butter, maybe tomorrow there will be more people in the restaurant.'


Monday.
'What do you want?' asks Cecil.
'My cheque.'
'What cheque?'
'Pay cheque.'
'You quit.'
'You still owe for hours worked.'
'Not if you quit.'
Wait it out. Wait it out.
Mustn't be late for Miriam.
Cecil out-waits.
Twenty hours. One hundred bucks owed.


At The Back Street Ukrainian Restaurant things are slow. The mountains whisper I told you so. Blank, eyeless, soulless, cautionary. They look like metal, forged by a giant smithy.

Eyes close. Leafy green tunnel, maple long john growing among the leaves, sausage and pyrogies, maple glazed, borscht, Boston cream.

Eyes open. Sunshine, Sunday. Eyes close.

Green water, swim, sink, rubber duck float, rubber duck whispers, whisper, whisper, air eases out of rubber duck, sink, sink, sink. Eyes open. Still Sunday.

Eyes close. Belly empty. Eyed close. Rubber duck re-inflated, swim, swim, hiss, whisper, swim, hiss, hiss, eyes taped closed, rubber duck repair kit, eyes hiss, hiss, shout. Angry rubber duck. Flap, slap.

Eyes open.

Dusk outside.

Voices in the wall, through the wall. Sounds. Male? Female? Silence. All calm.

Man smuggled in? Sleep with fingers in ears.


The Vending Machine Room.
NOTICEBOARD

Free plants—long term tenants only.

French conversation in return for English conversation.

Bear safety. A small pouch for information is empty.


Monday. Again.

'Don't tell me why I don't like Mondays, I know why I don't like Mondays.' Hum, hum.

'Why should I pay you?'

Cecil's nudging tummy points towards the street, like sheep dog with sheep.

'You owe the money.'

'You quit.'

'It's illegal not to pay.'

'Not true.'

'Looked it up. All work is paid.'

'Get out of here. I owe you nothing.'
Refuse to move, refuse to move.
He shifts his feet.
He licks his lips.
He hesitates. Sighs.

He takes a grubby wallet out of his back pocket and pulls out a twenty-dollar bill, licks his finger, flicks it to make sure there is only one. Stay by the door, still. He does it again. Screaming inside, *Don't lick the money*. He stares. Watch his wallet. Another twenty. Then a ten. Spittle glistens on the ten.

'Twenty hours, five bucks an hour, one hundred bucks.'

'You had breaks, you ate donuts.'

'One donut.'

He goes to the cash register and takes out a ten.

'Eighty bucks works.'


Canter to Miriam's.

Eighty bucks in pocket is victory enough. Knees are pistons, turn corner fast.

Stop!

Hopscotch!

Chalked in blue. Slow down. Right foot, both feet, left foot, both. Be kind to others written at the end.


The Vending machine Room.

Pour dish washing liquid in the sink, add water, hot water, steaming water, plop in eighty bucks, use fork to push down. Money laundering.


'Hello dear, are you new?'

'Hello Mavis, we met last week.' And the week before and the week before that.

'Toasted BLT with fries and coffee.'

Stare at him like he comes from Mars, then take the order into the kitchen.

Miriam reads the order and stares at the world like she's landed on Mars.

'We have no bread,' said Miriam. 'Or bacon.'

Stare at each other. Miriam's good for the fries because some people order a side with their traditional sausage.

'I'll give him coffee. You take money from the till, leave by the back door and go to the convenience store. Buy bread and bacon,' says Miriam.

Grab twenty dollars and run out of the back door. Freedom! A work-time run in sunshine to the convenience store, fingers crossed there isn't a line up. There isn't. Grab bacon and bread and run back.

Walk in. 'Fourth generation Canadian,' says Miriam.

The man nods. Take the coffee pot from Miriam's hand.

'Refill?'

'Haven't had much.'

'Warm up?'

'Sure. Got a newspaper?'

'Just the free one.'

'Works for me.'

He is a nice man, eats his bacon crispy just like Miriam cooks it. Reads the free paper, accepts multiple coffee refills, leaves a two-buck tip. Tempted to pocket it but Miriam has a system and it is fair. Two bucks in the cash register and at the end of the day Miriam gives $2.50 in tips. More than fair.


'I'm Mavis.'

'We've already met.'

'If you say so, dear.' Mavis walks down the hallway with her key, trying the doors. 'But I think you're making it up.'

Mavis was a temporary guest, waiting for a spot in a facility, her temporary shifted into permanent years ago. Amelia says remind her of shared history, it helps her memory.

If it works, stumbles along, then don't fix it.


Eyes closed.
    Cool green dream, soft, refreshing.
    Eyes open.


Scramble eggs swiftly on the Vending Machine Room stove.

EATING IN ROOMS IS STRICTLY FORBIDDEN

Eat quickly to avoid Debbie.
'Hi, I'm Natalie.'
'Hi.'
'I work in the Christian Bookstore.'
'Working with books must be nice.'
'Working with Christians is better. You?'
'The Back Street Ukrainian Restaurant.'
'Don't know it.'
'No one does. Used to work at a donut shop.'
'Cecil's?' says Natalie.
'Yep.'
'Good donuts.'
Natalie eats salad.
'Smells like eggs, sorry.'
'No worries. I like eggs.'


Mavis has escaped. Five of us residents and Amelia, search the streets. In pairs. Melanie, next door neighbour, stares at the mountains.

'They creep me out,' says Melanie.

'The mountains?'

'Totally, like some kinda supernatural fort.'

They are my security.

'Look at them, it's like they're peering into my soul,' says Melanie.

I look, I wrap my soul in barbed wire, I steel myself against Melanie.

'You need to leave while you still can,' says Melanie. (I don't want to leave.) 'I head back tomorrow. Never thought I'd spend my last evening searching for Mavis.'

The search adopts a competitive silence, interrupted with glances at the mountains. (I identify no menace and I am quick to identify menace.) Melanie's shoes squelch against the sidewalk. She is sombre, like the mountains in dusk and winter, halfway home already. Our eyes swivel from side to side. Melanie's eyes swivel to me and to the street and to me to the horizon, me, the street. No sign of Mavis. Melanie walks closer, I nudge towards the road.

'Ever hear noises at night?' says Melanie.

'Like music?' Melanie interrupts sleep with night-time noise, causes exhaustion, exhaustion means less tips. 'Like music?'

'Guess again.'

'Mavis!'

'Where?' asks Melanie.

'There.'

Clatter down the street, Melanie behind, Mavis stands and smiles and doesn't run away.

'We've been looking for you everywhere,' says Melanie.

'Do I know you?' asks Mavis.

'I'm Melanie,' says Melanie.

'I don't know a Margaret,' says Mavis.

'Not Margaret, Melanie.'

'Why did you say your name's Margaret if it's Melanie?'

'Are you ready to come home, Mavis?' My voice.

'You know,' says Mavis, 'there's a Melanie lives down the hall from me.' And then she winked. At me.

'I'm the Melanie lives down the hall from you,' says Melanie.

'Would you like some tea?'

'Tea would be very nice,' says Mavis and takes an arm. Melanie follows.

'Melanie from down the hall,' says Melanie.

'Is that woman following us?' asks Mavis. 'Should we be worried?'

At the corner of the road stand Amelia and Natalie.

'You know,' whispers Melanie from behind, 'Natalie used to be a Nun and gave it all up for a man. Now she's trapped in the YWCA.'

'Is that Margaret still here?' asks Mavis.

'He left her,' said Melanie.

'Is Margaret bothering you?' asks Mavis.

'The church won't have her back and she doesn't make enough at the bookstore to move.'

'Good job,' says Amelia. 'Everything alright, Mavis?'

'We're being followed by a Russian spy,' said Mavis. 'Her name is Melanie, she looks like Margaret who lives down the hallway from me.'

'Did she come willingly?' asks Natalie.

'I think so.'

'She doesn't much like Melanie,' whispers Amelia. 'Too much noise at night.'


Seven neatly packaged takeout orders.

Smile, grab order from serving hatch, ring up, take money, make change, hand food to customers, smile. Sour Cream? Extra onions? Plastic fork? Extra napkins?

'Who worked here before me?'

'No one,' says Miriam.

'Why did you hire me?'

'I thought I'd be busy for summer.'
'You should fire me.'
'You need a job.'
'I'll apply for a one.'
'I'll give you a good reference.'


Bluff Falls.
Bears in the mountains, slumping into town, cautious, curious, ravenous, greedy, staking out garbage cans in alley.


BEAR BELLS, GREAT PRICES
The Mountain Outfitters Emporium.
Curious. Like cowbells? How do you get a bell around a bear's neck?
There are pictures in the window, happy hikers on mountains.
Bear bells too appealing. Must conserve cash.


Help wanted.
Help wanted!
Must have experience.


A bear has been apprehended and removed to the back country.
Once more, the alleys are safe.


Bluff Ridge burns in the sun. People nudge each other, slurp ice cream and frosty drink treats, smell of coconut sun lotion.
Streets switch to paved path to gravel to dirt, small hill, large mountain, meadow. I walk out of town, hesitate

on the edge of the gravel. Ahead there be back country, ahead there be bears.

The mountains lean towards me, like giant staggering chess pieces, closer, closer, crowding me. Lowering. Ominous.


The Valley Family Restaurant is attached to a hotel and serves all kinds of liquor. Application form is lengthy. Must take care.


COMING SOON! GOODWILL!
Quality used clothes and household items.
Exciting!


Eyes closed. Blue skies, mountain flowers, green grass, picnic sandwich, sun soft on my skin. Bear eats other half of sandwich. Does he like cream cheese? Bear! Run! Bear runs! Down, down, falling down. Eyes open. Sex sounds, humble, apologetic, no danger. Close eyes. Endless tunnel of donuts. Bear runs paw down my Eats List, bear looks at me, pelts me with Maple Glazed. Run! Bear runs faster, down down, buried in donuts.

Eyes open.


Samantha is responsible for both the French conversation and the plant notices. She is returning to Quebec. Can't learn French but newly adopted aloe vera plant will heal external injuries.

'Phone call,' says Amelia. 'Valley Family Restaurant.'


'Waitress!'
    'Waitress.'

'Can you help us?'

'Are you our waitress?'

'I want pop.'

'Milk, dear. Is milk included with the children's special?'

'It's fifty cents more.'

'What's your name?'

'Don't bother the waitress dear. Milk is extra? But surely if you want children to be healthy, the pop should be more expensive.'

'What's your name?'

'I told you. It doesn't matter, she's only the waitress.'

'Can I have pop, please?'

'Don't talk to her. Mummy and Daddy talk to the waitresses, you talk to us. Don't talk to strangers.'

'She's not a stranger, she's a waitress.'

'Exactly.'

'Can I have pop?'

'Would you like crayons and pictures to colour?'

'Don't ask me, I don't want to colour, ask the children.'

'Would you guys like pictures to colour?'

'Yes please.'

'Can I have pop?'

'What's your name?'

'Don't ask her name, she's only the waitress.'

The Valley Family Restaurant serves fish and chips, veal cutlets, hot beef sandwiches, burgers, spaghetti, fried chicken and pizza. The children's menu offers all the same in smaller portions with ice cream and pop. Fifty cents extra for milk.

'Most of the guests are on holiday and don't go for the milk,' says Julia, my boss.

Julia wears jeans and a white T-shirt. All wait staff wear jeans and white T-shirts, with bib aprons over top. Band and movie T-shirts are okay if covered by the bib.

Today: Boomtown Rats.
$33.00 tips! Enough to live on for three days.


Eyes closed. Emptiness.
Eyes open. Need to pee. Too much pop at work. It's free. Get up, unlock room door, lock room door, pad down the hall like a thief in the night, use toilet, wash hands, back down the hall, unlock, lock.
Sex in the night sounds.
Tired. Eyes closed.


There are two Danny's at the Valley Family Restaurant. Danny B. and Danny S. Danny B. is nice and kind and funny flaky. Danny S. takes other wait staffs' tips off the tables when he clears them. And keeps what he takes.
Julia acts all big sister.
'Danny S. asked you to a movie yet? Be careful.'
Danny S. is no threat, even though his hair hangs floppy over his left eye.


Night sounds from every room on my floor.
All the residents shriek in joy at the same time.
Fingers in ears.
Closed eyes.


'Wanna come to a movie?' asked Danny B.
'Where I come from we don't do dating.'
'Who says it's a date?'
Shit!
A friendly laugh cuts through skin, bones, hidden thoughts.
Sit as far away from him as possible. Not far enough. His fingers explore and poke. Saved by popcorn.

Disentangle to eat more popcorn. Consider moving to the next seat.

Afterwards:

'Thank you for the movie.'

'You paid your own ticket.'

'For asking, I guess.'

His eyes, pallid and pale, anaemic, brown, resemble badly fried eggs.

Run.

The Mountain Equipment Emporium. BEAR BELLS ON SALE! Hover outside, nose to window.

'Heard you bolted on Danny B.' said Danny S.

'I knew you'd forget something,' said the father at table 19. He laughs and his whole body jiggles with joy at waitress forgetting.

'I can't believe you told Danny S. about last night.'

'I didn't, he's winding you up,' said Danny B.

Slosh salad dressing onto the salads that get served before the veal cutlets and fish and chips. Blue Cheese for her, Thousand Island for him. Thousand Island is lumpy and smells bad. Pretend to mix them up and then reverse at the last second, jiggling man grins.

The Mountain Equipment Emporium.

SALE. BEAR BELLS!

'Can I help you?' asks a woman.

'Saw the sign about bear bells.'

'Over in the corner. Feel free to try them on.'

The bells are on bracelets and designed to be worn on wrists and ankles. They scare bears away.

'Any questions?' asks the woman who wears her clothes in a reassuring mountain woman kind of way. Her baggy green pants teem with pockets and metal hooks hang from her belt loops. Is there a future as a mountain woman?

'Do they work?'

'Humans scare bears. Bells are human-like. If bears hear bells they run. Especially black bears. Of course, you can always sing.'

'Sing?'

'Make noise. Here.'

*Safety in Bear Country.* A pamphlet.

Grizzlies have smaller ears, longer claws. Black Bears can be blue-black, dark brown, light brown, cinnamon coloured, or white. Back away slowly from a grizzly, stand your ground against a black bear. If you can't back away from a grizzly curl up slow and small and put your backpack on your head for protection. What if you don't have a backpack? How does it fit on your head? If you see a black bear, make lots of noise, wave your arms, jump up and down, fight back.

Never climb a tree to escape a bear.

The metal rhomboid hanging from the woman's belt clip glitters in the sunlight.

Black bears come in a range of colours.

'Carabiner,' says the woman.

It's a hook.

'How do you spell carabiner?'


The Goodwill is huge and bright, and organised.

ALL CLOTHES WASHED OR DRY CLEANED.

Imagine giant appliances out the back.

Purchase blue tablecloth, or maybe a bedspread, with elephants skipping around the edge and tree growing in middle. Hang over open blind and window. In sunlight the room glows indigo.

Mavis left today. She has moved to a house that accommodates forgetful seniors. She will have all the care and support and locked doors she needs. She'll be missed.


'Waitress!'

The skiers have arrived.

'Waitress!'

They step through the door and yell.

'Menus?'

'Beer, we want beer. Who wants beer? Hands up. Eight beers.'

Rainbow snowsuits, cluttering every booth, dragging on the floor.

'What's good tonight?'

'Special's fish and chips.'

'How about you?'

'Are you on the menu?'

'I want the waitress!'

'With fries on the side.'

'Waitress! Where's my beer?'

'Give her a minute.'

'She's forgotten my beer. Waitress!'

'Someone want beer?' Hand around beers.

'I love you, waitress.'


Goodwill.

There are bookcases in the corner, ignore them. Do not want novels.

A tiny book on a table by the cash register. *The Young Woman's Pocket Guide to Self-Pleasure*. Not a novel.

The woman behind the counter stashes jeans and a black hoodie in a large Goodwill—*Helping Your Community*—bag.

Flip the book open. *MASTURBATION* is written on the first page.

'Oh!' The woman at the cash register sniffs and stares at the book, stares up, book again, up again.
*You're selling it.*
She accepts money, counts out change, refuses to look.


Consider faking a broken leg, skiing accident, to avoid staff Christmas party, but it's on Christmas Day and the Y has a party too. Work party the bigger of two anonymities.

Julia's gift from the owner is a Swiss Army Knife.

Unwrap a chicken jug.

Everyone's gift different, carefully chosen to complement personalities. Oohs and aahs as paper crackles and rasps off the presents.

I am Chicken Jug woman.


'Waitress!'
First table.
'Waitress'
Second table.
'Don't take the beers off my tray.'
'Pardon me!'
'Naughty, naughty.'
'It's balanced.'
'Balanced, you heard the lady.'
Later cleaning their table. His arm out and behind, closes in, feel the warmth of a lingering hand, grab his wrist.
'I don't think so.'
'Ow. She attacked me. You attacked me.'
'Uptight bitch. I'll complain to the management.'
'Go ahead. Let me get the manager for you. Julia. Gentleman here wants to complain.'
'You got a problem with my waitress?'

'Apologise, Quentin.'
'Yeah, apologise.'
'Apologise to the 'lady'.'
'Sorry.'
'Everything okay then?' asks Julia.


Glenys smiles a lot and shuffles when she walks. She likes snacks but isn't allowed to use the vending machines. Amelia warned me not to buy Glenys chocolate bars or hot chocolate. Glenys lives in Mavis's room.


*The Young Woman's Pocket Guide to Self-Pleasure* has three sections:
    Section One: Skin on Skin
    Section Two: Helpful Household Objects
    Section Three: Custom Devices


There's a new restaurant in town. Carrots and Peas. Vegetarian. It's where all the cool kids work, live music on weekends, a real fire in winter, a patio with twinkle lights. Press nose against the window—not literally, that would be gross—and peer at the dessert case. Looks good. There's homemade bread and a tea bar with jars of teas and mis-matched teacups.


Julia, wannabe big sister, gifted with Swiss Army Knife, understanding manager, protective co-worker, has fired me.
    Two weeks' pay in lieu of notice.
    Quentin, whose arm I grabbed, complained. The complaint moved through management, to head office, to owners.
    It's unfair dismissal but Quentin's father is a judge

and owns shares in the Valley Family Restaurant.


Bake.
    Molasses. Cloves. Cinnamon. Ginger.
    'Gingersnap?'
    'Thank you. I'm Lydia.'
    'Just arrived?'
    'Temporary. How long have you been here?'
    'Almost two years.'
    'You can't find a job with accommodation?'
    'Don't want a job with accommodation.'
    'You can save more.'
    'Lose your job, lose your accommodation.'
    'Where's home, dear?'
    'Here.'
    'Your real home.'
    'Here.'


Sleepless, mind wanders, *The Young Woman's Pocket Guide to Self-Pleasure* smoulders on the bed side table.
    Room is sadly bare of household objects.
    Pillow on my bed is a leading man from an old-time movie when men said little and women spoke only when spoken to. If this was the cover of a romance novel the bed would be a meadow with sunlight and daisies and unnaturally green grass.
    Pillow has been around the block. His stuffing has shifted, overused and worn out. Section Two: Helpful Household Objects suggests a pillow can be a young woman's best friend.
    What is that smell? Borax? Or a cheap one-month-wonder detergent?
    He looks tired.
    He needs to rest.

WANTED: Waitress.
    WANTED: Waitress.
    WANTED: Wait staff. Full silver service.
    WANTED: Servers.
    WANTED: Girl for tables.
    WANTED: Money for rent.

Kim moved into Mavis's room. (Glenys has been moved to a group home.) Kim wears dresses and cowboy boots and a jean jacket and looks a like a country and western singer. Her glossy red hair is straight to her shoulders. She is graceful.

I am the girl for the tables.
    It's a tavern. Some regulars wear lumberjack shirts and work boots, some are skiers, others hikers. Nobody questions my right to remove hands or talk fierce when necessary.
    The tips are good.
    Cecil arrives with a lady friend.
    'Good evening,' all chipper, words from an imaginary script that says 'add pep and smiles in greeting'.
    Lady Friend smiles back, Cecil glowers.
    'Cecil,' says Lady Friend. 'What has she ever done to you?'
    'Quit after two days! Insisted I pay her.'
    'It was longer than that.'
    'And now you're working here,' says Lady Friend. 'Good for you. I suppose he told you there'd be tips? And half price donuts too, right? You're so tight-fisted, Cecil.'
    'Shush, Charmaine,' says Cecil.
    'Do you like working here, dear?' asks Charmaine. 'It's very friendly.'

They fork-out a three-buck tip. Bet it was Charmaine.

Fields is a practical store with inexpensive clothes and household items. They have canvas running shoes, perfect for waitressing, in all known and some unknown colours. Eight bucks a pair. Red.
HOUSEHOLD SECTION, THIS WAY.
Pillows. New. Seconds. $3.00.
Second to what? Or is it seconded? Enough with the words.
Pillowcases. Black with white edging, a leather jacket and white T-shirt pillow equivalent.
'I always think it's a special treat to get a new pillow,' says the woman behind the cash register. She is small with tidy mouth, ears, eyes, and hair, all neatly glued in place; a well behaved women in sensible shoes. Her name tag says *Weronica—Here to help!*
'Is that your name?'
'It's meant to be a V.'
Her nose bubbles out her face with magnificent style and peeks over the cash register. She is short and should stand on a stool.
'Such a sign of hope,' says Weronica. 'The whole world seems different in the morning when you've slept with a new pillow.'
'Yes,'
'And such a fine pillow. Pillowcases too! Would you like a little tip from an old woman?'
'Please.'
'Give them a good wash before you use them, the pillowcases. New cotton, especially when dyed dark colours, is stiff against the skin. It can give you a rash.'

Hey Eve! Four more beers.
 Hey Eve! A plate of wings.
 Life is good. Most Tavern regulars gentle.
 Cecil is a regular. Every Wednesday. With Charmaine.


Seen from the doorway of the Vending Machine Room:
 'There was bear sighted in our back alley,' says Kim. 'Did you hear?'
 'Was it relocated?' asks Amelia.
 'I bought honey,' says Kim. 'In case it wants a snack.'
 'I don't think so,' says Amelia and takes the honey away.
 Kim looks like she will protest.
 'Ah,' says Amelia and holds a finger in Kim's face.
 Kim, subdued, leaves. Impressive Amelia.


Slink to the communal washroom in the middle of the night and lock the door.
 Tip filched dish liquid from the Vending Machine Room into the basin and run warm water, agitate for bubbles. Submerge the pillowcases. Like a thief in the night without stealing, except for the dish soap but it's for general use. The fabric billows.
 There are acres of foam and much rinsing, must not risk a rash from soap in the pillowcase. The world of bedding is fraught with skin disease.
 Footsteps.
 Wrap pillowcase in towel and stealthily unlock the door.


The Tavern.
 Reserved as 'Girls' Night Out'. All women, all drinking draught.

'She really said that?'
'Louisa was telling the story when you got there.'
'I babysit the grandkids on Thursdays.'
'… her mother was washing her hands in the Mystical Lake Hotel and shook her wedding ring off!'
'It was my story. Word for word. I'd told it to her a month earlier.'
'What did she do when you arrived?'
'Ate a breadstick. But she stole my story!'


'Can I have my honey?' asks Kim.
'Why do you want it?'
'For my toast.'
Amelia considers.
'There hasn't been a bear sighting for days.'
'Bring it back when you're finished. It'll be safe.'


Too excited to sleep, count footsteps, door closures, bathroom visits. All my YWCA roommates appear to be sleeping.

'Back soon,' to Old Pillow and New Pillow.

Head to The Vending Machine Room with Fields bag. All stealth. Could apply to the Canadian Spy Agency, need a trench coat and trickily disguised listening gadgets. Do they take people without high school diplomas?

Silently pull ironing board out of the wall, slyly plug in iron. Absolute discretion, no one must know these are personal pillowcases. Worse than a man in the room, personal bed linens. Buying my own pillowcases. Saving them for a move or too stuck up to use YWCA bedding?

Footsteps. Light off, fingers crossed, sink into the shadows, hold breath. Footsteps head to the washroom. Imagine lights bright in the eyes. *What was your purpose in the Vending Machine Room? Your purpose! Tell us!* A sign above the sink says *Please Do Not Wash Undergarments in These Sinks.* Underneath, in felt pen, YES! PEOPLE CLEAN THEIR TEETH IN THEM. A third person has written *and mine are false.*

Flushing, water running, footsteps. Sound carries well at night. Make note.

Flick on the light and hold my breath. Nothing.

The iron is really hot, sizzles.

Back to room. Dress pillows with soft ironed pillow slips. Both of them.


'Waitress!'

'Give her a minute,' says Cecil. 'She's with us. Show her some respect.'

'I see the skiers are here,' says Charmaine. 'We'll have our usual and take your time. Don't worry about us.'

Cecil and Charmaine smell of vanilla and ginger.

'I'll see to them, if they're disrespectful,' says Cecil.

Skier guy reaches for tray.

'Don't take the beers off my tray.'

'Pardon me!'

'It's balanced.'

'Listen to her,' yells Cecil.

Charmaine has a chocolate sprinkle in her hair.

'Is that...?'

'Oops,' says Charmaine. They blush.


Kim attacks Natalie with a pair of scissors.

Walk into the Vending Machine Room, thinking hot chocolate, see Kim's arm curve through the air, glittering. Natalie screams. The glitter scissors. There is blood. Kim screams, footsteps in the hallway. 'Get help!' Want to bolt but Natalie has don't-leave-me-eyes. Kim frozen with rage.

'Would you like some hot chocolate?' Desperate for

ordinary.

'Yes,' says Kim. Natalie nods.

'Can I go to the machine and get some?' Kim nods, Natalie's eyes says yes. Walk sideways to the machine, change for the hot chocolate swimming in hand sweat. It clatters into the machine.

'That's not chocolate,' screams Kim.

Pushed the wrong button. Shit!

'Sorry. Tea for Natalie'.

Gently set tea on table and return to the machine.

'Get her chocolate now,' whispers Amelia from the hallway.

Dump all the change in machine, eyes can't unglue from Kim. Breathe deep, heart pounds, glance at buttons, press hot chocolate. Kim licking her lips, hand on scissors, scissors buried in Natalie's arm. Sound like the roof was falling in. Cops on ropes breaking through the Vending Machine Room ceiling? Kim points at money clattering into the vending machine change tray.

Offer hot chocolate to Kim. Natalie leans away from Kim—difficult, still has scissors in arm. Kim takes chocolate with both hands. Natalie shrinks into the wall and yanks at the scissors. Head feels light, knees funny. Kim sips her hot chocolate.

'Don't forget your change,' says Kim.

Smile. Hold breath, turn, scoop up change. Covert shadows tip toe into the Vending Machine Room.

'Come along, Kim,' says Amelia.

'Thank you for the chocolate,' says Kim.

'You're welcome.'


Lay on side, head propped up in sunny meadow pose. There is no sunshine. The sky is lowering, and the wind is wuthering. New pillow is made of the wrong stuff. Have decided to return *The Young Woman's Pocket Guide to Self-Pleasure* to Goodwill.

'You're quite the hero.'
'Well done you.'
The regulars in the Tavern are supportive.


Amelia has gone. Kim was the last straw. She has retired.


Home.
Social services covers the cost for one bed for women with mental health issues. They pay even if no one's in the room, Diana, replacement for Amelia, says. She is young with curly hair and freckles and has courses in restraint and dementia care.


Work.
Alabaster Pete has the palest skin and tallest body ever seen, compensates with more muscle than any man deserves. Dark hair flows through a black floral bandana onto leather jacket and ancient T-shirts, jeans with a studded belt. Alabaster Pete has a surprising face, robust chipmunk cheeks, wise eyes, and a smile that worms its way across his face. His nose is think and gloriously upturned.


Natalie is home from the hospital.
'Thank you.'
'I didn't do anything.'
'You intervened. Might have saved my life. I must take you out for dinner.'
'I should have done more.'
I wobble inside.

'This isn't what I ordered! How could you get it wrong? Take it back. No onions.'

'It's a special pizza. Only comes with onions.'

'And I ordered hot chocolate.'

'No, you didn't.'

'I don't eat onions!'

'Hey!' says Alabaster Pete from the kitchen. 'Leave the young woman alone. I don't do pizza without onions. You got a problem with the pizza talk to me.'

'I never meant to make her cry.'

Who's crying?

'Kitchen closed for ten minutes,' says Alabaster Pete. 'I'm driving Eve home.'


Eyes closed.

Eyes closed.

Eyes closed.


'Guy called Pete phoned, says to rest, take some time, the job's not going anywhere,' says Diana.

Does Alabaster Pete own the tavern?


Eyes closed.

There are no dreams. Only a dragging, clutching, shaking darkness. Drag, drag. Clutch, clutch, shake, shake.

Eyes open.


Carrots and Peas has closed. There's a note. *We thought Bluff Ridge was ready for vegetarianism, apparently not.* Where have all the cool kids gone?

'Come to a movie with me.'

It's an intervention, not a date.

Alabaster Pete is younger than he looks.


Charmaine and Cecil are having Christmas at their place. They insist.

They have a tree.

Presents. Swiss Army Knife for Charmaine and a book of donut photos for Cecil. Worry about Cecil's present. Who wouldn't want a Swiss Army knife?

'Just put them under the tree,' said Charmaine.

The apartment is small. Cecil makes beer in the storage room, Charmaine knits and sews in the tiny spare bedroom.

'This is our bedroom,' says Charmaine. 'Have a look.'

'It's very pretty.'

Cecil sleeps under a pink rosebud quilt?

I have brought cake. Wacky cake with cherries.

Mountains peek through each window. There is no need for art on the walls but there are flowers everywhere and a single donut. All cross stitched.

'By Charmaine,' says Cecil. Proud, his arm around her shoulders.

We eat turkey and toast with wine. Then plum pudding and chocolate cherry wacky cake.

'This pudding is amazing.'

'Thanks,' says Cecil.

We open presents.

Charmaine made me mittens, they are dark green and soft like small friendly creatures.

'Thank you, they're beautiful.'

Cecil gives me an alarm clock. It's bright red and has two little clappers on the top.

'So's you'll never be late,' says Cecil.

'It's perfect.'

'I think I got yours,' says Charmaine.

'I don't think so,' says Cecil, flipping through his donut book.

We watch television and Cecil snores.


Four more movies.

'I don't want to take up your time,' says Alabaster Pete. 'Not if there's something you'd rather do.'

'I love movies.' It is not the answer he wants to hear.


'We still have to go out for dinner.' said Natalie.

Stare at her.

'Reward for you saving my life.'

'That was… a long time ago.'

'How about breakfast?'

'Castle Hotel Brunch Buffet?'

'Mountain Pancake House.'

'Deal,' says Natalie.


The pancakes are excellent. They are whole wheat covered in peanut butter and honey.

'No bacon? No sausage? No maple syrup?' asks Natalie.

'This place is nice.'

'They're looking for help,' says Natalie.

'I think I'm becoming a vegetarian.'

'Is Bluff Falls ready for you?'


A day off.

Tourist shuttle to Lake Mystical.

Three dollars return.

'Bear,' says a voice.

Hopefully return.

'That's not a bear, it's a bush,' says another voice.

'A moving bush?'

The bus slices through mountains, three lanes in both directions, pulls off the highway at Lake Mystical village. A hotel, another hotel, a motel, a small plaza with a vegetarian restaurant, liquor store, burger stand, donut shop, no houses, a gingerbread cottage—actually a hotel—tourists. More tourists, all making noise. This is good.

Grizzlies have snoutier noses. Or is that Black bears?

Check bear bells. One step, jingle jingle. Two steps, jingle, jingle.

Scrunch down to protect yourself from a grizzly. Or is it a black bear? Check identification page.

PLEASE DISPOSE OF UNWANTED FOOD AND FOOD WRAPPERS RESPONSIBLY

'I told you, you shouldn't bring sandwiches,' says a voice.

BOAT RENTAL, hourly and daily rates.

Something inside unfastens and I walk to the water. A breeze jingles my bear bells, comfort and music. The lake is blue green and sparkles. Magical, No, mystical. A canoe heads to a spot where two mountains meet and disappear into the water. Except they don't, they fan out in reflection. The best painter in the world couldn't paint something this good. A hard but friendly grey, rippled in a sheer rock face sort of way, ugly bit of mountain. But magnificent.

Nestled beside it two near perfect mountains, leaning to the right, whispering, like the gossiping cool girls in school, dip sharp, rise sharp.

TODAY'S CAPPUCCINO IS MINT CHOCOLATE CHIP

NEWSPAPERS FROM AROUND THE WORLD

The hotel is built close to the ground, ornate with carved patterns edging the eaves, delicate like lace.

TODAY'S CATCH OF THE DAY:

## CUTTHROAT TROUT

Walkers amble a broad paved path close to the cool girls' mountains. Bear bells jingle from back packs and ankles. Pity the poor bear that stumbles into this group.

The air is scented with mint and coffee and cinnamon. Underneath, way underneath, heady natural fresh mountain air crisps up heart and skin.

LAKE MYSTICAL TEA HOUSE 3.5 km

The path shifts quick, to gravel.

Behind voices and footsteps. Ahead flashes of colour.

Hum. Practice the words, *The bear went over the mountain...* The trail agonises into a blind right turn.

'Morning.'

'Hi!'

'Hullo.'

And gone.

The lake peeps through forest. People colours, red and orange backpacks, distant, ring bear bells. Sing.

LAKE MYSTICAL TEAHOUSE 2 km

Less people. Shout out the words. Deep forest tickle-your-lungs smells, salt and pine. A crack. Freeze and listen. Too silent. A creak. Another crack, another, echo in the silence. Trees toppling? Ring right bear bell. Ring left bear bell. A flash or purple above.

Plan is to walk upwards to Lake Mystical Teahouse. Arrive, use washroom, drink coffee, use washroom again, follow big group down, at a respectable distance.

TEAHOUSE 1 km

Gravel path becomes rock path becomes a pile of rocks, disappears. Someone has stolen the path. Maybe a bear has camouflaged it, misdirecting people to their pantry. Which is more intelligent, black bear or grizzly? Black bears. Make a lot of noise, long snouty faces.

TEA HOUSE. Wooden sign and arrow. Points to other side of the rock pile.

Scramble over the rocks and there it is. The path.

Forget to sing. But jingle, smell coffee.

Movement in the trees. No orange, no red, no backpack colours, only trees. Dark green, shadowy, piney foreboding. Long snout, short snout, black bears can be other colours. Grizzlies can be black. Move backpack onto head. Casual. Cautious. The shadows move.

Voice stifled. The trees creak.

A shape behind the trees. Big shape. Brown, definitely brown. It moves, it crashes. Sudden urge to climb a tree.

The bear crashes towards me.

'Hullo,' says the bear.

Talking bear? The flyer doesn't mention talking bears.

'I hope I didn't scare you,' says the bear.

'Of course not.'

'You're going to have to wait for a table at the tea house. It's packed with people,' says the bear and crashes off towards berries.

Talking bear with a green backpack. Definitely a bear. Unquestionable. Indisputable.

A real wooden manmade staircase. I touch it, the wood smells human, all the way to my heart. My skin prickles.

'Hullo.' 'Hullo.' 'Hullo.'

A herd of humans races down the stairs. Clinging to the stair rail I see the tea house.

I rattle my bells. I am a mountaineer.

Equanimity.


'Waitress!'

Stack beer glasses in the dishwasher, cross the floor with cups and a coffee pot on my tray.


'Maybe we should go for a meal before the movie?' suggests Alabaster Pete.

'No thank you.'

I drop off a résumé at The Mountain Pancake House.

All quiet at night in the YWCA. No bears. No donuts. No night noises. Could be I am exhausted.

Goodbye Tavern. Goodbye Alabaster Pete.
The Mountain Pancake House is flooded with early morning moonlight. I wake at 5.30 a.m. to shower and dry my hair. Skiers lurk and totter to 7.00 a.m. tables. I serve coffee immediately to tame their hurly rude burly hangovers.
And yes, the tips are good, very good.
'Good morning! Menus? Coffee to start?'
They slink into booths with red greased faces and morning hair, eyes bleared, racoon white circles inside the greasy red.
'Yes ma'am, coffee.' He is curled up into himself.
I fill coffee cups.
'Don't you work at the Valley Family Restaurant?'
'Used to.'
'Must you talk so loud? Is she talking loud or what?'
'Today's special is huevos rancheros.' I say it with a lilt and rolled rrrs. 'Served on two mini pancakes each topped with a fried egg.'
'Oh god, fried egg.'
'Topped with warm salsa, sour cream, scallions and grated cheese.'
'Whisper!'
'Ready to order?'
'Are you going to remember our order.'
'I am.'
'Pancakes.'

'Whole wheat, regular, sourdough.'

'Sourdough?'

'House specialty.'

'Why don't you work at the other place?'

'I was fired.'

'Seasons ago,' says a belligerent sleepy head, could be Quentin.

'Why?'

'What sort of pancakes did you want?'

'Is there anything other than pancakes?'

'We are a pancake house. But there are waffles. And a grilled cheese.'

'Is the grilled cheese on pancakes?'

'No, bread.'

'I want an order of pancakes and a grilled cheese. Regular pancakes.'

'Me too.'

I look at the fourth and he nods. 'Four orders of pancakes and four grilled cheese. Hash browns on the side?'

'Yes! Hash browns! They have hash browns!'

'And coffee. More coffee.'


I am officially a YWCA long long-termer. Rent is governed by a complicated hierarchy of rates. Daily, weekly, monthly. Louisa, who worked in the bank and stayed many nights with her boyfriend—most thoughtful, thank you, Louisa—has moved into his apartment. Permanently. I was offered her month to month rate. I have a shelf in a cupboard in the (long long-termer) Vending Machine Room. Same room but I have a key to the cupboard.


My day off.

I review the ears on bears and lengths of noses and

get it wrong.
 I stay home and bake cookies.
 I offer all the long-termers cookies.
 'You are such a doll,' says Diana.


Another Christmas with Charmaine and Cecil. I wrap a log book for home brewers for Cecil and a dictionary of embroidery for Charmaine.


Summer.
 Athens Pizza.
 'Waitress, waitress, where are the pitchers of Greece?'
 'Pitchers of grease?'
 'My place mat is plain, there used to be pitchers of Greece.'
 'We ran out of pictures of Greece placemats. More next week.'


YWCA potluck tea.
 I make gingerbread and applesauce.
 'You need to sweeten this applesauce,' says Jenny who is our mental health room occupant and actually a nurse in the mental health unit at the hospital, waiting for the apartment where she lives to be cleaned. 'Bed bugs,' she said when she arrived.
 At night I scratch my arms and turn the lights off and on, quick and sudden, stare at my walls. Again, and again. Covert light attack for identification purposes.


I am the proud owner of a Genuine Curling Sweater. The label says so.
 'Are you sure you want this?' the Goodwill cash

register woman snarls. Her glasses, blue frames, rhinestones, bounce as she sniffs disapproval.

'Absolutely.'

'It's got a zebra on the back.'

'I know that, Sharon. It's why I want it.'

SHARON, VOLUNTEER, says the badge above her left breast.

'It's been mis-priced. It's vintage…'

The label inside, complete with fresh dry cleaning ticket, is yellowed with ancient writing.

'It's worth more than three dollars, I must increase the price.'

'Aren't prices honoured at face value?'

'You switched the price label.' She staggers with excitement.

'The label's stapled on,' I say. 'Do I look like I have a stapler?' I hold my arms out and turn around, all the way round. I wear a Kurt Cobain T-shirt and blue jeans, wallet in my back pocket.

'That doesn't mean you didn't switch the price.'

'How?'

'Is everything alright?' asks SHEILA, MANAGER, a woman in shiny high heels, big hair, and a tartan skirt that's pleated outwards from her hips. She might break into song, County and Western, something Dolly Parton about her hair.

'She switched the price on this.'

'I did not. I don't have a stapler,' I say and hold my arms out—again—to demonstrate. Sheila smiles and looks at the label.

'No,' says Sheila. 'I priced this. It's accurate.'

'But it's a Genuine Curling Sweater with a zipper up the front and a Zebra on the back.'

'It's already priced,' says Sheila.

Sharon slowly rings up the sale. I take a handful of change out of my pocket and count out two dollars in quarters and one in nickels and dimes.

'I'll give you twenty for it,' says Sharon, when Sheila leaves.
'No.'
'Thirty.'
'I like zebras.


Charmaine and Cecil are gone. They have a small house in a Temple City, a prairie city many miles away. They say come visit but I stay in Bluff Falls, not rooted but comfortably wedged.


Winter Solstice.
I stare at the motionless sun from the window of the Mystical Lake bus. I have cleats and a thick jacket, a backpack with supplies. I wear extra warm gloves that are like a second skin, warmer still with Charmaine's knitted mittens on top.
Only skiers ride the bus with me, cross country skiers, they will ski the lake.
Mystical Lake. There are bright lights in the hotels and motels, gift shops and restaurants. More people cluster at the lake than expected. I wear dark glasses to cut the snow sparkle. I have read a pamphlet on how sun on snow can be dangerous to eyes. There are skaters. The air crunches into my lungs. I walk. The snow is solid and packed on the path. My cleats chomp down. Black tree trunks creak and crack—I am not scared I know that is what they do in winter. The sun is large, orange redness spreading out in waves. Cold but not freezing, my face stays bare; skin will not freeze quickly today. The snow is grubby with foot prints.
'Morning.'
'Merry Christmas.'
I will not celebrate Christmas.
I pause. It is solstice, the bears are asleep and I am

alone with the sun. There are small animal tracks and silence broken with a giant crack. Like a giant's bone has snapped. Somehow familiar. A breeze, more cracks, winter trees. The world slips back to silence, the trees black against a blue sky and white snow. I celebrate. Raging silence echoes my heartbeat. My insides tick over.

I turn a corner alone but on a path recently stepped by other feet, snow pushed down and mounded in the middle, near frozen mounds like eggs in white water. I walk on the fresh crust of edge snow. Crisped and glittering. Occasional steps break through the surface, ragged cracks, snow layers, like broken shortbread.

I turn and turn again and up and on in companionable outside air. Peaceful. Dynamic.

I see smoke, a snaking wisp disappears into the blue. Solstice celebrating bears? Christmas bears wrapping nuts and berries in sodden snow-buried leaves? Can't be bears they're all asleep.

The smell of fire.

The Tea House is open but not open. *Closed for Season*, says the sign. There are cars, evidence of humans. I am too curious not to investigate.

I open the door.

'Eve!' Mountain Family Restaurant Julia. Swiss Army knife Julia. 'Come in!'

'I'm hiking,' I say.

'We're not open but we're open. Staff party.'

I stay a moment. Refuse all offers of food and drink.

My silence is broken.


Moose Waffles (coffee, moose antler headbands, berry topping, piggy topping, cowsy topping).

Nick, waffle maker, catches up with me after shift. We walk till we run out of town and stand looking at the stubbly grass with daisies and yellow and pink flowers.

His fingers grab mine. I pull my fingers back.

'Don't be so detached,' he says.
'This is who I am.'


I make raisin cookies. I share with Jonquil, who reminds me of Glenys from my early days in Bluff Falls; with Katherine, who has replaced Diana who replaced Amelia, our new leader in chief; with a giggling group of early summer tourists.


Mountain Greek (Spanakopita with ten different salads).
    Original Pizza (Hawaiian, Mexican, Bratwurst).
    Mac's All Time Greatest Steak House (steak, steak, more steak, fish and chips).


Another winter solstice. I hike a canyon, absolute silence, no staff parties hiding out in closed tea houses.


Christmas. I help Katherine cook Christmas dinner. A different celebration. Warm and fuzzy and very indoors with all food remaining in appropriate areas.


Everyone at The Sunrise Pancake House, not to be confused with The Mountain Pancake House, has free tickets to the Castle Hotel Hot Springs and Swimming Pool. The Castle—as most service industry workers refer to it, often with derision, rarely with affection—invites local service industry workers to an annual party and head hunt.
    There's free food.
    I don't want to go to the party.
    There are seven swimsuits in Fields. I try each one on. Only one fits. Lime green but only five bucks. The

label says odd shaped. It fits me.

I have not decided to go to the party. The swimsuit is insurance. If I am prepared it might fall through.


Jonquil has been removed from the YWCA. She was caught with food in her room. There were mice. It was ugly.


The party does not fall through and I am out of excuses.

I wear jeans, a Nick Cave and The Bad Seeds T-shirt and my Genuine Curling Sweater. Zipper up the front. Zebra on the back.

The lobby of this hotel like a castle has tartan carpets, chandeliered ceilings, rock walls, and the staff wear kilts. A welter of patellas.

I clutch my swimsuit, towel, and bristling self-confidence.

One pair of knees pauses, huge knobs and nubs, kilt, shirt, stout neck, black blanket beard, censorious eyes. The eyes carp in my direction. He raises a bushy right eyebrow and points to a sign.

*Hospitality Industry Event. Please use side door.*

There's an arrow.

He nods, I nod. I leave and come back in the side door. I am in the same room as before.

Knees and beard nods, points to another sign.

Halfway down a small hallway, the carpet becomes functional and there's a table. *Hospitality Event.* A stack of job applications. The hallway slopes downward into stone and the air smells of rotten eggs.

*Staff Change Rooms*

Debbie, pleasantest waitress I've ever met—entering her fourth year of university in September—is in the locker room.

'Isn't this fun! We're in the staff baths. Do you want

me to wait for you?'

'Sure.'

'Great sweater.'

'Thanks.'

'Is it a Genuine Curling Sweater?'

'It is.'

'The one with the Zebra. Oh my god, I love the one with the zebra. You know that's probably worth three hundred bucks in the right vintage store.'

I lock my locker tight.

I almost wish I could swim naked since the lime green swimsuit is hideous and bags on the belly. Probably why it said odd shape. My body is not an odd shape and feels underused.

'I have three GCSs.'

'Huh?'

'Genuine Curling Sweaters, silly.'

'Right.'

'The bear, a puppy, and a bow.'

'A bow?'

'I know—who'd have thought there'd be a bow?'

'Maybe it's a knock off.'

'You think? You could be right. I'll phone my parents, get them to check.'

'Aren't you going home soon?'

'I need to know now.'

Debbie studies retail and logistics at university. She will sell and deliver the future.

The pool is half inside, half outside. Inside warm, outside hot. You are forced into the pool to get to the outside party. Debbie swims. I walk, knees bent and bum dragging on the pool floor, head above the water.

I am all talked out and head for the hot tub.

Debbie joins a cluster of service industry staff jumping into the main pool from a small diving board, beneath the NO DIVING OR JUMPING sign. The Grand Castle's haughty kilts wait on us. Few will be hired, I won't apply. No way I'm wearing a kilt.

I wrinkle up in the hot tub, delighted no one can see my lime green bathing suit.

'It's unhealthy to stay in there too long.'

Steve.

'Too hot.'

More Steve.

'You should go for a cold plunge.'

Steve, college boy, skier, good bones, floppy brown curls, big brown eyes, works two tip-heavy shifts at The Sunrise Pancake House. He's good; they'd hire him for more shifts but his heart is in his bartender job at The Mountain Bar and Brewing Company. We work well together Saturday and Sunday mornings.

'Can't swim,' I say.

'I'll teach you.'

'I like it here.'

'Look at your fingers and toes.'

My fingers and toes wrinkle and flake.

'I don't want to get out.'

'Lethargy. Your heart's collapsing on itself. A warning. I'm pre-med.'

He points to a sign.

HOT TUB GUIDELINES

*Recommended Soak Time: 30 mins max*

*Light-headed? Dizzy? Nauseous? Vacate pool immediately.*

Underneath someone has scribbled: *We don't soak in your toilet, please don't pee in our pools.*

I lie flat in the swimming part of the pool, Steve's hand against my lime green swimsuit.

'Keep your legs straight.'

'They are straight.'

Steve adjusts my legs. My tummy flounders. Steve gently props it up.

'I'm going to bend your arms now.'

He switches arms under my tummy.

'I'm going to move this arm. Like it's swimming.'
Gently he has my arm bat away the water.
'Now the other arm.'
His finger still holds up my belly.
'Do the arms on your own.'

I slap them against the water. His hand remains beneath my belly.

'Kick your legs.'

I kick. His hands straighten my legs. One smooth movement.

'Keep going.'

I move. He stands beside me, no fingers touching. I miss them. I am going to drown. My face panics.

'I've got you.' Steve pulls me by the hand. Occasional directional taps more than a pull.

'Good job,' says Steve.

We sit in the sun on the steps of the pool. Steve is on the edge and I am one step down, most of my swimsuit submerged.

'Hey!' He flags down a waiter.

'Steve. Hey man!'

'We were in high school together, me and the kilt.' Steve has two glasses. 'Red or white?'

'Red.'

'If I give you this you have to promise not to go in the hot tub again.'

I hate games. I dislike alcohol; I'd have sipped and held the glass. 'Give me the wine,' I say.

'I'm just looking after you.'

'I don't need looking after.'

We stare at the staggering and swaying and boozing hospitality workers.

I don't like wine. I choke some back.

'Food,' calls Steve and fancy crackers with fancier cheese appear on a plate on the hand of the guy who was in high school with Steve.

Like much accommodation in Bluff Falls, Steve's room is tiny and attached to his bar tending job. Rent is deducted from pay cheques. It's too shabby to be rented to tourists (summer) or skiers (winter). When he's fired, or quits, he moves. Permanent accommodation is hard to find. I am fortunate to be a long-termer.

Steve is quick and efficient. I remember the wet swimsuit and his damp fingered adjustments and keep up. Just.

Steve is flat on the bed grinning when I reach for my clothes.

'Stay.'

'The Y is pretty strict.'

'They can't throw you out for not going home.'

'They can. I signed papers.'

'You want me to walk you?'

'No.'

Outside I gulp air, relieved to be alone. Steve's a college boy. He will leave town soon.


'What does 'wuthering' mean?'

I bake Healthy Hiker Cookies. Tammy drinks coffee and reads at the kitchen table. She's new, we met last night.

'Wuthering? It means windy.'

She holds up the book.

'Why are you reading that?'

'I took a semester off to read.'

Decadent.

'Can't pass English courses. I want to be a vet.'

'Shouldn't you study science?'

'I'm great at science.'

'Cookie?' I ask.

I won't think novels. I walk through the YWCA offering cookies.

Steve watches Star Trek. I stare at a crack in his ceiling. Captain Janeway appears to collude with the Borg.

'I might pick up another shift at the Sunshine Pancake House,' he says during an ad.

'Aren't you going back to school soon?'

The Borg planet is destroyed. He is watching a rerun in anticipation of the new series.

A man on the television drives a red jeep through back country.

'That's just wrong,' said Steve.

'You're not going back to school?'

'Pollution,' said Steve. 'We must keep the wilderness pristine. I'm taking a year off.'

A year?

A kitten plays with toilet paper.

'You're staying in Bluff Falls?

'My year to ski.'

'You ski?'

A Borg cube tows the Enterprise through the credits.

'Yep. Why are you dressed?'

'I'm opening tomorrow.'

'See you tomorrow night?'

I let myself out quietly so as not to disturb a rerun of one of the 444—or is it 445?—episodes that came before Captain Janeway negotiated with the enemy.


Tammy and I drink tea at a shiny table with its own ivy plant in The Mystical Vegetarian Eating Experience.

'*Discuss the theme of regret in* The Stone Angel,' reads Tammy.

'I promised myself I wouldn't read while I was here.'

'I thought you lived here. Permanently.'

'I do.'

'She's ninety-one years old. Her life had ups and downs, the world had ups and downs. She's a practical woman, she survived. No guilt no regret.'

No guilt, no regret? Hagar is culpable, answerable for John's death, ever since I was fourteen years old. He was the first boy, man, to supplant Pony Boy and Darry (only after seeing the movie) in my passions. How could Tammy read the book and not know this? I am plunged back into pages. My heart races. I am under water in the restaurant, struggling to surface. 'She made choices, she chose John over Marvin and killed John and destroyed Marvin.'

'Marvin's sixty-five and sells paint.'

'She never saw him.'

'If I live that long I'll have no regrets.'

'But all the complications in Hagar's life…'

'That's why I want to be a vet. No complications. Animals are uncomplicated with their affection.'


The crack on Steve's ceiling grows, branches out. Little cracks creep away from the big crack.

'How old is this house?'

'Watch,' says Steve, 'Spock's mind melding.'


Many Step Valley is on the edge of town. The steps are built into the rock, straggle down one side and up the other. I fold my body into the steps to avoid joggers. Faded autumn grass, like bristles on an old man's chin, crackles underfoot. The valley floor is covered with phoney almost winter dying, like a magician's rabbit waiting to jump out his hat in spring.

I sit on a rock and mourn John Shipley. Do not get mixed up with the characters from books. I thought Tammy was safe to talk to, all science and no story.

I stare into the horizon and think I see a black shape. A bear? Half a dozen folk, running, walking.

I watch elk in the river. They pause as they wade

across. Like statues, waiting. Maybe they enjoy standing in the water, maybe it cools them, makes their blood run free. They stay for minutes. Longer. Then without collusion or obvious decision they leave. The valley walls darken in the afternoon light. I walk up a few steps and sit down. More rock than plant. Good hard rock, unforgiving.

Steve and I run dilettante through the shreds of Goodwill castoffs. Children playing at other lives. Trying on, checking out. Me, peacock blue silk dress future member of the wedding party; Steve, slate grey suited major from an unjust, unquiet war. Both in street jacket topped pyjamas, playing air guitar for invisible audience, benevolent smiling shoppers. Lampshade headed jesters. Faded silk flower mourners.

'Good morning! Coffee? Menus?'
'Rodney, Geoff, Sarah, Jane: this is my girlfriend.'
Girlfriend?
I wave, pour coffees. Steve stands behind me. I can feel the heat of his body.
'They just showed up this morning. Hammering on the door. We went to school together. And college. Still go to school together, I guess.'
I wince but it looks like a smile.
'Anyways, it's time you met my friends. They said I'd made you up. Let me help.'
I carry three coffees, Steve carries two, that way I don't have to use and wipe a tray, walk the tray back to the kitchen to be washed.
I set down my coffees, he sets down his, then he kisses me, chaste but proprietary.
'Does everyone know what they want?'
Rodney and Geoff leer at Steve.

The Mystical Vegetarian Eating Experience has a fireplace. So had Carrots and Peas. I return. Alone. I sit in the glow of the fire, the gleam of the varnished and polished wood tables and the twinkle of the fairy lights and imagine how I would deal with the Borg. *Fully vegetarian and vegan accommodated* says the sign. Enough people to suggest Bluff Falls is ready.

'We should go out for dinner,' says Steve.
I am happy to watch the crack in the ceiling. 'Have you ever noticed how much like a spider's web the ceiling is?'
'Nah. I should read some of these books. Get a head start on school.'
There are nine. I counted.
'These are seriously university books?'
'Yeah.'
'I've read them.'
'No one's read that many books.'
'Old woman looks back on her life with regret and guilt, spinster teacher finds love on the other side of the track, grad student...'

GOODWILL
I find an amazing coat. Fake sheepskin, only better. Tan. Seamed together in squares, a bit mountain, a lot western. Toasty inside. Goes down all the way to the ground.
I look like a guardian of the universe.
I feel like a guardian of the universe.
I am a guardian of the universe.
I walk with bigger steps.
Strides.

Steve and I eat dinner in a restaurant. I wear jeans and a Talking Heads T-shirt and my Genuine Curling Sweater, the one with the Zebra. Things don't start well.

'Nice sweater,' says Steve. 'Is it new?'

'When do I not wear this sweater?'

Steve is wearing jeans and a shirt and a bolo tie. A bolo tie?

'What do you think of my tie?'

'Very country and western.'

'Alt country and western.'

'There's a difference?'

'Natch.'

'Natch? Did you just say 'natch'?'

Things get worse.

'I'm going back to school,' says Steve.

'I know.'

'Not next year, this Christmas. My parents won't pay for another semester off.'

'You'll miss the best skiing.'

'Come with me.'

'Skiing?'

'Home. We'll get an apartment.'

'No.'


The Mystical Vegetarian Eating Experience has a help wanted sign.

I walk by and to the edge of town. I stand in the frozen meadow. Steve's parents promised him a year off school. To ski. Now the ski season is here and they are pulling out of the deal. I smell the November air, wood fire and exhaust from the trucks on the truck route. Not allowed in town unless they're delivering. Instead, they tear by the meadow.

'Do you think you should tell someone about the cracks?'
'What cracks?'
'The cracks in the ceiling.'
'There are cracks in the ceiling?'
'You want to be a doctor?'
'My parents want me to be a doctor.'
'These ceiling cracks are a symptom of the building's decay.'
'My parents want to meet you.'
'Doctors are meant to recognise symptoms. You told your parents about me?'
'Come home with me.'
'No.'
'We can get engaged.'
'No.'
'Let me buy you a ring.'
'I don't want a ring.'
'I can't believe you never finished high school.'
'Believe it.'
'You're so smart.'
'I'm a waitress. You know nothing about me.'
'Come to university with me.'
'They won't let me in.'
'Upgrade.'
'Still won't let me in.'

I have been offered a job at The Mystical Vegetarian Eating Experience. I almost didn't apply. My résumé clung to the insides of my purse, screaming, *Don't take me in there, no, no, no.* The wait staff wear jeans, cargo pants, long skirts. There is no uniform.

'Come visit me.'
'A clean break would be best.'
'You're wrong.'

'Hello dear, you're new?'
'Just started.'
'How do you like it so far?'
'A perfect half hour.'
'Excellent. I'm Gwendolyn Maeterlink.'

A shadow of a woman with a giant purse that could hold the world and a hat from a French fashion runway. Her hair flows thick and grey and half-way down her back, she wears button boots and a long velvet coat, green as an empty 7 Up bottle. She shuffles from old age and her thin face is pinched and transparent. Gwendolyn has spunk and charm but my gut churns like she is trouble.

She settles into a sharing table with two bear bell hikers, a businessman and a jogger. She waves me over.

'Just coffee, please. Black. And a muffin.'
'Pumpkin wholemeal, date bran, or rosemary sage flax?'
'What would you recommend?'
'I've only worked here half an hour but the date bran looks good.'
'Anybody?' She invites the table.
'Pumpkin wholemeal,' says the jogger.
'Date bran,' says the businessman and winks at me.
The healthy hikers shrug.
'Date bran, I guess.'


'There's a new bookshop in town,' says Linda who has replaced Katherine who replaced Diana who replaced Amelia as leader of the YWCA. Linda is a fully qualified Mental Health Support Worker, 'Just in case,' says Linda, 'you know, there's enough 'cases' to make it worth my extra wages.' Linda favours faded shades of pink and purple and has a hairstyle popular in women's magazines from the fifties. It is rinsed in blue. Powder pools in the lines of her face. Her eyes blink repeatedly. I think she might need glasses. She is a woman who looks like she should have grown up children but if she does she never mentions them. The role of YWCA leader is the last step before no work at all for most of the incumbents.

'It's not religious,' said Natalie with a sniff. 'The bookstore.'

We eat cake—Linda bought it at Safeway, she discourages baking in the kitchen because of 'vermin'—to celebrate Natalie's tenth anniversary at the YWCA in Bluff Falls. Linda and I are washing up after the modest celebration, Natalie as guest of honour sits at the table and sips from a teacup. Everyone else evaporated into the hallway and beyond.

Linda looks at me to join the conversation but I am preoccupied. I am closing in on eight years at the YWCA. Am I over connected?

'Eve doesn't read,' says Natalie.

'Really?' said Linda. 'You look like a reader to me.'

The Mystical Vegetarian Eating Experience. Live music Friday and Saturday nights. Real hearth, opening shift chops wood and sets the fire. I have never chopped wood before.

A dark eyed carpenter builds a spiral staircase from one floor to the other of the new bookstore. I watch through the window. Books fill the shelves and I find it hard to focus on the carpenter. He takes his shirt off and I notice a perfect row of Penguin Modern Classics.

'Hello dear.'

Gwendolyn.

'It's going to be a beautiful bookshop, isn't it?'

I blush and search for words.

'Actually, I was watching the carpenter.'

'Oh yes?,' says Gwendolyn as if she doesn't believe me.

'Hello.'
'You're new.'
'What's your name?'
'Is there a special?'
'Enchiladas, hold the cheese, no I don't want the vegan cheese, I'll have an extra enchilada, Davey in the kitchen knows me, tell him it's Al.'

'Hey Al,' yells Davey before I get to the kitchen, 'enchiladas, no cheese.'

'You got it.'

Today I work backbone. (Backbone shift: Mystical Vegetarian Eating Experience talk for mid-morning to early evening.) Music starts at eight. After shift I sit on the patio and listen, alone in a corner lit by fairy lights, the rest of the patio dark. I am unaccustomed to music. This is folky, a gravelly voice, a story about an old car. The voice burrows under my skin. My body feels light. I snuggle into my Curling sweater and eat a grilled cheese sandwich. Davey makes the best grilled cheese. Homemade bread and a mix of edgy cheeses. Afterwards, vegan chocolate cake. I drink rose-hip tea, traces of bitterness, tastes of roses.


I edge into vegetarianism. Soak beans at the YWCA and cook them stove top.

'Making beans?'
'Yes, making beans.'
'Same as in a can?'
'Close.'
'Why?'
'Because I want to.'

Briony is the new mental health room occupant. She talks much and listens little.

'But I really like the ones in the can,' says Briony. 'They always taste the same. Are yours going to taste like the ones in the can?'

'Probably not.'

'Why aren't they going to taste the same as the ones in the can?'

'Maybe because they're vegetarian. No meat.'

'I know what vegetarian is,' says Briony.

'You know those chunks of bacon in tinned baked beans?'

'The fatty pork? I don't like the fatty pork.'

'These don't have any.' I add ketchup, molasses, vegan barbecue sauce, salt and mustard and pepper, stir and simmer. Linda puts her head around the door. I can't see her body. It's like Halloween, her head floating in the air.

'Is it time I took Briony shopping, Eve?'

'She was just going to try my beans, there's enough for you and anyone else.'

'I hope I'm going to like these,' says Briony and sits at the table with Linda.

Satisfaction.


Gwendolyn dips into the largest purse known to humans, roots and rummages, hands over small change.

'Is that enough?'

'More than.' I hand a loonie back.

'Keep it.'

It rattles into the plaster wine cooler where we pool our tips.


I have purchased a slow cooker. I soak chick peas, then slip them into the slow cooker with onions and garlic. Make home made falafel.

Only Natalie has been at the YWCA longer than me.

'Play 'Casey Jones'.'
'I played 'Casey Jones'.'
'Play it again.'
'I played it again.'
'Three times.'
'I played it three times.'
'I didn't arrive until after you played it the first time, so I've only heard it twice.'
'The other customers don't need to hear it four times.'
Gwendolyn is the only other customer.
'Hey, lady,' calls the Dead Head.
'Are you talking to me?'
'Yes, ma'am.'
'I'm Gwendolyn.'
'Hello Gwendolyn. Do you mind hearing 'Casey Jones' again?'
'By the Grateful Dead?' asked Gwendolyn. I groan.
'The one and only.'
Please say no, please say no!
'I'd be delighted.'
They both sing along as does Marcus in the kitchen (Davey's day off—I will have soup, salad and bread for my meal) and Randell, the other wait staff. In fairness Randell is out on the patio having a cigarette because we are slow before the rush.

Gwendolyn rearranges charity chocolate bars stacked by the till as I make change. Too many skiers foraging for chocolate almonds. She sorts and separates, Crunch Bars with Crunch Bars, Chocolate Almonds with Chocolate Almonds, Smarties with Smarties, Milk Chocolate with Milk Chocolate. I yearn to muddle the candy.


I walk down a residential street with few cars and few tourists—it is no longer summer and not yet ski season. I cross a parking lot to the paved trail beside a riverbank. I walk in silence, bear bells in purse, enough people around not to need them.

The path climbs and the canyon falls, deep, deep to the left, its striped walls, reds, orange, green and browns, sparkle with silver.

Warning! Bear Sighting.

Grizzly or black, I wonder.

I walk upwards, one eye always scanning for other humans. Striped hill, like a humbug, falls downwards behind. Mica like sugar today. I am in wonderland. Today's people, silently identified protectors against bears, might be ready to turn around. I stand casually and look over the side. They sprawl across the bridge and take photos of each other. At canyon bottom there is a stream. Gurgle, spit, spray. I shift to spy a tiny waterfall. They take photographs, they lean a long way over the edge. I hope they will be gentle with me if we come across a bear. I am not prepared to lean dangerously from a great height.

Someone has stolen my Genuine Curling Sweater. We think, the Mystical Vegetarian Eating Experience staff, that it was a mistake. We have taped a LOST notice to the front window and another on the community noticeboard in the doorway.

I borrow a grey blue jean jacket from lost and found. Feel like a teenager. Hurry home in the fast-cooling night, worried someone might accuse me of stealing the jacket. The Mystical Vegetarian Eating Experience is softening my skin.

Last night I found *The Young Woman's Guide to Self-Pleasure* in the bottom of my drawer, beneath my spare pillow. Old friend. Forgotten but not forgotten.

I am not Portnoy.

Enough with the books his mother would say, if she were my mother. They only get you into trouble, his mother would say if she were my mother.

My mother wasn't Portnoy's mother. My father wasn't.


I hike the hidden valley. Alone. No protectors, no Curling sweater. I sing and ring bells.


I buy a sweater. In handwriting the label calls it 'rainbow blue' and lists the blues: *Royal, space, Egyptian, navy, sapphire, azure, cobalt, lapis lazuli*—only the bold blues. It is soft and baggy and cozy and has a high but not strangling neck. It doesn't stop until it is almost at my knees, I prowl the store and find boots and a dress that fits and is soft. I look a different version of me.

I miss my Zebra.


Davey whistles when I walk in in a dress. Even though I'm wearing boots—hiking boots, good lugs—and the dress falls close to the ground.

'That's sexist,' says Jace who waits tables with me and has already chopped the wood.

'You know I don't mean it. I'm sorry.'

I light the fire.

All day people comment on my dress and boots. I am close to incognito.

'I think you look beautiful, Eve,' says Gwendolyn. She stands at the tea buffet, looks beatific. Twenty-three well lined up cups and saucers, a mug half filled with coffee.

A young man in too high cowboy boots and a slow smile sidles up to the coffee mug. Takes it back.

'Pardon me, ma'am,' he smiles at Gwendolyn. 'Just

taking a bathroom break.'

'This is so kind of you, Gwendolyn.'


Natalie is moving. She is now manager of the Christian bookstore and with the job comes the apartment above the store.

'Imagine,' says Natalie, 'an entire apartment to myself.'

I will miss Natalie's inevitable presence in my life.

'Good luck,' I say.

'You must come to my housewarming,' says Natalie.


I wear a Grateful Dead T-shirt, from Goodwill's 99c clearance.

'Nice T-shirt.'

Davey nods at my T-shirt and makes a two thumbs up sign.


I hike a canyon in skirt, boots and sweater.

Green moss, clings to the rock like a tablecloth slipping off a table, barely maintaining purchase on the surface.

Would I rather climb down a canyon or fight a bear?

I reach the first bridge across Slot Canyon. *Up to 50 meters deep* the sign tells me. Underground springs cause bubbling and popping water, small waterfalls. At the second bridge a sign says *Beware Black Bears*. Black bears. Make yourself big. I am wearing a dress and won't be tempted to climb trees. A knot of rowdy hikers shamble onto the bridge. I peek over the side. It is spectacular.

Suddenly a staircase. In the middle of the wilderness. It can't be easy for bears, going up and down these stairs. I slip bear bells on my wrist. Some steps are carved in the rock, others are built of wood, in between natural earth ledges. The rowdy hikers peer at my bear bells and smile and follow. I smile. I am prepared, I am a back country hiker. I live in these mountains. I know these bears.

I tread cautiously down the stairs. Down, and down. Rushing water. Louder and louder. I see a deep ground swirling eddy. Then I see the waterfall, feel the spray. I look up. Water drops from the canyon peak, clings to the edge of the abyss. Water cuts into rock. Way at the bottom of the canyon, the rowdy hikers step behind the waterfall, two and three at a time. I wait on the walkway. My turn. I stand behind the waterfall. I have come a long way. And I do have bear bells.

It is as if the water were in my head. Roaring all around in this magical hollow, sheltered by rock, concealed by spray. Magical.

I hear the rowdy hikers from behind the waterfall. I stay long, walk up the steps as they point and shout and point.

'Bear!'

I freeze and look behind me and to each side.

'Bear,' they shout.

Calm. I look upward. On the other side of the canyon stands a bear. Lumbering along. Pausing to eat berries. Eating berries is good, preferable to humans for the average bear. I can tell from his ears he's a grizzly.

I have seen the grizzlies' ears!

The rowdy hikers run along the path for a better view.

'Stay with us, safety in numbers.' I smile appreciation. I stare and stare and want to remember the grizzly forever.

We ramble back slow and limp with excitement, up the down steps and down the up. I lift my skirts in places. I am myself but not myself.

Gwendolyn lines up the tips. Little piles. Toonies, loonies, quarters, dimes, nickels. And cups. On the counter. I smile my thanks.


I hike with the rowdy hikers. A tag along.
    'I know you,' says a girl. 'You work in the Mystical Vegetarian Eating Experience.'
    'That's me.'
    'Is it a good place to work?'
    'The best.'
    'Any accommodation?'
    'Nope.'
    'Shit. I stayed a while at the hostel. Cleaning rooms, paying for food, everything else free. But it's noisy at night and the cleaning can be gross. Do you have your own place?'
    'YWCA.'
    'Heard it's difficult to get in long term.'
    'I was lucky.'
    'How long have you been there?'
    'Almost nine years.'
    'Wow.'


Old Woman Gwendolyn grabs a bus pan and hauls it to a table. Clears an unfinished Buddha's Feast.
    'Gwendolyn, you mustn't exert yourself.'
    'It's my pleasure.'
    'Your coat, what if you get tamari on it?'
    'I could bring an apron.'
    Her face pleads.


We hike once a week. And always eat afterwards. Pizza or other shared food.
    'You hike in winter?'

'You haven't seen the canyon in winter and ice and snow?'

We meet every Monday at noon in the Castle Hotel parking lot. Walk or shuttle or car pool to the hike.


'What are you making?' asks Linda.

'Olive oil cake. With lemon.'

Four of us eat olive oil cake and drink orange cranberry tea.

Linda who replaced Diana who replaced Katherine who replaced Amelia as our leader, Briony who has eased up on the conversation and is upgrading to go to college, Tiffany who reminds me of Nikki from junior high and says very little.


Gwendolyn drags a chair halfway between fire and counter and sits with her lustrous black velvet hat, glittering with a sparkling rose. Apron covered in poinsettias, whispering winter. The wait staff detour around as they leave the kitchen.

'I thought,' says Gwendolyn, 'that since I'm almost working I shouldn't take up a table. This is much nicer, isn't it?'

The Mystical Vegetarian Eating Experience is ill-prepared to be manipulated by an elderly bag of bones. I am now shift manager.

'How about I pay you to clear the tables?'

'I couldn't accept money. My sons would be appalled.'

'Sons?'

'Three,' says Gwendolyn. 'Bane of my existence.'

'If you fell, hurt yourself…'

'Bar me at the door if you must but if the door's barred to me when I show up tomorrow, I'll sit on the sidewalk and protest.'

Gwendolyn busses tables and I let her. It agitates my shift-managing waitress cool. Customers don't. Shouldn't. Mustn't. Can't. Won't. But here they do.

I hike a gentle canyon. Little more than a path in town. Gwendolyn holds my arm at the stairs. Smiles at the mountains, the moss, the tourists, the sky. A moose pokes his nose through a brush.

'Moose.' I point.

'You don't have to shout, I'm not deaf.'

'It's to keep the bears away.'

'Do you have any hobbies?' yells Gwendolyn.

'No.'

'You should have,' says Gwendolyn. 'I read.'

We trudge in silence, her tiny ancient hand clutches at my arm.

'You're meant to ask me what I read,' says Gwendolyn.

'What do you read?'

'Books.'

I grin.

'Just joking,' says Gwendolyn. 'I like Margaret Lawrence an awful lot.'

Ice in my heart. '*The Stone Angel*,' I whisper.

'You'll have to speak up. I'm a little deaf.'

'I said, *The Stone Angel*.'

'I'm Hagar.'

'I don't think so.'

'I knew you were a reader. I could tell by looking. We should start a book club, you and me.'

'I've been offered a guide job for winter,' says Sara. 'Mystical Canyon. I was tempted but I love ski instructing. And skiing.'

'Are they still looking for a guide?' asks Noel.

'Yep. Interested?'

'How many hours?'

'As many shifts as you want. Everyone in this car is qualified.'

I am in this car.

'You should all apply, there's lots of work. Use me as a reference. Twenty-five bucks a hike plus tips.'

'Good tips?'

'Varies. I took a group of fifteen women last week. Everyone gave me two bucks. Fifty-five bucks for a three hour hike I'd do anyway. Pretty average.'


Edith is our new wanderer. She is in the room that so many years ago Mavis lived in. I sit in the lobby, one eye on a book of hikes and one eye on Edith, lurking by the door. She knows I will follow her outside. She is waiting for me to duck into the bathroom. I can hold for a very long time.


'This is our first book. For the book club.'

*Down Among the Women* by Fay Weldon.

'My treat. I think you might like it.'

I hold the book. Gwendolyn watches.

'I don't read novels,' I say.


Hike leader training takes three days.

First day in the classroom. It is odd to be at a desk, book open, taking notes and learning.

My heart hurts.

Second day safety in the wilderness. Bear identification, bear defence.

I get it right.

Third day a guided hike. We all narrate certain parts.

'I have three sons,' says Gwendolyn. 'Milton, Blake, and Eliot. You must meet my sons.'

I read 'The Waste Land' to her. I choke.

'What's the matter, dear?'

'This poem does that to me.'

'I didn't think you read.'

'A long time ago.'

'You? I can say long time, not you.'

'Different life.'

'Have you read your book yet? I want our book club to get started. Properly.'


I take the women from the Y on a hike. A gentle hike.

Nella (mental health bed, 16, runaway, streetwise), Lydia (replaced Linda who replaced Katharine who replaced Diana, who replaced Amelia, the green lady who first registered me), Maggie (cleans at the hospital, has children in another country, waiting for residency qualification so they can join her).

Lydia takes pictures of Maggie every few meters to send home. The grass smells of yesterday's warm rain and late spring. Almost home, lazing along the path to town, almost home and there they are. Two yearling grizzlies eating grass. Blocking our way.

'Stop,' I yell. 'Make yourselves big.' I can sense them behind me, cautious, nervous. I stretch and jump and holler. Cars stop. A trail biker is suddenly by my side.

'Holly fuck,' says Nella. Again and again. Too soft for the bears to notice.

Keep yelling, he tells me, wardens are on their way. We yell and jump and throw rocks short of the grizzlies, close enough to scare them into eating grass a meter further away. We lob more rocks, we yell, the wardens arrive.

'Were you scared?' asks Maggie.

'Terrified.'

'You didn't look scared.'
'I was.'
'You are our hero,' said Lydia.


'Present for you.' Gwendolyn holds out a small package wrapped with silver paper and night-sky blue ribbon. Not paper at all. A gift wrapped in gentle silk.

'I can't accept...' When I look up Gwendolyn is gone.

I bury my fingers in the softness of the fabric.

I walk to Many Steps Valley and sit, alone, to unwrap my gift. A rose, its petals carved in stone, each petal unique, tumbles out. Shimmering green leaves cling to the flower, a single dew drop sparkling like diamond.


I am offered a full-time tour guide job. It scares me to think I will not be waitressing. The Mystical Vegetarian Eating Experience tells me they will always have room for me. I can return whenever I want. A lump grows in my throat. I swallow. It disappears.


Gwendolyn and I sit in the back of the donut shop eating warm sugar donuts with jam inside. Gwendolyn feels the cold more and more and this is a warm cubby.

Cecil's manager has been charged to set up a table and chairs and coffeepot. Cecil still owns Cecil's, he just doesn't live here any more.

'This book is about an old man alcoholic.'

'Geoffrey Firmin is not an old man. He has a beautiful wife probably younger than you. It's a Canadian classic.'

'Set in Mexico, written by an Englishman.'

'Exactly.'

'It has nothing to do with me.

'You are not this obtuse, Eve.'

'You think the mountains are my alcohol?'

'The mountains are your escape. Escape is your alcohol.'

'No. Not reading was my escape. I came here to leave the stories.'

'And you fell back in.'

'You pushed me.'

'Then my work here is done.'


Maeterlink Law—Elliot, Milton and Blake, Brothers in Law, isn't difficult to find.

I stand on the doorstep.

'You must be Eve,' says the man who opens the door.

I haven't heard my name in a long time. It is not that no one speaks it, it is that I have not heard it.

'You must be Blake, Milton or Eliot.'

'Guilty.' His eyes twinkled, he doesn't say which brother he is.

I stand with Elliot, Milton and Blake as Gwendolyn, in a box, retreats underground. The process is slick and not particularly religious. In my mind she burrows happily, like an Alice with a backpack full of poetry. I watch with Elliot, Milton and Blake, dry eyed and cautious, and the stories fly through my head.


I hike a canyon.

I wear a Genuine Curling Sweater, one with a bear: Elliot, Milton, and Blake delivered a box of books, for me, from Gwendolyn, inside a Genuine Curling Sweater. With a bear.

The world is different without Gwendolyn.

Eyes closed: an endless hike. Bears with faces I have seen before, Mavis and Amelia and Gwendolyn and others. They follow me.

Eyes open: dawn.

Eyes closed: sleepless. Steps in the morning. Voices.

Eyes closed, eyes closed, eyes closed.

Nothing.

Eyes open. Up and out of bed.

# Stories from Inside the Wallpaper

# One

My mother and I disputed our situation behind the wallpaper bars.

'We're trapped,' she said.

'We can get out. Just let me figure it out.'

My mother exhaled, noisy and deep, and grabbed every shred of her courage and strength—and, believe me, they were well shredded—to bend the bars slowly back, forcing a small opening.

'Get out,' she wheezed. 'Get out.'

'I can't,' I said.

'Go. One of us has to be free.'

'Not without you.'

'I spit on you,' said my mother and, always one to make a point, spat on me. She missed. The spit mixed with stale wallpaper paste and created a foul smell. Like moulded paper. I coughed.

My mother and I are poor milkmaids stuck behind the wallpaper bars. We came to this house to sell our milk.

'We want to help you,' said the woman who managed the affairs of the place.

'How?' asked my mother. She smelled betrayal.

'I want to make something of you.'

'We're already something,' I said.

'We are,' agreed my mother.

'By making more money, of course,' said the woman.

'I'm interested,' said my mother. Making money always suited her. She nodded like a sage.

'I need your help. I have a wall to be painted and you look like women who can paint.'

'We're strong, we can do anything,' said my mother.

'You must paint this wall from the inside. Yellow as the sun.'

'How do you paint a wall from the inside?' I asked. My mother raised her eyebrows and shrugged. I rolled my eyes. My mother aped counting money. She looked like she was stroking a cat.

The woman gave us both small pots of paint, opened a door in the wall and we climbed in. It was a narrow passage, the other side of the wallpaper. She promised payment and she promised free food. We were content. I was enchanted. It's not every day you get to step into a wall and paint the wallpaper from behind. The first night she let us out to milk our cows. When we returned to sell the milk next morning she had two more pots of paint. In we climbed.

'This is a doddle,' said my mother. 'All we have to do is paint. These pots don't hold much.'

'They don't empty out fast.'

'Complain, complain, complain. What do you expect? Something for nothing?'

'She doesn't work.'

'She's a lady,' said my mother. 'Maybe someday you'll be a lady.'

And so we painted. Each evening we were released, paid, and invited back the next day. Our earnings increased. The pots of paint remained small and were slow to empty. We worked our way around the walls. The morning we thought we'd finish, the woman had large paint pots for us.

'We don't need this much,' said my mother. 'We're almost done.'

The woman smiled. My mother shrugged. The woman helped us in and we started to paint.

There were boxes in the room. Packing boxes. The

woman who paid us had dismantled everything, except the bed, and stowed it in the boxes. Maybe she wasn't a lady if she worked like this. Maybe my mother was wrong.

'This painting of yours is good. The new owners will be pleased,' said the woman.

We heard the movers bump and bang around the house and it was true, we were close to the end of our painting. The wallpaper looked fresh and sunny from the inside. I wondered what it looked like from the room. It was dark at the end of the day when the door was opened and we were paid. And, again, dark in the morning when we exchanged our milk for paint pots and climbed in. We never saw the wallpaper from the bedroom. We only knew it was yellow.

'We'll miss this money,' said my mother.

'Lucky we saved some.'

'I hoped we'd have more.'

'If people see what we've done here, they might want us to paint their wallpaper too.'

'You're right,' said my mother. 'We'll hang out a shingle. Mother and daughter wallpaper painting. But what if people don't have handy little rooms behind their walls?'

That night, the money woman who promised to make something of us didn't show up. My mother and I heard her voice in the courtyard. Hooves of horses and the wheels of a carriage.

'She'll be up to pay us now,' said my mother.

'She's late. It's been dark outside for some time.'

'Ssh—I hear her footsteps. Get painting. Maybe there'll be a bonus if we're still working when she comes back.'

We held our breath and waited. And painted a small section of wall that had faded with the light.

'Hey,' yelled my mother. 'We've run out of paint.'

'No we haven't.' My mother winked at me. 'We've

run out of paint,' I yelled.

But no one came.

'Hey, let me out. Let me out.' I had a pair of hearty lungs back then. I rattled the bars but they only cut into us more and more. As if the space behind the wallpaper was shrinking. 'She's forgotten us. Help. Help!'

'Easy,' said my mother. 'She'll be back in the morning. With a bonus, I shouldn't wonder. For making us stay all night. Settle down and think of all the things you'll treat yourself with.'

We scrunched down behind the bars and I thought of cherries, their sweetness, those perfect second morsels. I eat the first sweet half and scoop the pit out with my teeth, spit it in a field or lane, or spitting pot if there's one handy, and then relish that second mouthful. No pit to foul the joy. I ate several perfect cherry bites that night. Then an orange without seeds and a cup of chocolate, sweetened with honey. I ate a slice of fresh bread and dozed off. I woke with a slight sensation of indigestion and cramps in both legs. My mother was still asleep, crushing me under her weight. I wanted to move but hesitated in case I woke her. Instead, I lay and listened. Listened for footsteps. None came.

When my legs grew numb, I shifted my body and my mother woke with a snort and considerable quantities of night-time dribble.

'Those poor cows,' I said as I stretched. 'Their teats will be sore, their udders heavy with milk.'

'Poor us,' said my mother. 'Our purse will be light without milk money.'

We stretched and stood and walked on the spot to rid ourselves of night-time stiffness. I peered into the room, willing the woman to return.

'The boxes are gone,' I said.

'Can't be. I never heard anyone.' She looked. 'They were very quiet,' she said.

My mother picked up her paint pot. 'Hang on a

minute,' she said, 'look at this. What's yours like?'

I peeked in her pot and then mine. 'The same,' I said. Both paint pots were full.

'We might as well make ourselves useful,' said my mother and started painting.

'They've left us here, forgotten us.' I sat down.

'If we get another coat on this they'll pay us a nice bonus, that's what I think.'

'You think too much about bonuses.'

'Someone's got to pay the rent.'

I stood and painted. It was better than sitting and my mother could be right about a nice bonus.

And so it continued. By day we painted and at night I dreamed of food. In the morning I woke with indigestion and rarely felt hungry.

Days later we were asleep when the people came to view the house. They were leaving before we knew what had happened. I cried.

'They'll be back,' said my mother. 'They liked the place. You'll see.'

Before we became painters I might have believed her without question but painting had jaded my trust. I'd believe they'd return when I saw it. But you should listen to your mother. They did return, with horses and carriages and giant footsteps and the lugging drag of furniture and trunks. The feet came higher and higher in the house. Snaking around the landings. Mother and I straightened our dresses and brushed the hair from our eyes.

'Look at me,' said my mother. And when I did she pinched my face so blood and colour rose to the surface. 'Now you do the same for me.'

I took surprising delight in squeezing my mother's cheeks. I blamed her for us being in this prison. She had agreed to paint, not me.

When the door handle turned, we stood straight and near bursting from the smell of freedom. We looked as fresh as possible given the confines of our space behind the wallpaper. A woman entered. I waved.

'Hello,' called my mother, 'over here.'

I waved again and smiled. She was a pretty woman for all she didn't have colour in her face. I would tell her about the cheek pinching immediately she released me. She looked ill and a man half carried her to the bed.

'What was that noise?' asked the woman.

'You're imagining things,' said the man.

'No she's not,' cried my mother 'we're right here. Hello. Over here. In the wallpaper.'

The man settled the woman on the bed and left. We heard a key in the door.

'Did he lock her in?' asked my mother. 'Hey, over here.'

The woman looked startled. She came over and peered right at us. It was obvious she couldn't see us. But part of me thought she saw through us and noticed our chamber.

'Maybe she needs glasses,' said my mother.

# Two

'I think,' said the teacher, 'Linda would be a very good candidate for our new commerce programme.'

'Is there an extra fee?' asked Linda's mother.

'Maybe fifty dollars a year, Mrs Sch—'

'Just call me Tulip.'

Linda's mother changed her name to Tulip and grew her hair long when she was hired on to read the cards in a local coffee shop. She did palms and tea leaves too. It was 1969 and everything about Tulip was long. Her skirts, her crochet boleros, her boots, her mascaraed eyelashes, and her clear painted nails with miniature pictures of suns and moon beneath the varnish.

'The program will provide Linda with a marketable skill. When Linda completes grade ten she'll be able to walk into a job. Without further training. Or expense. Eventually a personal secretary. Between you and me, if a girl has secretarial training these days, then the sky is the limit. And our programme is the best. It's small and there's excellent attention to detail. We only have twenty-four student typewriters in the whole school and twenty are dedicated to this programme.'

'And there's a job at the end?' asked Tulip.

'And it lasts for all of grade nine and ten?' asked Linda who looked a lot like her mother except her long straight hair was light with natural streaks and honey brown whereas her mother's hair was dark and the honey brown came from a bottle.

'You won't necessarily start as a secretary but there are filing and typing pool jobs readily available.'

'What an opportunity,' said Tulip, playing with one of her many love bead necklaces. 'I wish I could learn to type. What do you think Linda?'

'Sounds okay. Is Rosie in it?'

Rosie was Linda's best friend.

'If she wants to be,' said the teacher.

'How about this, I'll go read the cards and if they say it's a go, we'll bring the form back tomorrow?' said Tulip.

'The cards?'

'Tarot. I do all the festivals, I'm very much in demand. I did Bob Dylan not so long ago. Or maybe it was a guy who looked like Bob Dylan. He had a guitar.'

Later that night Tulip read the cards.

'The cards say,' said Tulip 'that the secretary thing is good. What do you think?'

'I get to type. That is cooler than cool,' said Linda. 'I wanna do it, Tulip.'

'It says the painting's not so good. Have you been painting?'

'No. You must have misread the cards. I can't paint and don't want to.'

'The cards are never wrong,' said Tulip.

Two years later Linda graduated grade ten, the secretarial programme, and school and was hired on at a temp agency.

'We're sending you to a doctor's office. His regular receptionist is off with women's troubles.'

'Is there any typing?'

'Some. And you're going to meet with the public, so my suggestion is you wear shorter skirts and less jewellery. And ease up on the make up.'

'Okey-dokey,' said Linda.

The job was good. Linda enjoyed meeting the patients and by the second week she was back wearing mascara, rings and necklaces, her dresses were touching her ankles and she was tying a ribbon around her forehead. Like mother like daughter.

'Would you mind typing up these reports, Linda, before you go home?' said Dr. G. on Friday evening.

'I love typing. Of course.'

Linda started typing right away. Dr. G., a man in his thirties whose wife usually did the receptioning, watched for a moment.

'Very impressive, the speed you type at.'

'I was well trained,' said Linda.

'I can see,' said Dr. G and turned to go back to his office.

The job was going to last for a couple of months. Mrs. G. was home recovering from a difficult post baby birth experience.

Dr. G stopped at his office. 'One more thing... I don't suppose you paint?'

'Pictures?' asked Linda.

'Walls,' said Dr. G.

'Sure' said Linda who'd never painted a wall in her life but couldn't see how hard it would be.

'I need a bedroom painted.'

Linda was concerned. There's been a module at school on not letting bosses take advantage of you.

'You can bring a friend if you like. And, of course, I'll pay. Here's my address. Can you come tomorrow?'

'Yes.'

'What do you mean you're asking Rosie? I could come paint with you. Why give her the chance to make money?' asked Tulip.

It was early 1972 and most local people had already had their cards read by Tulip. And successfully. As a consequence of Tulip's success, the market was expanding. Even the man who delivered the mail pulled on velvet pants and a silk shirt and read a crystal ball on the weekend. No one realised that Tulip was the real thing. They didn't like it when she told them to ask their question. They preferred it when the postman flipped out cards and promised them a glimpse into a rosy future. Fraudulent, thought Tulip and considered changing her name back to Rhonda. Or maybe Maggie, like in 'Maggie May'.

'I already asked,' lied Linda who didn't want Mum crashing her secretarial dream.

But when Linda asked Rosie, Rosie was going on a date with Sam her new boyfriend who had long hair and looked like Roger Daltrey. Linda decided to go alone. By morning, Linda had changed her mind, relented, and let Tulip come too.

'We have a rather peculiar set up here,' said Dr. G., 'let me lead the way.'

'Ooh,' whispered Tulip, 'he's gorgeous, he can lead the way with me any day.'

'Mum—'

'Don't be such an old fart, if this lasts until tomorrow I'm wearing a low neck.'

'He's married.'

'He's educated. And a doctor. He understands all

about free love.'

'So, we have a bit of a scrim here, accessed from just behind the wall.'

'Scrim?' whispered Tulip in Linda's ear. 'Like a scrum?'

'Through this little door, after you ladies, and then we access the scrim. We'd like to have it a brighter yellow. Here's the paint. Just cover it from behind.'

'You know, Dr. G.' said Tulip, 'I do read the cards, if you're interested.' As she spoke she laid her fingers, topped with a set of nails emblazoned by most of the solar system and several phases of the moon, on Dr. G.'s arm. Dr. G. looked at Tulip's fingernails.

'Interesting,' said Dr. G. and left.

'I think he likes me,' said Tulip.

'Paint,' said Linda. 'These pots are heavy.'

'Is there anyone there?'

'What?' asked Linda.

'I thought I saw someone else in here.'

'Must be your imagination.'

'Second sight,' said Tulip, 'it's why I'm so good at reading the cards.'

'Paint.'

At the end of the day Dr. G. showed up, paid Linda and Tulip, and let them out.

'Same time tomorrow?' asked Dr. G.

'Sure,' said Linda.

'We're going to have to find time for a reading,' said Tulip.

'Reading?' asked Dr. G.

'The cards.'

'Maybe once the job's done,' said Dr. G.

'I'll look forward to it,' said Tulip.

Linda and Tulip walked towards their bus stop.

'Money's good,' said Tulip.

'Must you talk to him in that voice?' asked Linda.

'What voice?'

'That husky 'I'm gonna read your cards' voice.'

'It's musical.'

'It's a 'I want to read your cards in bed' voice.'

'How can I have brought up such a prude?'

'I'm not a prude. You're just so… you.'

'Aren't I just. Did you see him look at my nails? This is a good job.'

'So don't mess it up.'

'I made more in a day painting than at a whole festival reading cards. Course, the festivals are more fun.'

The job continued on weekends. Linda and Tulip made slow progress, but Dr. G. didn't seem to mind. He paid well.

'Can you arrive a little earlier tomorrow?' Dr. G. asked about four weeks in to the project. 'As early as you can make it.'

When they arrived at 7.00 the next morning, Tulip still blinking sleep from her eyes, Dr. G. was anxious and pacing. 'My wife comes home Monday. I'm hoping things can be finished.'

'Sometimes,' said Tulip, 'it feels like the wall goes on forever. Growing by the week. Like an ever changing yellow mandala.'

Dr. G. handed them the paint and raced off. They painted all day and in the evening, about the time that Dr. G. usually paid them, they heard a commotion. Horns honking and people yelling.

'Sounds like a fire,' said Tulip.

'Fire? This door is locked.'

'Figuratively speaking. I don't mean a real fire.'

'Are we almost done?' asked Linda.

'Close. He'll be pleased.'

'He's late. Maybe we can be done by the time he gets here.'

And they painted and painted and when they were within six inches of the end, Tulip shushed Linda. 'Listen.'

Both women listened.

'I think,' said Tulip, 'that they have gone and left us.'

'You could be right. Maybe he's excited about seeing his wife.'

'No need to be mean.'

'I was being a pragmatist.'

'Mean— Anyways, I'm over him, let's have a break. If he comes later, we'll leave and not come back. If he doesn't come till tomorrow, we'll finish before he gets here.'

'And if he doesn't come tomorrow,' asked Linda, 'and we're abandoned?'

'We'll sue. And don't be so morbid. Okay, come and sit opposite me. Cross legged, there's a girl.'

'I hate this Mum. What if he comes, now.'

'Om. Clear your mind and close your eyes.'

Linda closed her eyes but let her mind wander. She imagined going back to school and reading books or learning fancy math or maybe about maps. She dreamed of never having to type again. She flexed her shoulders and thought painting was better than typing. She remembered the teacher who said typing was a good job. She realised she made more temping than in a permanent job. And she didn't make much temping.

'I'm hungry,' said Linda.

'Picture a huge bowl of vegetarian chilli,' said Tulip.

'Seriously?'

'It's going to help. Think about the onions and chickpeas and black beans and corn and sweet potatoes and a piece of warm cornbread on the side. Only using your mind, take a spoon and dip it into the chilli and slurp up the goodness. Chew slowly and swallow gently. How was that?'

'Okay.'

'You're not trying. Have another spoonful.'

'Yum.'

'Don't be sarcastic. Butter your cornbread. The

cornbread is hot. Let the butter melt. Take a nibble of cornbread and a mouthful of chilli.'

'Mmm, that's good.'


We were deep in the shadows of the wallpaper, watching. My mother nudged me in the ribs.

'Go ask them if we can have some of what they've got.'

'They haven't got anything.'

'They've got our job.'

'They're milkmaids?'

'Painting. They've got something. Look at their faces and they're swallowing.'

'Excuse me,' said the daughter milkmaid.

'Aargh,' said Linda.

'I thought I saw people down there,' cried Tulip. 'You've been there all along, haven't you? Spying on me and my daughter.'

'We've been here all along, trapped,' said the milkmaid mother. 'Did they ask you to paint and then never show up to let you out? Happened to us.'

'When?' asked Linda.

'1892.'

'Thought so,' said Tulip. 'I could feel the auras move.'

'Just you see, tomorrow the wife'll move in. She'll see you but do nothing.'


# Three

They exited the undergrowth with caution, onto a large lawn. The deserted house had windows like eyes blinking in the moonlight and a boarded up door.

'You're sure it's not alarmed?' asked Mel.

'Positive,' said Lydia.

'We must be swift and silent and surefooted,' said Mel.

Lydia glared at her daughter. A shadow in combat boots and baby doll dress that could be a nightie, black because all her clothes were black.

'I don't know why I let you talk me into this,' said Lydia.

Mel rolled her eyes.

It was Lydia's idea. She'd heard the stories, thought it might be a way to draw closer to Mel, appeal to her spirit, a spirit that materialised in silence, brashness, loud music, determination, and the colour black.

'Let's go to the old estate,' Lydia had said, 'liberate the prison.'

There had always been rumours throughout Mel's childhood: women curled up underneath the floorboards and behind the walls. Throughout Lydia's own—'If you don't finish all your vegetables you'll end up in the old estate, buried behind the walls,' her father used to threaten her.

Everyone knew the rumours about the old estate but hardly anyone went there. Except Lydia. She had been offered the house to sell. She couldn't believe her luck but recognised it was a white elephant, a rock around her neck. Too big, too old, too abandoned, too decayed, but if she was successful it would make her reputation and the commission would be exceptional, the largest in her career to date.

Lucas Lucas IV, owner of Lucas Realty had showed her around himself. He was a man who smelled of too much cologne and too little deodorant and wore suits poorly pressed at home by 'the little woman'. He stood too close during the walk through but always the professional Lydia walked away to inspect a different feature whenever the grinning gold filled teeth and ruddy face crowded her: sash windows (so historic), working fireplace (filled with charm), antique range imported from Germany (pure class). French windows (or were they doors?) completely genteel. She needed one or two more sales, good sales, before she could offer him a piece of her mind without losing the job—and her income, her home, her comforts, and her daughter's future.

Recently, Mel had become distant, locked in study, pensive about university, abrasive about Lydia's job, embracing causes rather than her mother. And so this night-time raid on the old house.

Mel and Lydia edged towards the mystery, the glamour, the horror, and the decay. They paused on the rim of the night world. One last adventure together before stepping out in separate directions.

I should never have agreed, thought Mel. She's searching for some weird meaning or redemption, hanging on to her imagined youth when she didn't dress as cool as she remembers and didn't fight as hard as she claimed. I should be studying physics, thought Mel, instead I'm massaging guilt, hers and mine. Hers that she hasn't been a good enough mother, mine that I'm leaving, leaving her alone. Please, whoever may be listening, let me leave her in safety and happiness.

'Ready?' said Lydia.

'Ready.'

Lydia and Mel ran across the lawn in moonlight. Daisies tickled their knees, they almost looked like sisters. Dark hair, Mel's, short and tight to her head, gleaming in the night, Lydia's artificially large like an animal had fallen asleep on her head and must hold on for curly life. Mel's nose slightly more upturned; Lydia's smile a fraction wider. Eyes the same brown with the smallest hint of green. Same height, 5'5", though Lydia was boosted by ridiculous high heels—who wears high heels on an adventure, on a break in? not really a break in because Lydia has a key, some rights to the place, if only to sell it on to some poor sucker… Mel put the thoughts out of her head because Lydia (in her too-brown suit with the slinky peach coloured blouse with the bow at the neck) was, after all, her mother.

The key turned in the lock.

'Odd,' said Lydia. 'I don't remember these leaves.'

'It's hau-hau-haunted,' said Mel.

'That's not funny.'

'Maybe someone broke in. Wow!'

Mel danced. A clopping lopsided, skipping and hopping dance round the enormous panelled room. Lydia watched. As if it were day, light washed through the large window and sparkled on mirrors. It was stunning but best of all Mel was a child again, bounding from wall to window to mirror with her funny little dance. The panels were painted with milk maids and horses and a family eating a picnic and a woman with the furthest away eyes Lydia had ever seen—but then it was a painting and maybe those were the only eyes the painter could paint.

'It's perfect,' gasped Mel, 'let's buy it.'

Lydia laughed, 'If only.'

'I'm going to pick my room,' said Mel and headed to the hall.

Mel walked first on the black tiles, then on the white, all the way to the kitchen with its ancient stove and a huge space against the green painted wall for a fridge and a pantry bigger than their living room at home.

'All these shelves for food,' said Lydia.

And on to the stairs and upwards round the wooden curve.

'Imagine gliding down these stairs in a prom dress,' said Lydia.

'I'm not going to prom, Mum.'

A mother has to try, thought Lydia. She'd never finished high school, never had a prom, made it anyway, fully licensed realtor.

'My bedroom,' yelled Mel. The room had a wall of glass and beyond that a balcony and below the balcony the lawn with the flowers.

I must get that lawn cut before I show it, thought Lydia. And stage furniture for a slightly lived-in look. The ceiling was painted midnight blue with tiny stars twinking through. Real gold paint? She should check, could be a selling feature. The walls were creamy like butter but Mel was gone.

'I've found your room,' called Mel.

The one with the roses, thought Lydia and sure enough her daughter was smelling the rose bushes painted low on the walls like they were growing out of the floorboards.

'Like they're trying to escape,' said Mel.

They ran from room to room, their feet echoing. I need photos of this floor, thought Lydia, they'll spice up the brochure.

And then they were standing at the bottom of the attic stairs.

'Guess they ran out of the fancy wood,' said Mel. The stairs were painted red, like dried blood.

'It was the school room, or nursery, or maybe a gymnasium.'

'In the attic?' asked Mel, halfway up.

'Not much to see,' said Lydia, following, 'though I should get your opinion.'

'It's got good windows for an attic,' said Mel.

'Such a realtor's daughter,' said Lydia and Mel shivered. Was that a ghost skipping across her grave?

'It looks lived in,' said Mel, peering at the old bedstead and the peeling wallpaper.

'I wonder if I should paint it. Before I put the listing up.'

'You paint?' said Mel.

'Get the workman in.'

Lydia sat on the bed and surveyed the room, plotting the listing.

'Is this a door?' asked Mel. 'In the wall?'

'No. There's just the one room. But an en suite's a good suggestion. Maybe it could be a bed and breakfast or a small hotel.'

'It is a door,' said Mel. 'You can see the line.'

'Maybe there's a closet, or an en suite already here. Could be worth money, whatever's behind this door.'

'There's nothing to pull, no handle.'

They tried pushing

'It's a closet,' said Mel.

'Just piles of old clothes. Watch that paint can.'

'It smells of paint.'

Back in the room, Lydia took one last long look. A draft snuck its way through and gently closed the door to the landing.

'It's stuck,' said Mel, tugging at the handle.

'I hate these old houses, always something warping. Let me try.'

'It won't open. I have a physics test tomorrow.'

'Help me. Pull harder.'

'I'm hungry.'

'I've got some trail mix in my purse.'

Lydia and Mel sat on the bed and ate nuts and raisins and sunflower seeds with the occasional chunk of dried mango and papaya.

'We'll try again in a minute and if we can't get it open we'll just have to wait till tomorrow when the house inspector comes.'

'Are there any chocolate chips in here?'

'No, I got the healthy stuff.'

# Four

Mel kicked the door in the wall, the door to inside the wall, the door to behind the wallpaper. Her foot was well clad for kicking, a solid black boot whose pounding at the door echoed effectively.

'Don't do that, Mel,' said Lydia. 'I have to sell this place.'

'There are people in there, we must free them,' said Mel and kicked again. 'Can't you hear the voices?'

'What voices?' asked Lydia.

'The ones inside the wall.'

'You're hearing voices? What have you been doing?'

Mel kicked harder at the door until it crumpled. 'Ssh,' said Mel.

Lydia listened. Footsteps and mumbling, a bit like the hiss of a deflated balloon, grew louder and louder. Mel grinned, triumphant. Lydia tried to price the damage and hoped the hissing was a natural phenomenon and not break-and-enterers, though if there were unauthorised humans lurking in the walls maybe they'd be responsible for the damage. Unless the noise was rats… Lydia thought she might hyperventilate and wished she had a paper bag.

'You took your time,' huffed a creased Tulip as she exited the door.

'This is private property,' cried Lydia, 'look at the damage to the door.'

'I was trapped. A prisoner.'

'We all were,' said the Milkmaid Daughter, the Milkmaid Mother, and Linda.

'Moonlight,' said Tulip, sitting in rays falling through the window.

'Why are you dressed like this?' asked Lydia. 'Fancy dress?'

'If anyone's in fancy dress it's you,' replied Tulip.

Lydia paused to consider whether this might be a compliment, decided in all likelihood that it was—the blouse was pure silk, purchased on sale—and joined Tulip in the moonlight.

'I think,' said Tulip, 'that we should all sit in a circle and get acquainted.'

'Great,' said Mel, squatting down beside Tulip.

'Nice boots,' said Tulip.

'Thanks,' said Mel. 'Are those the planets on your finger nails?'

'Look at that,' said Tulip, 'all those years trapped in that closet and still my nails haven't grown any. Don't look bad though. Come and sit with us, Linda.'

'What do you mean, years?' asked Lydia, beating Linda to the spot beside Tulip.

'We've been in there since 1971,' said Linda.

The milkmaids joined the circle. '1892,' said the Milkmaid Mother.

'What year is it now?' asked her daughter.

'You don't want to know,' said Mel.

'How is this possible?' asked Lydia.

'We were conned into the wall,' said Linda, 'by a doctor I was working for as a secretary.'

'You worked as a secretary?' asked Lydia. 'That's very... outdated.'

'Mum!' said Mel.

'What about us?' asked the Milkmaid Mother, 'we've been here since 1892. What about those poor cows? Who's been milking them?'

'They're probably dead by now,' said Tulip.

'Mum!' said Linda.

The Milkmaid Daughter snivelled a few tears for the cows.

'We need to bring them down, the people who did this to us,' said Mel.

'Us?' said Tulip.

'The door to this room is also locked,' said Mel. 'We

are all prisoners.'

'But I'm sure we'll be rescued tomorrow,' said Lydia. 'I am the realtor for this house and—'

'You, a realtor?' said Tulip.

'We're all locked in then?' cried Linda.

'Yes,' said Mel.

'Well I, for one, am going to have a stretch,' said Tulip, lying flat on her back in the moonlight. Linda lay beside her. After a moment, the milkmaids joined them.

'A bit like corpse pose,' said Lydia.

'You do yoga?' said Tulip.

'I do,' replied Lydia. 'You know Mel, if you can't beat them…'

The six women lay next to each other, half a dozen worry dolls in a moon-illuminated matchbox.

This is kind of cosy, thought Lydia, but I've got places to be, things to do. Better try that door again.

'I can't get up,' said Lydia.

'I think,' said Milkmaid Daughter, 'that we are trapped on the floor, like rats in treacle.'

'Go with it,' said Tulip, 'let the floor accept you into its heart.'

The six women lay in the moonlight as the floor rippled slightly, as if an invisible hand were trying to flatten it. There was a collective gasp from the six women as a giant black stick streaked across the room and tapped against the floor beside the window, an inch from Milkmaid Daughter.

'Can anyone move?' asked Mel.

No one could move.

The pointy stick flew over their bodies. Like they were on a flying carpet, a ripple sent each woman an inch to the left and a small distance in the air. The black pointy stick banged down one more time.

'I,' cried out Tulip.

'Your eye?' exclaimed Linda.

'What do you mean your eye?' asked Milkmaid

Mother.

'It got her eye,' said Linda, 'the sharp pointy thing.'

'Can you see?' asked Lydia.

'Not my eye,' said Tulip, 'my *i*.'

'You definitely said eye,' said Milkmaid Daughter.

'No,' said Tulip, 'you heard *eye*. I said *i*. It's a pencil and it dotted my *i*, the one in *Tulip*. Can't you see?'

All six women peered at the pointy stick.

'I think you might be right,' said Mel. 'And I think she might be stuck.'

'Who?' asked Linda.

'The writer,' said Mel.

'How do you know it's a she?'

'I just picked a pronoun.'

'Nice,' said Linda.

'Stuck?' asked Lydia.

'Yeah. She can't think of a word and is tapping her pencil until she comes up with it.'

'So why did she dot my *i*?"

'Ow,' hissed Milkmaid Mother. 'She's tuning me into a flower.'

'Just the *o* in your *mother*,' said Lydia.

'It's making me feel peculiar inside.'

'All of this makes me feel peculiar,' said Lydia.

'It hurt when she dotted my *i*,' said Tulip.

'She's written herself into a corner,' said Mel.

'I think she's doodling, over there by the window,' said Linda.

'What she needs to do,' said Mel, 'is write us an ending.'

All six women lay in the moonlight, waiting with varying degrees of optimism and hope, though in all fairness the milkmaids were a little unsure of Mel's hypothesis and Lydia was experiencing a significant portion of motherly pride.

Nothing.

They waited some more.

Still nothing.

Until the six of them were scooped up in a smooth move, to perch in the air a moment, all still in line. Suddenly the moonlight went out and they were smashed between two crackling surfaces.

'Oof,' said Lydia. 'Everyone okay?'

'I think she's closed the book,' said Mel.

'So, if our book is closed, then what?' said Linda. 'Oh my! Wheee! It's like being on the merry round.'

'I think she's closed the book and put it in her suitcase,' said Mel.

# Return

Eve journeys home by train. She eats scrambled eggs with peppers and onions, brown toast, and hash browns in a VIA dining car as the mountains flatten and flatten some more.

'More coffee?'

'Please.'

'How's waiting tables on a train?'

'Better than most places. Excuse me, Ma'am.'

Ma'am. Eve bristles inside her jeans and boots and Janis Joplin T-shirt, and touches the Mountain Curling Sweater soft beside her. Gwendolyn.

The world shifts from mountains to greeny brown stubble prairie, the sky giant and blue. Cloudless. Birdless. Moundless.

The train pulls into Bedford. Grubby and grey under the stark sun, a broad river and low flat buildings. The rail yard is in the north end, permanently settled with a thin film of dust. More freight than passengers, the platform bare, not even a bench.

City smells are different from mountain smells. Oil and dust and cigarette smoke and perfume. She breathes them in, they clog and cleave, she coughs them out. Sounds are different too. Drills, sharp soled shoes on pavement, screeching brakes, a distant siren, constant chatter. Other peoples' words just below the surface of the world's skin, sometimes breaking through.

She's booked a room at the Transit Hotel, unknown territory beyond the double doors. It looks like a saloon, something from an old Western with its veranda and hitching posts, an elegant, three-storey rectangle, broad side flat against the street, short side almost as long, with shared balconies across the front. It stands on its own small triangular island with busy roads on three sides. A sign says *Gerbil Races Nightly*.

There's a green door right inside. It's almost blue green—Gwendolyn might have called it aqua but the Transit isn't an aqua sort of place. Behind the door a desk and behind the desk a blue green board full of room keys.

'Nice T-shirt,' says a voice. 'You registering?'

'I made a reservation.'

'That was you? Just fill out the registration form. Sixty bucks for two nights plus GST.'

Eve fills in the form and pushes her sixty-three bucks across the ancient wooden counter without looking at the face.

'Good math,' says the man. 'Upstairs, third room on the left. This here's your key—you've got to leave it on the board when you go out. Need help with your bag?'

'I've got it.'

The hall smells of stale smoke and staler beer. The shine has worn off a wooden floor that bristles in places with brown carpet. The old-fashioned key, glamorous with age, unlocks a single room with window, bed, and closet (bathroom down the hall, an inconvenience she is used to). Brown paint sucks the light out of the room. Eve touches a dried paint drip, the skin of the Transit. Beneath her finger beats a seriously long life.

Downstairs, the city holds no pull. Exhaustion diverts Eve and she opens the door to the bar instead of the door to the street. Large and murky, filled with the smell of roasting potatoes and round wooden tables, aged and scarred—initials, hearts, messages, scratches.

'Hey honey, you Room 222?' He's the oldest waiter she's ever seen, a white apron tied around his waist, a cowboy hat that has to be too hot, and a check shirt. A metal tooth gleams in the middle of his smile. 'Heard you made a reservation.'

'Yep,' says Eve. 'That's me, Room 222.'

'You look like you can handle things. Don't get me wrong it's a safe place... for the brave.' He cackles. 'What can I get you?'

She orders veggie burger and fries ('Doug's famous grilled and spiced home fries,' according to the cowboy waiter), both good. Eve looks at the table: *Brian loves Doris, 1962*, scored inside a heart.

'And it's Simkins by a lettuce leaf, edging to his apple,' yells a man, voice static-laced.

Gerbil racing nightly.

The gerbils are stacked in a set of metal trays, the sort bakers or fudge makers might use, only narrower. Each gerbil is placed in its slot and lured to the other end with a pile of rotting fruit and vegetables. Run, gerbils, run.

'Come on Simpkins,' screeches a man with a beery voice and half empty glass of draft, a nervous finger tapping a nickel against the table. He sits close to Eve and smiles when she looks in his direction but doesn't stop the tapping.

'Come on Duster,' chants a group of men, older than the nervous tapper.

A couple in the corner are backing Trail Ride. The woman rolls her eyes at Eve and smiles. They sit in shadow, making out in old age. *Way to go*, thinks Eve and wills Trail Ride on.

Elderly Tapping Guy catches Eve's eye. 'I used to come here when the roads were gravel and the city wasn't called Bedford. Come on Simpkins! You can do it, Simpkins.'

'How were the fries?'

'Best ever.'

'More hot water for your peppermint tea?'

'Please. Is there a paper anywhere?'

One appears from the pocket of his apron, like magic. The rental ads for apartments exhaust Eve, demands for references and guaranteed income. Welfare okay. Employed only.

Next morning, Eve hands her key in at the desk.

'Thank you, ma'am.'

'Eve.'

'Rocky. Nice T-shirt, Eve.' (Joan Jett)

The emptiness of the sky prickles Eve's skin. New stores—Babies R Us, Home Sense, Chapters—square and large, squat in parking lots. Dust covers the window of a tiny vacuum repair shop. Unchanged.

Small, almost well-looked-after houses and yards and low-rise apartment buildings with vacancy signs operated by rental companies. References. Proof of income. Welfare welcome. One application at head office. Don't apply without a steady stream of income.

Eve hops a bus south side. Downtown high rises, the bridge across the river and over the Valley Swimming Pool, the university, scene of her mother's dissolution. University students don't have proof of income. Or welfare. Walk up apartments, trees growing out of the sidewalk in a well-organised grid, a veneer of caring.

Eve prowls the streets, stopping to press manager buttons on apartments.

'You've got an apartment for rent?'

'Nope, gone…'

'You've got an apartment to rent?'

'Yep. Meet me in the lobby.'

The lobby smell of yesterday's cooking disappears as a cloud of Old Spice drags in behind a shadow man, small with a sideways slant to his walk and a downward looking face covered in caramel coloured fluff. His eyes are so pale his pupils look like pushed out matchsticks. Eve remembers last night's racing gerbils. They take a staircase to a small landing with battered gold mailboxes.

'Just you?' asks the man.

'Just me.'

'No parties. I don't like parties. We're a quiet building.'

'I don't party.'

'You working?'

'Looking for work. Just got here from the mountains.'

'You'll need a job to get the apartment.'

'I'll get one.'

'What do you do?' He unlocks an apartment door.

The room surprises. It has a large window, sun everywhere, and the floor in the small living room is hardwood.

'Waitress.'

The kitchen has white appliances and grey speckled lino. Everything looks clean. The bathroom is white and shiny, the bedroom has hardwood with a rug.

'You don't have to keep the rug if you take it, it's a left over from the renter before. It's good quality, didn't want to throw it out.'

'I'll keep it.'

'Management company'll want references.'

Sound of a buzzer. The man presses an intercom.

'Here for the apartment? I'll be right down. Wait in the lobby.' He turns back to Eve. 'Interested?'

'How much?'

Eve calculates. Assumes she'll eat on the job. Wages on rent, tips for everything else. 'I'd like it.'

'You got furniture?'

'Some,' says Eve, 'in storage.' A Formica table and chairs and cement blocks and planks. Books, the collection kicked off with a copy of *Wuthering Heights*, the pages stuck together with banana.

The buzzer sounds again, a group of people on the sidewalk, all there for the apartment. 'You better get that job quick,' the man tells Eve.

Slav's Diner, *home of the best pyrogies this side of Kiev*. There's a cardboard cut-out of a jolly woman in the doorway. She has pink cheeks and her hair is in a fancy roll on the back of her head. In her hands a sign says *Help wanted*.

Eve has copies of her résumé, decorated with steaming cups of coffee and plates of food. She hands the young woman at the cash register a version with a grilled cheese sandwich and bowl of soup.

'Gimme a minute.' The young woman's skirt is barely as long as her uniform top. Eve wonders how she wipes the tables. *I'm getting old*, thinks Eve. Eve admires the pale green milk shake carousel behind the counter. A classic. An old friend.

A woman in black yoga pants and T-shirt covered with a diner shirt—Slav's written on the back, Bessie on the front—walks to the cash register, holding Eve's résumé.

'Cute,' says the woman waving the resume in the air. 'Let's me and you sit down.'

'That's you in the sign,' says Eve.

'Years ago.'

'I like it.'

'You've got lots of experience. All in the mountains. You ski?'

'Just like mountains.'

'You going back there?'

'No.'

'What brings you to Bedford?'

'It's my... home.'

'Where you staying?'

'The Transit.'

The woman peers real close at Eve. 'Gutsy.'

'I'm looking for an apartment but I need references and a job first.'

'Why the Transit? If you don't mind me asking.'

'Really? I used to walk by it when I was a kid. On my way to junior high. I thought it looked cool. Hot and cold water and bathrooms.'

Bessie laughs. 'When can you start?'

'As soon as you want me.'

'Tomorrow, 6.00 a.m.'

'Perfect.'

'Any questions?'

'Is there a Slav?'

Bessie laughs loud and rich like double chocolate fudge.

'He's long gone. This place is all mine.'

'Nice,' says Eve.

Eve figures The Transit suits her more than the cut throat rental market. Rocky curls sideways into an ancient rolling chair of leather and tired wood, reading, his cowboy boots—crossed at the ankle—rest on the desk. He has Roy Orbison hair and Buddy Holly glasses.

'Nice T-shirt.'

Leonard Cohen, 'Bird on a Wire'.

'Thanks. I need the key for 222.'

Rocky steps his boots down one at a time, rolls his chair closer to the desk, searches out a blank reservation slip and places it between the pages. Eve looks down on the top of his hair, it is shiny like plastic toy's snap-on hair. He rolls back and sets the book on the desk. Leonard Cohen, *Stranger Music*.

'You got monthly rates?' asks Eve.

'Need a job for an apartment these days, am I right?'

'I got a job.'

'Thought you'd just arrived in town.'

'Hired on today. Slav's Diner.'

'Good place.'

'You got information on these monthly rates?'

Rocky rolls backwards and rustles a sheet of paper out of a plywood pigeon-hole, rolls back to Eve.

'They're good,' says Rocky. 'And no commitment. Third week of every month you decide to renew. Or not. Only one week's notice needed.'

'Good deal.' Eve closes her eyes and pictures a small apartment with a wooden floor, sunlight, and bookshelves. Her tables and chairs have been stored more than ten years, $45.00 a month rental on a tiny metal locker accessed from a back lane—a small price to keep her past at a distance. Now she's ready to unpack but has no room.

'I'll take a month.'

'No need to pay now. Rent's due on the last day of this month.'

'Tomorrow.'

Rocky shrugs and slips a key on the counter. 'For you. Cupboard in the kitchen, same number as your room. Please don't keep open food in it, don't want to attract the rodents.'

'There's mice?'

'Not if you keep your food in containers.'

'Is there a fridge?'

'Not so's you'd notice.'

Eve inspects the cupboard and heads to the discount store for plastic containers and supplies. It's little more than a cloakroom cubby, the sort you kept your shoes in in school. But clean. She fills her containers with crackers, and mini tins of tuna along with a pack of Red Square Happy Colon cookies (with raisins and five grams of protein per serving), stashes the containers in the locker before setting a can of instant hot chocolate beside her newly purchased, quickly rinsed and now air-drying on the counter, mug. Tomorrow she'll buy tea towels. She plugs in an ancient but clean electric kettle and waits.

An elderly man walks into the kitchen and politely coughs into his arm. 'Excuse me,' he chokes.

'You alright?'

'Nothing a little water won't fix.'

Eve watches him shuffle to the sink, left foot dragging. He is thin to transparent, his leather belt cinches too-big jeans that bag around his bones, its tongue is peppered with holes professionally punched and more, handmade, to reduce its size, the excess curls downwards like a perforated worm. His skull, translucent skin and no hair, dominates. All his features are buried beneath the rising spectacle of old bone, head held high and forward, he looks like a man pushing forward into another world.

'You've got a cupboard,' says the old man. 'Must have signed up for the month.'

'I'm Eve.'

'Crispin. People call me Old Man Crispin, on account of me looking old. But I'm only fifty-nine.'

Eve removes the foil from the top of her tin of instant hot chocolate, her back to Old Man Crispin.

'Nice bird,' says Old Man Crispin as he shuffles towards her.

'Thanks.' Eve turns around too quick and his head is almost touching the bird on the wire.

'Pardon me,' said Old Man Crispin. 'I never meant to... I...' He turns humbled eyes towards the door.

'Will you drink a cup of hot chocolate with me?'

'That would be champion.'

They sit at the table and wait for water to boil.

'Champion,' says Eve. 'I like that.'

'Had a foreman used the word. That's just champion, Crispin, he'd say. Just champion. Guess I picked it up. I was a miner—asbestos, Thetford mines.'

'Where's that?'

'Quebec.'

'You speak French?'

'Not really. Nobody cares what a miner speaks. Came to Bedford looking for work in the oilfields but the asbestos poisoning turned them off me.'

'Poisoning?'

'Works its way through your body, you breath it in same time it's squeezing through your skin. When I was a kid—my dad mined too—white dust covered my toys, our house, the street, the town, pretty little downtown, and the tailings. Tailings looked like hills hemming us all in, pretty but they were covered with the dust too. Like my lungs, squeezing out the oxygen.'

Eve watches Crispin cough and learns about asbestos mining.

'What room are you in?'

'222.'

'224. We're next-door neighbours.'

'Good to meet you neighbour.'

Eve is reading *Barometer Rising*. She picked up the book in a junk store halfway between the Transit and Slav's Diner. Small paperbacks, ten cents said the sign. *Barometer Rising* just sneaking in although it was 219 pages long. Number eight in the New Canadian Library, a list at the back of the book saying there are ninety three in the series. Some are old friends. Eve resolves to read them all.

That night she's in a corner of the Transit's bar, eating a salad and unsettled by Penny's life in Halifax. She admires her for designing submarines but it nags that Penny's success is based on Neil's design. Eve knows Neil will be a hero, she figures him and Penny will end up together if the explosion doesn't kill them, but who really designed the submarine? She feels outside the novel, arguing with it instead of living it.

'The lady's with me!' says an old man with a brown suit complete with waistcoat and a ten gallon hat. A lazy length moustache hides most of his face.

'I stand.' A second old man, also in a suit—grey pinstripe—with a black turtleneck and baseball hat that says Bedford Beavers on the front. He has sparkly blue eyes and a similar moustache. 'I stand to correct you. The lady is most definitely with me.'

Rocky, fake snakeskin boots and bolo tie, slouches on over.

'How's it goin' boys?' says Rocky. 'Don't suppose you fine gentlemen would be interested in helping with the beer?'

The fine gentlemen are Bart and Benedict, twin brothers and never married, in their seventies, quarrelling over which one of them has asked Molly to the bar that evening. Molly sits between them in velvet and lace. Eve watches Bart and Benedict follow Rocky to the cellar for some slow beer unloading and smiles her appreciation of Rocky's ability to defuse a fight before it starts. Eve turns back to Halifax 1917 and doesn't notice Molly gravitate to her corner.

'Can I join you?'

Eve smiles. 'Sure.'

'Always duelling over me, those boys,' says Molly. 'It's Eve, isn't it, dearie? Lovely name. Got class and longevity that name.'

'Molly does too.'

'And the hint of a roll in the hay, I hope,' says Molly. 'Seventy-eight and shacked up with two younger men! Twins! I like your jacket. Real leather, is it? Buy it local? I'm morphing my style and on the lookout for places to buy new crap.'

'Value Village.'

'My favourite,' says Molly. 'You know it's environmentally friendly to buy second-hand.'

'And cheap,' adds Eve.

'I've always been velvet and lace and the boys appreciate that. I used to mix it up with denim—blue jeans, like. But these days I slip in a little polyester. So much more comfortable and the boys don't seem to notice. But I need to find my happy place. Somewheres between denim and polyester. Oh, here's my boys…'

Eve smiles and Molly is on her way back to the table, grinning at her boys.

'Now you've met Molly, you're practically a regular,' says Rocky. 'I hope she wasn't bothering you.'

'Bothering me?' says Eve. 'She's a sweetheart.'

'They're good people,' says Rocky and heads back to the bar.

Eve is distant from but curious about Marian's life (*The Edible Woman*, New Canadian Library, #93) when

Rocky taps at her door.

'Wondered if you might want to take a drive into the country. I don't mean nothing by it. Just thought you might like a drive. I'm not coming on to you.'

It's a Sunday afternoon in spring and she's been at the Transit for almost a year.

'Thank you. I'd like a drive.'

The car is pink outside, cream inside, and bigger than Eve's room at the Transit. "58 Impala, same car Buddy Holly had.'

Rocky's wearing dark glasses and sitting beside him Eve can see they're hiding a seriously black eye.

'Never walk into a fight,' says Eve.

'Who told you that?'

'Always known it. Good advice.'

'Had no choice. Hockey fans, half from Bedford, others Apple Valley. They'd have wrecked the place if I'd done nothing.'

Rocky rummages in the glove box. 'Eight Track,' he says. 'Don't mind music, do you?'

'Nope,' says Eve, curious and ambivalent. She enjoys music when she hears it but doesn't need it at her fingertips; she has no music system of her own.

Tinkling piano plunks out of the chrome speaker in front of her nose. She'd expected rock and roll. Almost laughs. This isn't music to add to her life. This is music to ride up in an elevator.

'Where do you want to go?' asks Rocky.

'Me?'

'It's a Sunday afternoon drive. Speak your destination. Where's your favourite place?

'I've only ever been to the mountains.'

'My choice then? North,' says Rocky.

The voice from the speaker is like coarsened chocolate and curls into her ears and makes her shudder. The songs are small stories. This is no elevator music.

'Who is this?'

'Tom Waits. You want I should change it?'
'No!'
They head north to *Blue Valentine* and her heart grows so big she thinks she'll explode. She's found a musical home. They stop for gas and she offers to pay and Rocky laughs and tells her to keep her money. They drink coffees from an instant machine where you press a button and get cappuccino with or without milk. They find Coffee Crisps in amongst the flashlight batteries, antacids and fishing lures. Coffee Crisps will forever mean Tom Waits and a frisson for life. She must have seen small towns and low buildings and trees and fences and isolated farmhouses on that drive, but those are not what she remembers.

Eve is reading *Beautiful Losers*, #153, when Old Man Crispin's cough shifts. His grating hawk regularly crosses the thin walls that might be cardboard for all the sound they stop. Eve makes cocoa in the mini kitchen and knocks on Old man Crispin's door most nights.

'Champion,' he says.

The wall shudders as if it were clearing its own throat. Eve slips last month's rent receipt between the pages and listens. A sawing joins the grating.

'Are you okay in there?' She raps on the door. The cough wheezes and hacks some more. 'Can you answer the door?'

She races to reception.

'You look like hell,' says Bessie next morning.

'Old Man Crispin went to hospital last night.'

'You need a moment?'

'I'm fine. Gonna visit him after work.'

'Where is he? St. Mary's? Need a ride?'

'Got one.'

'You ready?' Rocky walks in just before shift's end.

Bessie raises an eyebrow.

'I'll get my jacket.'

Bessie raises her other eyebrow.

Rocky drives them back to the Transit.

'I thought we were going to the hospital,' says Eve.

Crispin left precise instructions for his farewell. Cremation, no service but music chosen by Rocky, a drive in the '58 Chevy to somewhere pretty, windows open, and a resting place in the lee of a coulee on an anonymous stubble-covered field.

'We'll never remember this place.'

'That was Crispin's plan.'

Eve stands, a tin of instant hot chocolate in her hands, her fingernails tearing and peeling the label, Rocky turns up the eight track and a jangly guitar filters across the breeze.

'Ry Cooder,' says Rocky.

They listen to the music, stare at the prairie. Eve senses her insides shift, the flesh tumbles and churns, a prisoner making to escape through her skin. The fence between who she was and who she is melts one stake at a time, her insides made ready for a new entrance. She stands on the edge of the world, almost ready to dive in.

The music vibrates all around as if it stems up through the prairie itself and into her hands and the hot chocolate tin, now gleaming in its thin slivery metal unglory, the wrapper shreds in her hand.

The music stops and Rocky heads to the car, returns with the cardboard box of Old Man Crispin's ashes. He's about to disappear with thin memory and little trace. Rocky and Eve stare long at the box. As the light fades beyond clouds, almost into darkness, Rocky eases it open and nods towards the hot chocolate can.

'That wasn't why I brought it,' says Eve.

'I think you should.'

Careful not to spill ash or chocolate on the breeze, Eve sifts the smallest amount of chocolate into the ashes. It is right, her and Old Man Crispin were all about the hot chocolate. The breeze strengthens and Rocky pours the ash and chocolate into its maw and they watch the old man shower his way across the prairie.

'Why here?' asks Eve.

'Graveyards made him think of a mouth with rotted teeth.'


This afternoon.

Home, my feet are near marble from the cold, a temperature inversion, should have seen it coming, should have worn warmer socks, winter boots. I crank up the heat and crouch over the vent, pull the fabric of my cords away from my legs to make a heat trap. The warm air billows up and my hands search for my ankles. I knead my toes.

I unpack my groceries, line them up on the counter. Set out mixing bowls. It is overwhelming. Too many people to feed. Too much disorder. I list the tasks, pen on paper.

Music in the background. My music. Nina Simone. First the T-shirt, then the music.

The squeak of a knife against a pepper. Washed. halved, quarter, scraped out, rinsed again, seedless, chopped, sparkling shreds.


Steam from the Slav's Diner coffee machine clutches at the street windows and heightens the warmth inside. Customers glow with indoor relief as they edge to their favourite tables, blinded by fogged over spectacles, or spectacles thawing in hand.

First table is the once upon a time, almost farmers. Eve opens five minutes early as they gather outside, stamping feet and clapping mitted hands. They sit in the corner, waiting for refills.

'They sold out!' says Ty Ditton.

'Na,' says old Wilbur Nefstead. 'They joined the Saskatchewan Wheat Pool.'

Ty has to be the youngest at seventy plus. Wilbur might be ninety and he's wrong. Eve isn't going to say the Alberta Wheat Pool merged with the Manitoba Wheat Pool, but she knows it did. She's been pouring coffees to the same stories, the same squabbles and grievances for years. She'd be upset if she didn't know the conversation, but she won't join in. Coffee pouring shadows don't.

'Manitoba,' says Jens Jensen.

Eve sends Jens a silent thank you.

Eve warms her back against the Bunn coffee maker and keeps an eye on all the tricky customers.

Yesterday, after shift, Eve went to the library and googled novels about waitresses. *Wait staff* the online catalogue hammered back. All she got was a bunch of biographies and training manuals and a series with a cocktail waitress who dates a vampire and solves mysteries. While this career anonymity suits her she'd like to think her kind were noticed if not notable.

'Fill 'er up' says the dark stranger from the Ford 150. His smile and jeans are too tight and the points on his high heeled boots a touch too sharp.

'You got it,' says Eve as he leers and his left-hand brushes against the top of her blue jeaned thigh. Eve shifts a fraction of a fraction of a centimetre in case the brush is accidental. It isn't. The hand trails back and Eve dodges.

'I wouldn't if I were you,' says Eve.

'Whatcha accusing me of?' asks the hand.

'You tell me.' Eve stands full height, in his face; her eyes flash and glitter and her fearlessness pokes through. The would-be farmers place their money on Eve's spine over the stranger's. Every time.

'Pardon me?' says Eve.

'Nothing.'

Eve keeps him in her sights. He tosses cash on the counter but a loonie rolls for all its straightened edges and falls on the floor. His eyes on Eve's face, hers on his.

She folds her arms, eyes still in place, and he bends to pick it up. All the time Eve watches and as he heads for the door he freezes and throws an aggressive stare.

'You'll know me again,' says Eve.


This afternoon.

Flour against my skin. Gentle like velvet and smooth like a small landscape in a bowl, consistency soon to be changed by sugar, salt, and baking powder. Coarse with the addition of butter, softened not melted. I flatten the edge of the butter between my fingers, create an unstable butter ridge. Cut in butter, knead, don't knead, knead, mix together, crumble apart. Gone too far? No, a perfect slurry. Mix egg and milk, add onions, green onions add milk and egg. Shape, bake, rise, success.


'I need a favour,' said Bessie.

'No problem.'

'Look through these job applications, would you? Pick three and interview them.'

'Me? I'm not a boss.'

'I'm not saying you are but I value your opinion.'

What people write on paper about themselves and what they are when they turn up in person can be different, vastly different.

Janice sounds like an orderly librarian but lolls across the table from Eve with a cigarette in her red claw fingers.

'Please don't smoke,' says Eve.

'Not planning on it.'

'Why did you leave your last position?'

'Customers were fighting over me.' Janice flicks her lighter.

'Please don't smoke.'

'Was that me?' asks Janice. 'What the fuck. I must be

more nervous than I thought.'

'We rotate shifts here. 6.00 till noon, 11.00 to 5.00. and 3.00 to 9.00.'

'Is that six in the morning? I'm not an early riser.'

'Please don't smoke.'

'Oops.'

The second interview is a no show and the third is Clover.

This afternoon.

The chilli pepper is a risky creature, has a dangerous heat. I cover my hands with olive oil before chopping. One dish with ribs and seeds, one without. Wash hands with soap and water. Then wash tomatoes, cilantro, wrap cilantro in a clean tea towel. Knife against soft, forgiving, tomato skin. Onion, top, tail, chop. Romaine. Roll the lime, slice, squeeze. Oregano, cumin. Mix. Split in two. One side gets the chilly pepper, one doesn't. Smell of cilantro breezes through the kitchen. Clean in winter.

Sam teaches at the local junior high. Sam doesn't look tough. He has a face like a rubber ball, all mashed up. His eyes are too pale to be soft and too dark to be piercing. He wears jeans and shirts with sweaters on top and the hint of a tie. None of it fits together but all of it adds up to Mr. Jenkins. The students, when they cross paths with him in the diner, are respectful and even friendly with a side of caution. Eve has seen the students greet other teachers. Mr. Jenkins is special.

'Sit with me,' said Sam. Years ago. She'd probably served him forty times by then. He eats at the diner once a week. Usually Thursdays but a different day occasionally if he has a field trip or a student needs to work with him during lunch. He likes to eat out on Thursdays because he has a prep block immediately after lunch and can lounge with a second coffee.

'What do you teach?' asked Eve.
'Literature.'
'My favourite,' says Eve.
'Favourite books?'
'I liked *The Stone Angel* in high school.'
'Why?'
'Hagar. Felt like a real person. All that guilt.'
He laughed.
'What?' asked Eve.
'Sounds like you've read *The Stone Angel*.'

They talk books, Sam and Eve. Comfortable conversation, until Sam transgresses, some months after he first said sit with me, a respectable time from when they first talked about Hagar and *The Stone Angel*.

'How was the sandwich?' asks Eve. 'More coffee?'

'Sandwich was great. Sit with me?'

The coffee pot's empty and Eve sits, expects Sam to ask her what she's reading, unsure whether to lead with the Gail Bowen mystery or *Half-Blood Blues*. She's reading both from the outside in, a visitor taking in a story. She sits, innocent and unsuspecting, open to Sam and the world. Content. And then Sam places his hand on hers. It's a small and unexpected gesture and as her blood runs cold, her mind empties of every word she has ever known. She is blank and terrified. She thought Sam her friend.

Eve feels the warmth drain from her hand, her skin chill. Sam watches. His eyes search for her happiness and her shock at his transgression registers. No one goes cold with happiness. Both Sam and Eve have read enough to know that.

'Sorry,' says Sam removing his hand.

'I have to…' Eve gestures to the coffee pot, the coffee machine.

They never mention it again.

Over the months and years they broker a fragile peace that grows with time. They discuss taste. Formica over laminate tables. Hardwood over carpeting, though Sam thinks there's a place for carpet and Eve disagrees. Bookcases vs planks with bricks, department store art vs. postcards or personal photographs or home done paintings. They agree on most everything and the few things they disagree on, Sam's opinion moves closer to Eve's than hers to his.

Today.
Solstice, official start of winter, seven hours, twenty-seven minutes and forty-two seconds of daylight. This afternoon, daylight is half finished. Seize every second. Revel in every moment. A ray of sunshine through snow cloud sparkles the already bright kitchen.. Daylight drips through the sand clock. Today.

Clover is well settled into the workings of Slav's Diner and room 224 has been empty for months—except for the occasional one-nighter or salesman in town for a week—when Eve hears coughing.

It's her second night with *The Double Hook* and she is unable to will James to shake off his gullibility. She pauses and listens... Coughing. Has to be her imagination. Stay awake and be done with James. She leans back to let the words stew in her brain and her eyes close and suddenly the coughing has her sparked awake. It isn't a cough, it's a sob.

Already in her sleep shirt, all she wants is to close her eyes but the sobbing pierces her skin. She pulls on the long grey overcoat with the torn lining that doubles as a dressing gown and pauses at the door to 224.

'Are you okay?'

More sobs. She taps on the door. More sobs.

'Are you okay?' she shouts.

'Who is it?' The voice is small and hoarse.

'Your neighbour.'

There's a shuffling and sniffling and the door opens. 'Eve. I'm sorry, am I keeping you awake?'

'Molly?'

'You better come in.'

Molly snuffles and splutters and stretches her back with her head tilted upwards, blows her nose, but the tears bank up in her eyes and are ready to fall.

'Wow,' says Eve.

'I couldn't live with the brown.'

Lacy shawls hang from the window and light shade and a huge piece of red velvet covers the bed. Scarves are pinned to the walls. Everywhere colourful flaps of fabric. Eve shudders; it's as if the room has peeling flesh. She prefers the brown paint.

'They threw me out,' sobs Molly. 'After all these years, they said leave. But I had nowheres to go and had to come here. They wanted me to choose, you see, and I couldn't.'

'Between Ben and Bart.'

'I need them both, I've always needed an extra man. Just to spice things up, you know. But they said they couldn't go on. Fighting with each other.'

'Did you explain that you needed them both?'

'They had to know. Sixteen years and it was always the two of them. We made a team. I wasn't much older than you when I met them.' (Eve is forty, Molly was sixty three when she met the twins.)

'Can I get you something? Hot chocolate, milk?'

'No, I think I need to sleep. Maybe you could come to the washroom with me, stand outside of course, while I get ready for bed?'

Eve watches the hall lights of the hotel. It's a high passageway and the light reflects off the brown walls in an unflattering way. The rooms all have false ceilings.

Rocky says some are used for storage, old furniture, old dishes, nothing has ever been thrown away. The owners think it adds insulation. Sometimes, when Eve can't sleep, she imagines furniture falling on her head. The storage areas are filled up and sealed off so rodents can't get in. Eve shudders.

Molly exits the washroom in mismatched pyjamas. Green and white striped bottoms and blue and white top.

'Benedict favours green and Bart blue. I snuck them out. I couldn't sleep without the smell of my boys.' Molly tethers herself to Eve's arm and totters down the hallway. They make slow progress. 'It's not so bad here, not really, is it dear? Not when you've got good neighbours.'

Eve settles Molly into bed, tucks her in.

'Now you get some sleep dear. You've got to work tomorrow.'

'If you need anything bang on the wall. I'm right next door.'

'Molly's in room 224.'

'I know,' says Rocky. 'I registered her and gave her the key.'

'Well?'

'She asked to be next to you.'

'What are we going to do? Benedict and Bart threw her out, because she wouldn't chose between them.'

'That what she told you?'

'Why would she lie?'

'Because she was coming on to a young cowboy and they said enough's enough and she had to take a break. It happens every two or three years.'

'She sounds heartbroken.'

'She does. She is. It'll blow over and she'll go home.'

Molly is tireless.

'Let's you and me hit the dollar store for snacks.'

'Let's you and me have a bite at Tim Hortons.'

'Let's me and you have a night on the town.'

Molly magnificent in an off the shoulder gown with

an uneven hem and heels, all purple tulips on a white background and sequins like dewdrops on petals.

'You look wonderful,' says Eve.

'I'm dressing for two,' says Molly taking in Eve's Ramones T-shirt and black jeans.

Molly dances till sweat glistens and threatens to make a paste of her sparkling face powder.

'Let's me and you take in the gerbil races.'

'Let's me and you…'

'Let's me and you…'

Rocky and Bessie stage an intervention.

'She's running you ragged,' says Bessie.

'You're exhausted,' says Rocky.

'You were late last week. Twice.'

'You have to say no to her.'

Even Clover joins in.

'I had to remind you three times about coffee refills. I'm writing it down. Keeping track.' She holds up her order book and on the back cover there were three lines drawn in pencil. 'When you get to five I make a cross through the first four.'

'I know how it works,' says Eve.

'It has to stop,' says Bessie.

'Tell her tonight,' says Rocky. 'Tell her you need an early night.'

'Maybe I'll talk to Ben and Bart.'

'You stay out of it,' says Bessie, 'it's not your business.'

Eve resolves to talk to Ben and Bart.

Eve dreams, the night before her planned chat with Bart and Ben, about Old Man Crispin. He's coughing and she's making hot chocolate. The cough thunders through her dream, wakes her. She shakes her head. The cough is still there. It has a wheeze and a bang. The cough becomes a knocking on her wall.

'I'm not feeling so good,' says Molly.

'Rocky!'

Next day Rocky picks Eve up from work and they head to the hospital. Rocky eases into a parking spot and stares at the parking computer. Eve hauls tips from her pocket and feeds the machine. At the door of the hospital Eve hesitates.

'Never been in a hospital.'

'Not even when you were born?'

'Maybe.'

'Don't you know?'

'My mum wasn't big on stories.'

Not true. Mum loved stories, she'd never seen a novel she didn't want to read.

'You don't have to do this if you don't want to. Molly will understand.'

Eve runs up the stairs. Ben and Bart tag team their attack on her.

'It's your fault."

'You exhausted her.'

'You should have said no.'

'It's not Eve's fault,' says Molly.

'Molly's right,' says Rocky.

Molly, stick figure in an orange fleece two piece, is held up on either side by her boys. Bart holds a small suitcase, Ben a pot of flowers.

'And we'd appreciate it…' begins Ben.

'Eve's my friend. She didn't keep me from you.'

'… if you'd send her things to our place,' finishes Bart. 'Don't encourage her Moll. You wouldn't have worn yourself out if it wasn't for her.'

'This hospital…' says Bart.

'This hospital stay is all your fault,' says Ben

'They only kept me in overnight.'

'They'll come round,' says Rocky.


This afternoon.

I pause in my work, my list half checked off, all items

planned and sorted. I listen to hearts beating. My own, the walls, the air nestling against this home, this street, these houses, Bedford.


'Can I ask a favour?' says Sam.

'Depends,' says Eve. She's almost forgotten the hand incident—but not quite.

'I'm buying a house, maybe, want your opinion.'

'Sure. Got pictures?'

'Come with me, to see it.'

Eve looks him straight in the eye. He doesn't blink. A good sign or no? Eve has no idea. Sam holds his hands up in surrender.

'I want your design eyes. That's all.'

Eve lolls in the passenger seat as Sam drives. A rainy Bedford morning slides by. Late April and she can't remember the last time it rained. Bessie is convinced Sam wants more. Eve needs to trust him. And if she can't, she can take care of herself. The rain cheers her.

As they cross the river the city greens up.

'You never told me it was south side,' says Eve. She watches the park—the one her and Chasity, Nikki, Tamara, and Lisa hung out in—disappear. She never sees them, not since she's returned.

Not true. Chasity came in the diner. With Sam. The same but different, less sharp, less glittery, less pink.

'Eve!'

'It is the same Eve. I told you it was,' said Sam. 'She didn't believe it was you.'

'It's me.' Eve prowled over to their table with her coffee pot, order book in hand.

'I can't believe it's you,' said Chasity.

'It's me,' managed Eve. All other words choke in her gullet.

'Chasity's my student.'

Sam teaches junior high. It doesn't make sense.

Chasity is way too old. Could she be a student's mother?

'Not that sort of student,' says Chasity. 'Some kind of explaining for an English teacher, don't you think? I'm on my practicum, learning to teach.'

'Not much I can teach you. She's a natural,' said Sam.

'No. But I am close to done. Next time this year I'll be teaching. English and Art.'

'Gonna be a hell of an English teacher,' said Sam…

There's a South Side familiarity that Eve drinks in like water. Bedford is two cities. South of the river crammed full of coffee shops and gentility, north of the river remains a frontier. There are attempts for one to bleed into the other. Most fail. After they see the house she'll ask Sam to drop her on Moore Avenue to check out Recycled Books. She was a teenager when it burned to the ground. Now rebuilt, she carries a list of titles of books she'd like to read.

The trees are thinly green in the spring rain, impatient to be hurried into summer thickness. Familiar. Eve steps out of the car and into the rain ready to be impressed, ready to sprint towards dryness, and instead freezes in a puddle.

'What do you think?' asks Sam.

Eve stands in the rain, her heart beating faster than any heart could possibly beat. She is soaked and dissolving. Her body is clammy from the inside out, not from the rain. Her mind slows down. Her legs rebel, refuse to move. The world buzzes. Even Sam becomes a bee she is tempted to swat. And in the middle of the fear, she adds up the numbers. Has she saved enough to rent a room for the rest of her life? Can she find a safe space and stay forever? Can she buy enough books to always read? How will she buy groceries? Can she grow food on the windowsill? Can she disappear?

'I know this house,' whispers Eve.

'Good memories?'

'The worst.'

Stephanie's house. She thought she had pushed her far away. She thought she had started over.

Sam is chivalrous. Takes her by the arm, talks in a soothing voice.

'Do you want to wait in the car?'

Eve looks at him, peers at the house. Minutes pass. They are soaked. Sam's some time curls are unwound and flattened against his skin. Must she forget all over again?

'No. I want to see the fucking house.'

Inside the house has grown a skin. The whisperings and ghosts of old time owners disappear beneath crisp new surfaces. New floors and walls and ceilings stretch tight over old histories. Eve steps into shiny surfaces, white walls and wood-but-not-wood floors. It's a shell without memory. The walls have disappeared. She sees the kitchen through the living room from the front door. Each old room cracked open to the visitor on the doormat. Echoes of her and Stephanie are sealed behind renovation. Outside rain, inside all is bright and sunny. There are bathrooms where there were no bathrooms, a basement clean and bright. Upstairs small rooms have regular sized closets with sliding doors and the bathroom is white tile and walk-in shower. Harmless. The past subdued. No mismatched style, no dust, no books, no bricks, no story. Maybe this is the wrong house.

Outside the window squats a dripping yard. No flowers, not even a spring crocus, gasp for air. Sticks of sodden plants tangle together, wait for their future.


This afternoon.

Blossoming aroma. I am attacked by garlic and onion and turmeric and cinnamon, in through the nose and in through the skin. I am brought to my knees by smell. This common, rarely uncommon—sometimes dull, skin sack is assaulted again and again in the best possible way by the itch of the exotic. I breath deep, ease into sweet and savoury. Loved aroma but overwhelming.


The Transit is closing.

Rocky has long had a passion for Slav's veal cutlets and has become a regular over the years.

'How's it going?'

'It's going.'

The Transit is no longer the home of gerbil races.

Eve has never known Rocky so closed. And she's known Rocky for years. She watches as he chews nothing except the inside of his own face.

Rocky looks at Eve. 'I've got news,' he says. 'They found a buyer for the old place.'

The Transit has been for sale for three years, limping on. Lots of tire kickers, Rocky figures, no buyers. Until this.

'They're gonna close her down and renovate.'

'Where will everyone live?'

'All the permanent rooms stay till they find somewhere else. You okay?'

'What are you going to do?'

'They've hired me on—manager. And until we open, I help with renovations and consult, keeper of the Transit Hotel history.'

Eve stares at the table. A coffee stain hints at a tree trunk cut crosswise, runnels of coffee dried in concentric circles, if she counts them she'll have the age of the imagined tree. She counts and counts. More important than life itself, to age that imagined tree. If she gets it right they won't renovate the Transit.

'Will there still be rooms to rent?'

Rocky shakes his head.

On Friday Slav's Diner serves salmon.

Brian waves at Eve from the corner table. A man of habit, always the corner, always his back against the wall.

'What's Mel doing with the salmon today?'

'Broiled. Grainy mustard, garlic, finely minced shallots, fresh thyme and rosemary, lemon,' says Eve.

'Shallots or onions?'

'Shallots. Bessie wanted onions. Mel argued for shallots. Greek salad?'

'And—'

'Water?'

'Must you finish my sentences?' asks Brian.

'Good memory. Can't help it.'

Eve meets Brian after Stephanie contacts her but she's known him for years. Always Friday, always the salmon, a man of few words. At first.

The message comes through the Slav's Diner's Facebook page. Bessie claims the page is advertising but spends hours talking with past employees, congratulations and commiserations. She writes the message on a pink Post-it note.

*Eve!*
*Friend!*
*Ur back!*
*Stephanie*

Eve shoves it in her pocket and pours coffee. The past is exorcised. But the note sits in her pocket and radiates ill will. Stephanie has found her. Stephanie is buried, forgotten. It is time, says Stephanie's note.

'You okay, honey? You're shaking,' says old Mrs. Anders, eighty and all dolled up in green leggings and a purple puffer jacket.

'I'm sorry!'

'It's okay, you missed me.'

'Ow,' says Emily, Mrs. Anders adult daughter, also in green leggings and a purple puffer. 'Didn't miss me.'

'Let me get you an ice cube.'

'No worries,' says Emily, 'I don't need an ice cube. But I'd have a cinnamon bun.'

The rest of the day is graceless, all spills and mostly merciful customers, occasional ice cubes and complimentary desserts.

Back at the Transit—bar closed and gerbils long gone, with luck to a gerbil retirement home—she searches out Rocky.

'I'm borrowing the kitchen,' Eve tells Rocky.

'No problem,' says Rocky. 'I'm out for the night.'

There are seven left in the Transit and they share the small commercial kitchen that used to feed bar regulars. Eve fills a steamer basket with cauliflower flowerets, rinses them under the tap, sets them on top of a pot of boiling water, and instructs herself to ignore the note's incessant throbbing. There's a small but joyful sound system in the kitchen, Rocky's idea. Eve chops onions and sings along to 'Whistling Past the Graveyard'. *Stephanie won't get me, not here.* She breaks eggs into a bowl, whisks and adds milk, onions, pepper, salt and garlic; *I'll go to the police if she harasses me. I have rights.* Eve flips the stove on to 375 F, sprays a pie dish, grates some cheese. *Stephanie has lied before she'll lie again.* Don't, Eve cautions herself, still singing. She spoons cheese, then cauliflower, into the pie dish, pours in the egg mixture, more cheese on top, and puts it in the oven. By the time the potatoes and carrots are washed, chopped, spiced, and roasting she's singing 'Blue Valentine'.

'One more time, Tom!' She re-starts the album and waits for dinner to cook.

Eve swallows the last of her quiche, stores the leftovers in the fridge with a note that says 'help yourself', and washes the dishes. *Friend.* It's still early and Tom isn't helping. Eve wants a cigarette but doesn't smoke. *Friend?*

There's only one solution. Swimming. Eve hates swimming with all her heart and most of her soul. She grabs her low-income attractions pass—free entry to swimming pools for those close to the poverty line but capable of tax returns. She shudders with anticipation, water stinging her eyes and nose and mouth and trickling down her nasal passages, but swimming will tire her and sleep is worth it.

The local pool is anonymous, and stinks of old socks and chlorine. Surprising since all swimmers do is wash. Foot bath, full shower. *She really called me friend?* Backwards down the metal staircase with its artsy flourishes and into the shallow end. No hesitation, medium speed, backward steps down. Eve's tough but not tough enough to jump in, too dangerous—spray in her eyes and nose and mouth.

Front crawl. Her arms arc out of the water like wet noodles but her legs kick in a close to front crawl kinda style. She can't resort to doggie paddle, not this early in the swim. The lifeguard has his eye on her in a reassuring, not flattering, sort of way. *Friend!*

She reaches the far end and holds on. The lifeguard waves. She doesn't wave back in case he thinks she's drowning. She smiles and salutes, a couple of fingers against her forehead, like a giant boy scout.

Eve flips onto her back and float swims to the other end. Her legs kick desperately, her arms pasted to her sides. She has a thing where she flaps her hands in the water like they know a secret way to propel her from one end to the other. They don't but flapping hands give her arms a chance to relax after the flimsy front crawl. *Ur back?* Her arm muscles relax as she peers at the ceiling. White metal girders like a stack of ribs without barbecue sauce. Huge bolt heads, industrial size. Ugly, not ugly, brutal and then small clouds through endless windows and more clouds and the tiniest shred of early moonlight trickles in.

The shallow end is humiliation. She stands briefly, a chilled, lime green streak with an un-curving body. (The lime green, still serviceable, stands out in the event she needs rescuing.) Eve is proud of her body, tough like a boxer, should have been a boxer. *Ur back.* Straight up and down without much waist and minimal padding. But strong. *Ur back*. She ducks under, knees bent, only her head above water.

*Ur back*. Eve swims to the deep end. Breast-stroke but she does it wrong, feels like a frog dissected with every stroke. *Ur back*. She returns to front crawl, shifts her head from side to side to side without rhythm, gasps at air, resorts to doggie paddle. Her element. Head strained up and out of the water, legs kicking, hands pawing through the water. Faking her way across the pool. Arms exhausted, water her biggest enemy, sleep on the horizon.

Eve swims three lengths and languishes at the deep end, one arm clutching the side in an offhand way. She's a swimmer. The guard nods, she smiles and nods back. Less military and more professional than a salute, grown up.

Eve twists, fully on her back now, and heads for the shallow end. *Ur back*. Exhaustion sets in. She no longer cares that Stephanie knows her whereabouts.

A coracle—one of a fleet of small round boats rented by the half hour at the front desk—bumps into her. Eve sinks, water in her nose and eyes and mouth. She jerks upward. Safe. She sinks. Not safe. She breaks the surface and shakes her head. Water in her mouth. Spit, spit, disgusting. The lifeguard is half out of his chair. Eve floats, smiles, continues to the shallow end. Her nose is raw with chlorine, every shred of frail sinus skin whines in discomfort. Her feet touch the bottom of the pool.

'Sorry,' says a voice. 'I bumped you.'

Familiar voice. Back to the wall salmon?

'Brian.'

'I'm Eve.'

'I know.'


Today.

This afternoon. I chop winter vegetables and grate cheese. Mix together the same ingredients. Solstice dinner. No swimming necessary.


'Another message,' says Bessie. 'Might be time you got your own Facebook.'
'No thanks.'
*Eve.*
*Slav's Diner!*
*I see you in your little uniform. (You know it's unbecoming, right?)*
*Get back to me.*
*Steph*
*Steph?* Suddenly she's Steph.
Eve heads straight to the pool. She kicks her legs and mutters 'Steph' with every kick. She flaps her hands and brisk talks common sense to herself. Fails to listen.
In the deep end, she stops the kicks and flapping and waits to sink. Eyes closed, heavier than lead. Nothing. She opens her eyes and the lifeguard is standing, ready to leap in and save.
*Steph?*


Today.
Earlier, at the market, I invited Chasity to dinner. An act of bravery.
'It's informal, a few friends, people from work.'
Chasity looked uncertain, then smiled and nodded.


'What's Mel done with it today?
'Baked.'
'And?'
'Green onions.'
'Okay.'
Above the order pad Eve's eyes laugh.
'And?'

'Pineapple.'
'Sacrilege! Salmon and pineapple? Mel!'
Brian is halfway in the kitchen.
'Mel! Pineapple on my salmon?'
Eve laughs. But there are only six of them left at the Transit and another message.

*Eve*
*Get back to me*
*Get back to me*
*Get back to me*
*Stephanie*

'You swimming tonight?'
'You betcha.'
Steve taught her to swim, Brian perfects her style.
The lifeguard sits, Eve lays flat on the water, stares at the ceiling. Her eyes swivel from side to side in case of danger, Brian front crawls up beside her.
'You should point your toes,' says Brian.
'Huh?'
'Point your toes. Try it now. It'll help your front crawl.'
She points her toes.
'Excellent. And keep flat.'
'I am flat.'
'When you're swimming.'
'I am swimming.'
'No, you're not.'
'I'm getting from one end of the pool to the other.'
He laughs and back on her front she flattens and points and he is right. It helps.
'Your fingertips have to lead,' says Brian.
She is swimming. Just swimming. No Stephanie in her head.
'You know front crawl is exhausting.'
'I swim to sleep.'
'It's easier to slice through the water if you point your fingers, of course if you want to sleep don't bother.

Make it harder on yourself, slap the water.'

Steve was all hands on when he taught her to swim, Brian is all hands off. He slips her a tip to improve her style. She works it. Next week another tip. Eve still hates swimming. The water, the chlorine, the goosebumps, the stinging eyes. But she is a swimmer.

'How's the salmon?'
'Broiled.'
'And…?'
'Blackened cajun spice.'
'Yum.'
'With rice and pecans.'
'Good for Mel.'
'Peppermint tea?
'Why not?'
*Eve.*
*Why don't you talk to me?*
*Stephanie*

She lays flat on the bottom of the pool, skin puckered from water. The world is silent. Her hair floats. *Why do you think I don't talk to you? I purged you.* The water moves in time to the blood thudding in her head.

There are five left at the Transit.


Today.

I bake wacky cake, raisin cookies, gingersnaps, chocolate chip cookies. Then I pour frozen blueberries in a pie plate, drizzle them with honey, powder them with flour. I add a spoon of margarine to oatmeal, a scoop of flour, cinnamon and brown sugar. The spice in its place, placid, subdued. I settle the topping on the blueberries and check there's ice cream. There is. No need to check.


'Another Facebook message yesterday.'
    'Shit.'

'I deleted it.'

'Thanks. Was it…?'

'Same as all the others.'

A young guy in a cowboy hat and Nike high tops heads to the cash register, careful not to slip. 'I need change. For the cigarette machine.'

Eve makes change, watches him pour his coins into the machine in the lobby. Not really a lobby more a boarded-in area with a mat and cigarette machine and the life-sized stand up cardboard cut-out of Bessie. There's a loud clunk and he collects his cigarettes.

'You know you can't smoke those in here or right outside?' shouts Eve.

'Yes ma'am.'

'He's a rodeo clown, that one,' says Bessie. 'Gonna to get hurt one day.'

'Aren't we all,' says Eve.

Bessie watches Eve watch the rodeo clown exit and stroll down the sidewalk. 'Some more than others,' says Bessie.

Eve heads for the door, arms folded, and checks he's gone far enough before lighting up, always protective of Slav's Diner, doesn't want Bessie fined.

There are four left at the Transit. Rocky staying. Luke and Al getting a place together.

After work Eve and Bessie decorate the diner for Christmas.

'Tradition is so important,' says Bessie.

Eve and Bessie frame the windows with phoney holly complete with berries and thorn and prickly sticks.

'You know what we need?' says Bessie. 'Some of those acorns on strings. We'll hang them in the window.'

'How?' asks Eve.

'Where there's a will there's a way. Come on.'

They drive down town in darkness, blowing snow glowing in the headlights. Bessie parks on Main Street in a free after 6.00 P.M. space. Main Street is a wind tunnel.

Cement high-rise hotels and business towers—offices deserted following the drop in oil prices—hem them in. Wind howls and cuts through flesh, Eve's wrists bare between sleeve and pocket. Bessie wisely wears arm covering gloves. I am not wise, thinks Eve. I am not dressed for the weather. Every inch of her bare skin is chapped. What price acorns on string?

The mall is a sad shindig of faded Christmas glory. The lights are too bright and constant renovations leave some areas boarded up, others humming with construction, no one knows where the new washrooms are, the only washrooms working. They head for Dollarama, a half basement of bargains, once a parking lot, before that a food fair. Eve looks up.

'What are you looking at?'

'Birds trapped inside.'

Bessie and Eve stare up, at skylights and mall rafters. Beyond glass, night-time clouds.

'There's no trapped birds,' says Bessie.

'Haven't been here for years,' says Eve.

'Best Dollarama ever. Come on,' says Bessie.

Inside, rows and rows of glittering shit. Eve wanders into stationary and searches notebooks. Her current word book is three quarters full.

'What do you think?' shrills Bessie from across the store, swinging string garlands with pinecones and false red berries.

'Okay,' says Eve. Did Mum ever decorate at Christmas? Maybe once. She remembers a small tree and chicken breasts for dinner. Mum swearing from the kitchen area. Maybe they blew up balloons.

At the trial, Mum and Hilda and Janet were in the dock together. Ursula was almost dressed up, giving evidence, half smiling at Frank sitting in the gallery, a timid smile, a guilty smile, a smile tethered to Frank.

Hilda and Janet were given probation and suspended sentences. Mum got six months but was freed because she'd been on remand even longer. How was Eve meant to bail her out? The cops had the teapot full of money, confiscated as the proceeds of crime.

They mentioned Eve in the courtroom. Said her mother was a bad mother.

'That's not how it was,' Eve yelled.

'Silence,' ordered the judge. Mum shook her head. Eve sat back down.

'Now we need something to hang them from,' says Bessie. 'We can't staple them direct to the window, can we?'

'We could tape them,' says Eve.

'How unclassy is that? How about this?'

'More fake holly?'

'No. This is better. Longer. See how long it really is. Your eyes are younger than mine.'

Eve peered at the label. 'Four point five meters.'

'What the…?' (Bessie doesn't do metric.)

'Fourteen to fifteen feet.'

'Perfect. Grab two.'

Back in the diner Bessie is efficient. 'Okay, you get on the windowsill.'

It's broad and Eve agile.

'Can you reach the top of the window?'

Eve reaches with ease.

'Perfect. Here's the staple gun and the garland. Start with the two ends.'

'Why don't we just staple them to the wood?'

'It's going to look way classier with the garland.'

The garland is stiff fake fir tree with spiky mini branches that Eve has to pull outward and into place. The wire middle is solid and Eve straightens and pulls its branches and straightens again, confident it won't break. The coarseness of the branch scratches her hands, worse she suspects than if it were living. She staples the ends and it falls way too low in the middle. Even for Eve.

'Maybe a loop in the middle?' says Bessie.

Eve holds the garland up.

'Perfect. Left a little. More, further. Back right. Half an inch left. A tad a tiny, tiny, tad left. Perfect. Staple there.' Eve does as she is told and repeats on the other window. The fake garland is dashing.

'While you're up there,' says Bessie, 'sling one of these over.' She hands Eve a series of pinecones on string with fake berries. They are tangled and knotted.

'What's taking you?' asks Bessie.

'Knots.'

'Let me try. I've got nails.'

'I've got nails too.'

'Mine are Pomegranate Passion, my friend Delores gave me testers. I've got a spare if you want one.'

'Let me see?'

Bessie holds up her nails.

'Maybe not,' says Eve.

'The good thing about the dark colours is they hide the dirt.'

'Charming.'

'Okay,' says Bessie. 'Curl that one over the middle of the garland on this side. Lovely. Now this one on the other side.'

Done, the windows startle Eve. They look… nice. Christmassy, but subtle.

'Fancy a drink at the Casino bar?'

'Huh?' says Eve.

'I'll take that as a yes. My treat.'


Today.

Twinkle lights decorate the plate rail. A yule log sits on the table, decorated with pinecones, and mistletoe on the window sill.


Eve is startled when she sits down in the Casino bar, still

shocked she didn't refuse. But then she rarely says no to Bessie. Bessie is a good boss.

'You should have a gin and tonic,' says Bessie when the waiter appears at the corner of their table. 'You'll be less likely to feel hung over.'

'She's right,' says the waiter. 'It's the mix of white liquor and the tonic.'

'Or maybe it's the lemon,' says Bessie. 'Good to get your fruit and veg.'

'Okay, I'll have one,' says Eve, her hand on her purse. 'And a club soda.'

'Okey-doke,' says the waiter.

'He didn't card me,' says Eve.

'About time.'

'My mum used to come here.'

'You don't talk about your mum,' says Bessie.

'She was a cleaner, came here with her cleaning friends on special occasions, they talked about books and ate the burgers.'

'The burgers are a good deal,' says Bessie. 'And it's nice to hear you mention your mum, you know sometimes suppression isn't enough.'

The Casino bar is little more than a place to go for a drink. Old memories, tangled up with Mum, have faded. Me and Mum against the world, Eve thinks.

Today.
Cooking. Life scratches at skin. A comfortable scratch, soothing, as if there's been an itch for a long, long, time.

But yesterday.

The house is modern. It sits lumpen, in a new suburb with

new streets and new gardens sparkling with sprinklers and new grass squares patched together with straight and almost invisible lines. From the outside the home is almost imposing, modern with yellow curtained glass and a supersized garage door. A balcony at the top looks too narrow for a human to perch on. It is the same but not identical to other houses in the street. There are small differences. A peak on Stephanie's house is stubbier than its neighbour's peak, the bulging window that pops out over the newly seamed grass is curved in one house, squared in another. Stephanie's door has black bolts and nail tops on the edges, is made of planks as if it belongs to history or in a stable. The door is painted a watered-down grey, a colour at odds with the green grass and orange bricks. The door is unwelcoming and Eve is ready to turn and bolt.

Inside, Eve expects empty rooms with shoes and clothes scattered as decoration. Will she be asked to iron?

When Eve's mum died, Stephanie sent a card and flowers.

Eve scrunches her eyes closed and rings the doorbell. She expects chimes but there is only silence. She holds her breath, patient, hopes no one answers.

A man opens the door. He is square faced and wears glasses. His hair loops across his cheek bones and his skin bounces around at unusual angles. Eve can't shake off the movement of his face. Strange affliction or ordinary tic? No, a glass wind chime reflects off his skin. He is normal but the glassiness hanging off the sapling, already tall but still spindly, forces movement into his skin.

'I think I've got the wrong house.'

'You must be Eve,' says the man who answered Stephanie's door. 'We've been expecting you.'

For how long? Stephanie expecting her? Since the first message? How did they know she'd come? Eve's poise, mustered together by swimming and loud music, frays at the edges. What confidence has Stephanie and this man that they knew she would come to the door?

'Yes, I'm Eve.'

'Max.'

Max invites Eve into a marbled entrance hall. The ceiling is two floors away, a bit like the mall, there are phoney lilies on ledges and skylights. The house smells of Dettol and decay, stale food and the secret ceremonies that shore up failing bodies. It is a jaundiced home, a sense of yellow pervades.

Eve remembers walking by a dress shop with Mum. She was a small child and the window of the store was covered in yellow cellophane, like a Christmas chocolate with an orange filling.

'It's so the clothes don't fade in the sunshine,' said Mum. 'The ones in the window.'

'Don't people buy them before they fade?'

'Apparently not,' said Mum. 'They're out of fashion and no one wants them. Sooner or later the shop will close.'

Eve felt an affection for the shop that didn't sell enough clothes to stay open. It rumbled into her heart in a sneaky sort of way. Her small child self wandered down the street to see if the shop was still there, again and again, curious to see if the clothes on the mannequins ever changed. They didn't. The same tweed suit and cotton floral frock were trapped behind the cellophane until the day she walked by and it was all gone. All except the cellophane. That stayed for weeks, slightly torn, occasionally flapping when the furnace kicked in. Fascinated, Eve peered into the empty store, waiting for the tremor of air that sent the tattered plastic flapping for the smallest moment. Then she carried on to wherever her eight-year-old self was heading. After what seemed like a long time the shop became a liquor store and was busy for the first time in years.

Stephanie's house is wrapped in invisible cellophane.

'She's ready,' says Max. 'This way.'

Eve follows Max down a carpeted hallway. Her feet disappear in its thickness. Did Stephanie choose the carpet herself? Is it a Venus Fly Trap carpet? There is a narrow table against the wall with an empty vase. She walks by a dining room with a glass table and chairs with brown padded seats, an empty bowl on the table. The kitchen, briefly glimpsed, glitters with shiny appliances. Eve misses the tattered bookiness of Stephanie's house south of the river.

Stephanie's bedroom smells of pinkness and medicine. Cough syrup or worse.

Stephanie rolls her gaze up and down Eve. Eve does the same to Stephanie. Stephanie lies in a four-poster bed with pink curtains. She has ribbons and lace tied into her golden yellow (dyed) hair. An elderly child waiting for a party.

'I'm Eve.'

'The Cleaning woman's daughter.'

'Yes.'

'Did you see what we did then, did you? That's exactly what we said the first time we met. Happy times, right Eve? Happy times. Do you want to sit or would you rather iron, no sit, sit, that was a joke. Let's have coffee. Max! Max, can we have coffee?'

'Of course,' Max peeks around the door. Does he know the story? Is he, Stephanie's husband?

'Isn't Max lovely? I'm a very lucky woman and his coffee is better than yours.'

Everything in the room bleeds sugar pink. Stephanie's princess bed, as wide as it is long, the sheets and blankets. A white dressing table with a mirror is hung with pink lights, turned on and reflecting into eternity, every moment a celebration. Pink pots sit on the surface, possibly full but there are no make-up crumbs or open nail polish bottles. Eve thinks of other dressing tables—she herself has a chest of drawers and bathroom mirror—most of them are places of work. The shared washroom in the mountains where the summer tourists and short-termers spent precious minutes stretching to hours, painting and altering and teasing and lengthening and heightening. Bessie too has a dressing table of litter. Eve has visited more than once, the first time a baby shower for Clover. Bessie gave them a ceremonious tour of every inch of her smart condo but still the dressing table was a work surface. All matching lipsticks and nail polishes, a random almost-mess.

Stephanie wipes spittle from the corner of her mouth, her face has come loose from its earlier doll prettiness. Stephanie's jowls wobble and her tongue has difficulty staying inside her mouth. She wears a crocheted bed jacket, heavy with multi pinked and purpled frills, a warm yarn. Does she wear pink when she teaches at the university? What do her students think?

'Coffee?' asks Max.

'That was quick,' says Stephanie.

'I had everything ready, waiting for Eve.'

'Good man,' says Stephanie.

Eve watches as Max balances the tray of coffee on one hand and opens a collapsed table with the other.

'Let me help,' says Eve.

'No worries, I'm practiced,' says Max.

It's the sort of table that people eat television dinners off in old television shows.

Max pours two cups of coffee and leaves. Eve waits for Stephanie to drink first, in case it's poisoned.

'Lovely coffee,' says Stephanie.

Eve's cup is thin china with pink roses.

'Pretty cup.'

'My best,' says Stephanie. 'Special occasions only.'

Eve sips the coffee, which is instant. She doesn't mind instant coffee. Thinks of it as a drink apart from coffee, not the real thing. As a waitress Eve has high expectations of coffee. She waits for Stephanie to speak. And waits. And sips. The air in the room is heavy and not the place to drink instant coffee.

'Why am I here?'

'Isn't it obvious?' says Stephanie.

'No.'

'I want my clothes back.'

Eve is confused. 'What clothes?'

'I was doing inventory and realised some were missing. Took me a minute to remember you had them.' Stephanie rummages under the bed clothes and Eve waits, constantly checking for signs of life and wondering if Stephanie is suffocating. There's a jangling sound from under the bedclothes, like two saucepan lids being banged together. Eve is about to call Max for help when Stephanie emerges. 'Here we are!' She opens a serious, black leather accounting journal and runs a broken nail down a page. 'Pin stripe skirt, white cotton shirt, cream linen shirt, white embroidered shirt, tweed skirt, and a kilt. The shirts are all men's, funny sense of style you've got.'

Eve laughs. Unbelievable. 'I threw them out.'

A ceremony. A shuttering of all things Stephanie. After the vice principal expelled Eve, after the world slipped beneath her feet, cracked and pulled her down. She'd needed a statement to underline the acceptance of her unwanted destiny. The ritual tossing, of each shirt and skirt into the dumpster was a blow for freedom. A recognition that she was who she was and fuck anyone who tried to change her. Twenty-seven years ago, her first step into invisibility.

'What?'

'I threw them away. I didn't want them anymore.'

'You could have given them back.'

'I didn't want to see you. I didn't want to be in the same room as you.'

'But I forgave you. Completely. And you are my friend.'

'No.' says Eve, 'I'm not.'

Stephanie rumples into herself. The skin on her face sinks into the bone, further and further. A whole-body slump. There is no animation.

'You know,' says Stephanie. Eve is startled, almost falls off her chair. The voice rasps at her in a lazy pink whine. 'If you'd left everything as it was… as it was meant to be, things would have turned out much better for you.'

Eve stares at a bright eye piercing through the slump and bedclothes.

'Credit you my story?' says Eve.

'Let slipping dogs lie,' says Stephanie.

Eve snorts. Sleeping dogs! she thinks. 'My life is fine,' says Eve.

'You could have had it all,' says Stephanie.

'All what?'

'All this.'

Intractable, thinks Eve. My story, from inside my head.

'I should go,' says Eve. Stephanie melts further into the bedding.

Eve places her coffee cup on the television tray with care. She turns to leave and there is Max. Nose to nose with her. His footsteps muffled by the carpet. For a moment Eve is startled enough to breathe fear. Then Max smiles. A thin voice wheedles its way from the bedclothes.

'Do you know what she did, Max? She threw my clothes away. The three shirts and the three skirts and there was a dress too. I didn't have it on the list but there was a mini-dress. I was going to let her keep the dress, Max. An inheritance.'

Max, his face still too close to Eve's but Eve unwilling to back down, smiles. It is an unpleasant and proprietorial smile. 'You threw her clothes away?'

Eve wants to scream. It was twenty-seven years ago! 'I didn't need them, so I threw them away.'

'It's very upsetting, Max.'

'I know.' Max hauls his face away from Eve and sits beside Stephanie. Stephanie rocks, a gentle, barely perceptible, back and forth. Max massages Stephanie's shoulders from the front. A soothing, mental massage connected through the shoulder. Eve's mouth tastes bitter.

Stephanie is still. The stillness a gash in the air. It owns a rigidity that is antagonistic and brutal in its silent calm.

'You should go,' Stephanie snarls, a small pink animal.

'Good-bye,' says Eve.

Max follows Eve out of the room and down the hallway. Eve senses his soft footsteps and suspects he is working up to intimidation. She turns, prepared to attack, ready to be attacked.

'I'm sorry,' says Max. 'I didn't know about the clothes when she asked me to find you. I thought you were an old friend and might do her some good.'

'Do her some good? How?'

'Lead her back into the world.'

'Me? I don't live in the world. I survive. Stephanie doesn't want my world.'

'You've seen her.'

'She teaches in the university?'

'No, she doesn't.'

'She does. It says so on Facebook.'

'Lies. Check with the university. She never taught.'

'Never? Who paid my wages?'

Eve knows it is true. She knew from the first smell of Stephanie's house, she knew it from the first glance at the pink at the dressing table, she knew it when Stephanie's skin slipped.

'What wages?'

'When I cleaned for her.'

'You were her cleaner?'

'At first. Then I helped her. With reading and stuff.'

'I suppose her mother paid your wages.'

'She said her mother was dead.'

'Not when she was in university.' Max gazes at Eve, curious not intimidating. When he speaks his voice is low with pauses between his words. As if surprised by his own words. 'She stole the ideas for her thesis from a girl who helped in the house.'

'Are you her husband?'

'Nurse. Keeps a bed free in the hospital for another poor sod.'

From Stephanie's house Eve walks into a sullen December morning, a morning punctuated with low cloud and dreary wind. She walks past the almost identical houses that remind her of a too-perfect set of dentures.

At the end of the road, a traffic circle. She crosses cautiously to the middle and then again to where a bus stop stands outside a short row of shops. Domino's Pizza, a pet shop, a Greek grocery and a shop with so many Christmas ornaments buried in holly and pinecone fakery she can't see what it sells. There are camper vans with Christmas trees on top, skiers with mistletoe, a surfboard with a Christmas elf, purple bells, a tiny record player with a record and Santa's face in the middle of the record, there are birds and pieces of cake all hanging in the window. Eve, mesmerised by the ridiculous, opens the door.

It is a bookstore. The books are second-hand and in the middle an overstuffed and battered leather couch from the fifties, bright red with matching chair.

'Coffee?' asks the woman behind the counter. Eve opens her mouth to refuse, hesitates, her tongue still soured by Max's coffee. A cup of any other sort of coffee might wash the bitter away.

'Thank you.' Eve places the coffee on the table, sets her jacket and hat on the chair. She inhales the dust and must and woody earth smell of the books, it seeps slow into her skin, all the way to her core. She touches the spines, smooth and exact under her fingertips, endless words folded into themselves.

Old favourites and new strangers. She closes her eyes and is a girl searching for a kind look from the father of the baby she carried, a girl woman eating a woman shaped cake, a young woman designing a submarine. She searches for New Canadian Library editions, then removes a book with an inviting spine, and another and another. No new books for her collection, she has more NC books than this store.

Eve smiles. She has a goal, a new need. She searches. American literature, no, short stories, no. She is not desperate but she is determined. A Solstice present to herself, if not here elsewhere. She searches some more, anthologies, academic resales, *The Heath Anthology of American Literature*. Her finger traces the index through centuries. *Success.* She takes the book to her chair and sits, holds onto the book as if it were a beating heart. She opens it. Cautious. She knows what she will find. 'The Yellow Wallpaper'. She reads, she tips over the edge and into the pages. She is back in the wallpaper.

Eve is too full of excitement to notice the coffee cooling.

She remembers the thrill of being seventeen and under the skin of her own people, her own writing. Knowing the words the characters would speak, the way they annoyed each other. Excitement bubbles through her body. It rakes through every inch of her flesh. It brings a long unknown promise. Eve dives head first into her story.

'Excuse me.' Eve looks up at the woman in the store. 'I didn't want to disturb you but I'm closing soon.'

Eve pays for the book and heads to the bus stop. Text 222 for bus information. Both information and bus are a long time coming. Her feet itch to dance on skiffs of snow dust. The world is extraordinary in front of her, larger than she had ever noticed before.

Today.
This afternoon.
My skin is fraught with anticipation. Inside organs tick over, glisten in blood and muscle and tendon and tissue. Ordered, pulsing, beating, all present and correct.

I stand by the window in dress and Genuine Curling Sweater. It is newly purchased but second-hand. A sweater with a hawk on the back and blue snowflakes on the sleeves. A beautiful blue, an historic blue. I recently re-read *A Jest of God* that used to be *Rachel Rachel* and I was overwhelmed, my heart sank low in my gut. At school I ridiculed the slow burn of Rachel's life. Re-reading it with its original title I was delighted.

I am not a new woman. I am a woman waking up.

The sweater gives me courage. I look out the bedroom window and am tempted to climb out, down the naked branches of a winter tree, and run.

But, it is time.

Dinner is cooked. The doorbell rings. My doorbell rings.

I walk along the landing. Hundreds of photographs and postcards. So many places from the world pinned on my wall. Mountains and sea and temples and windmills and women dancing with bottles on their heads and small children and family pictures, old weddings and elderly people in uniforms from distant wars. Life and history and roots blatantly displayed. Unravelled for the world to see. There are small children behind birthday cakes and chicken dinners and Christmas turkey. There are pictures of the sky at night and photos of Bedford. My mother.

Home.

When my mother came home she was broken. She looked and sounded the same but she is like an ancient, cracked, once fancy figurine, the kind you see amongst the dishes in Value Village. Her sparkle had gone, her eyes shattered, hollowed out inside. It was like the books and the tips and losing her authority and job had taken her insides away.

The small house creaks and expands with my mismatched friends. I have set the food on the red Formica kitchen table. Some friends slouch against the wall comfortable, others perch on chairs.

'Eve,' yells Bessie, 'I'm gonna put on some coffee, okay?'

I play host. 'I can do it!'

'It's my pleasure,' says Bessie. 'Lovely place.'

'Door,' says a voice.

Chasity is on my doorstep. My flesh curdles with the door bell's ringing, curdles like vinegar in milk. But vinegar in milk brings buttermilk.


When the police came for my mother I was surprised. I knew she read books on her break, I knew she made fast and light of the beginning and end of that break, and I knew some books found their way into our house. For a while. But she always returned them. She looked upon the university as her own private lending library.

The money in the teapot was a whole different matter. I knew it was there. I thought it was her savings. I knew people tipped her. I didn't believe she extorted the money, I believed it was freely given. The police took the teapot as evidence. There was a lot of money inside.

'You're arresting me for reading?' asked my mother.

'You can't do this,' I said.

'How old are you?' asked the young cop.

'Eighteen.'

'Old enough to be here on her own,' said the older cop.

'Can't I come with her?'

'We're arresting her not taking her to a fancy hotel.'
And they took her away.


Chasity lingers by my bookcase. Reads titles, drags a pink nail across the spines of my books and I flinch for them.

'It's like an old school library,' says Chasity. 'All these books they urged us to read. All these books you urged me to read. And more. I brought you a present.'

'It's not that sort of party.'

'I know, I know. I should have brought food. Made a cake. Like I could do that. I'm a worse cook than my mum and she was shit at it.'

'You didn't have to bring anything.'

'Here.' Chasity pushes a package into my hands. 'It's not a real present anyway because I need it back.'

The package is wrapped in a plastic grocery bag and taped awkwardly, the packaging rippling against a solid inside.

'Open it. My fingers are so crossed you like them.'

Books.

'It's only library books,' said Chasity. 'You'll have to give them back to me so I can return them. Or you can drop them off at the university.'

'Thank you.'

'They're books from my courses. Stuff I'd never have read if I hadn't gone back to school. Not a real present.'

'Doesn't matter. It's perfect.'

Milton Keynes UK
Ingram Content Group UK Ltd.
UKHW010838240823
427411UK00005B/127